I0607605

Cleat Chasers

CHALLENGE ACCEPTED

JAQUELINE SNOWE

Challenge Accepted
ISBN # 978-1-83943-737-3
©Copyright Jaqueline Snowe 2021
Cover Art by Erin Dameron-Hill ©Copyright September 2021
Interior text design by Claire Siemaszkiewicz
Totally Bound Publishing

CHALLENGE
ACCEPTED

Dedication

To the hubs.
Your Toledo Mud Hens hat inspired the story,
your love of baseball is contagious and writing
about love is so much easier because I have you.

Chapter One

Callie

"Get your gorgeous ass in here and give me a hug." Greta slammed the door open with her foot and jumped into my arms. She smelled the same as she had done in high school—floral and sweet. God, I had missed the hell out of my girl. She'd always been a violent hugger and the tradition continued. My lungs were gasping for air by the time she let go.

"Sorry I'm late." I lugged the suitcase into the apartment and grinned at her motherly expression.

"Unless the reason is some hot guy or some awesome story, then I'll remained pissed at you for another two minutes. I got afraid—"

"That I backed out? Me?" I held up my hands in surrender. "I wouldn't back out of our pact from ten years ago. I wouldn't dare."

"Glad you learned something from your year off," she mumbled loud enough for me to hear. We both had a mutual hatred of the deal my parents had forced me to accept and I understood her anger disguised the worry about this not happening. We'd dreamed about living together since we'd become best friends in fifth grade — when two kids get caught cheating on a math test, it forms a bond that's hard to break.

"I learned, like, two things," I replied to her comment and she skipped to my bedroom for the next year. "This is my room?"

"Yes!" she cheered. I'd expected the room to be small and I gasped when I saw a dresser, a built-in desk and a twin bed. "Wait here, I have a present for you."

I obeyed her command and set my cases on the floor. I could fit every piece of clothing I owned in the closet, and maybe a little more. It could even serve as an extra bedroom if needed. I'd lived in my childhood home my entire life. The last year…it had been hell taking a year off to prove to my dad I could make it on my own. Pure hell. But I'd made it and it pleased me to be on my own for the first time.

"Here. I bought it for you." She waltzed back into the bedroom with a package wrapped in sparkly paper. Greta *would* buy sparkly paper. "It's nothing big, just a welcome present."

"You didn't have to get me anything, Greta. Come on." I frowned at the gift, damn well knowing her kindness knew no bounds. She shoved it into my hands, despite my reluctance. "Fine."

I opened it up to find the very first picture of the two of us, taken when we'd been in our band in high school. I met her eyes and we shared a smile. "Good lord. Why did we name ourselves the Crazy Gals again?"

"Because our names start with C and G. Obviously that made sense when we were fourteen."

"I regret the name choice, but still dig the outfits." Closing my eyes in shame, I swallowed down the memory of gaucho pants, clogs and popped-collared shirts.

She shuddered. "Oh, lord. Not me. I regret the outfit, not the name." Greta's legs had more style than I had in my entire body. She'd won best dressed in high school. Even now, she wore a trendy sundress with a hat while I was wearing ripped jean shorts and a vintage band tank top. "I have another gift for you, but you cannot get mad."

"That's a great opener. No promises, G."

"It's kind of small." She bit her lip and pulled out something from her pocket. *What the hell? Sundresses have pockets?* A shadow of apprehension crossed her face and I worried what the fuck she'd gotten me.

I took the sticker from her hand, already planning where to put it. "I freaking love it."

"I know you really don't play in bands anymore, but you still have the same case." She motioned her head to the guitar case I'd set down earlier.

"Of course I do." I collected stickers from everywhere I went or from any large moment in my life. I peeled back the paper and placed the new college sticker on the front of the case, right in the center. *Big. Freaking. Deal.* "Thanks, Greta."

"Phew. I'm super happy you love it. I'd been nervous, like, what if you hated it and used your guitar to beat me senseless? Or, what if you assumed we were getting back in business?"

"Greta. Am I crazy?"

"I've seen you punch two girls in the face. At the same time, I might add." She bit back a grin and pointed down the narrow hallway. "Kitchen is down the hall to the right. I already know your first question."

"Obviously." I eyed the tile and large counters, sighing in pleasure. They were perfect. "Those girls deserved it, though. Sure, we were in a mosh pit, but they pushed a girl in a cast." I smiled at the memory.

"Your smile alone is why you're crazy."

I flipped her off and she closed the distance between us with open arms. "I'm damn glad you're going to be my roomie. I'm proud of you. You beat your dad at his own game and I love you more because of that."

"Love you, too. Now, that's enough affection. I need to paint my room black or something." I blinked away the emotions that bubbled up. Those words, coming from her, meant much more than she might ever realize.

"This is going to be hella fun!" she squealed and squished me for another hug.

* * * *

A couple of hours later, I'd gotten my room set up with all my favorite band posters, some twinkle lights that gave the place a nice touch and the oldest, goofiest picture of Greta and me from third grade. The temperature had changed from pleasant to hot as hell and damn, I must have stunk. Thank god I had my own bathroom to hit the shower whenever the hell I felt like. I loved Greta to death, but as an only child, I'd never had to share. I refused to start now. As I belted out the words to *Smells like Teen Spirit*, waves of happiness flowed through me. I'd worked pretty damn hard, saving money to be at my dream university. *Dad and his crazy take-it-or-leave-it deal. 'Prove you can make it on your own – pay for your own school. You'll never survive on your own.'*

My parents had attachment issues—understandably, as I was their only daughter. But more, they didn't think of me as college material. I hadn't gotten straight As. I'd done okay in school, but my focus had always been sports. I scoffed. *Huh, odd, isn't it? My dad's been a baseball coach his whole damn life, yet I've gotta choose a different career path.*

Hypocrite.

Not caring that I still wore a tiny robe, I shuffled into the kitchen to grab a drink before making a list of class materials. We had two full weeks of chilling until classes started and I intended to take total advantage of every free minute, but I needed to get settled in and figure out where the hell the Bookstore was, because I wanted good grades. I needed it more than the average person because, if I could pull off straight As, my parents planned to help me out with payments. *Thanks a lot, Dad. For your unfair twofer deal of proving myself to get here and also making me do it again.*

"Hey, G?" I hopped up onto the bar stool and flipped through the magazine on the counter. I never read any gossip mags and it didn't pique my interest, but I saw something about Blink 182. That definitely caught my eye. "Get your tiny ass out here and have a drink with me."

No response. I took a large swig of water and bent over the magazine. I was reading about the latest tour schedule when someone cleared their throat and I glanced up to find two pairs of eyes staring at me. My heart kicked up, shooting adrenaline down my body. I held the bottle tighter, in case I had to use it as a weapon. I glanced back and forth between them, hoping to figure out who these guys were and what they hell they were doing there. "Neither of you is Greta."

"G? I like that." The shorter one with perfect teeth smiled at me as he rubbed his jaw. I'd never seen such a large forearm before. Like, the size of my leg. He could have killed me with one punch. Before thoughts of getting robbed or murdered overtook my brain, he held out his hand. "You must be Callie."

"Maybe." I stood and backed up a couple of steps, ignoring his hand. The taller one stared at me with intense blue eyes. Or maybe they were green. I couldn't tell and should not have been thinking about his eye color when two strange yet attractive guys were in my apartment. "Don't make me throw a bottle at you."

The tall one's lip quirked so quickly that I almost didn't catch it. I clenched the bottle tighter as the shorter one introduced himself. "I'm Aaron. This is Tanner. Sorry if we scared you."

"Cool." If they were robbing me, they were kind about it at least. "Forgive me for being rude, but why are you here? I don't really have money if you're burgling me."

"Shit." Aaron shared a look with Tanner before smiling. "We're friends of Greta and we usually walk in. We heard you were moving in over the weekend and we wanted to meet you or see if you needed help."

His smiled appeared nice and safe, but I'd never heard of an Aaron or Tanner before and I knew of most of her friends. "Listen, guys, I have no idea who you are and G's my best friend, but if you're messing with me, you win. You should go."

"We'll leave, but you and Greta should start a band up again. Your voice is pretty good."

I blushed, wanting them to leave that second. *Great first impression, idiot. These strangers heard me singing in the shower and know how much of a dork I am.*

"Johnson! Hilly!" Greta's voice carried from the hallway and I smacked a hand to my forehead. *Damn.* I knew of Johnson and Hilly, Greta's baseball friends. "I see you met my best friend for life." She handed a chocolate cupcake to me and I moaned in pleasure. "Isn't she hot?"

"Greta. *Jesus.*" I choked on the dessert at her question.

Aaron laughed and nodded. "She lived up to every expectation I had. Although, is she normally violent? She threatened to throw a bottle at us."

"Hell, yeah, she is. She's gotten into fist fights a couple of times. She always wins, too." Greta put her arm around me. "That's why I love her."

"Shit. Don't tell them that. I'm not that bad." I set the bottle down on the counter. "I just definitely assumed these two were going to rob or kill me."

"Please. They're harmless." Greta ignored them as they flipped her the bird.

"Do they have keys? Should I be worried about them trying on my clothes or something?"

"Hell no. I love them but not that much."

Relief filled my chest but I didn't express it out loud. "I'm sorry I thought you were bad guys. I've heard a lot about you. Nice to meet you."

"You as well." I eyeballed Tanner and smiled at the pair. They were both way too good-looking so I had no idea how Greta remained just *friends* with them.

"You realize you were in the shower and if we were good robbers, we would've taken every penny you had and slipped out without you knowing?"

"Great point. Okay, he has brains and looks. I'm surprised." I totally checked Tanner out and he ate it up. Flirts I could deal with. The younger kids in my classes worried me. I hated feeling insecure, and already being a year behind put me at a disadvantage. "I only knew of you guys as Johnson and Hilly. I never guessed last names…" I stopped talking. Tanner's eyes had dropped to my chest. I forgot I was wearing only a robe and it had come undone, revealing a sliver of skin all the way down my body. I quickly tugged at the hem and pulled it together. "I make really good first impressions, if you couldn't tell."

Greta chuckled and opened up a beer for herself. Her parents were the cool ones, always buying drinks for her in the summer. Mine, not so much. Tanner continued grinning at me. "I'd say I'm going to remember our meeting…your robe forever etched into my mind."

I put my face in my hands and laughed. "I'll be right back. I don't want to embarrass myself even more." I threw on the same cut-off shorts and a different band tank top before heading back out there. I rarely wore makeup or did my hair, making my prep time less than five minutes. Greta drove me crazy with her hour-long routine. *But to each their own.* I came out to see them in the same position reenacting something that had happened the weekend before.

"So you two are the baseball players, right?"

"Well I'm also an Aries and charming as hell, but yes." Aaron hopped onto the counter and pointed to Tanner. "This guy is totally a Virgo. Shy, cranky and modest."

"Dude. Not the sign thing again." Tanner rolled his eyes and sipped his beer. "The latest chick he's been hooking up with is into astrological signs. It's all he's been talking about lately. She's nuts, meaning he is also nuts."

"She's not nuts. She's curvy in all the right places and her mouth...damn." Aaron closed his eyes and shook his head as if freeing it of a memory. "But the stars shit is super interesting."

I stared at Greta and she closed her eyes with a slight stiffening of her shoulders. *Hmm.* We needed to talk about that later. "I forgot to mention that Aaron here is the biggest flirt on campus. He'll try to get in your pants at least twice every time he sees you."

"Greta. Rude." He gave a sly smile. "It's more like three times."

"Great." I almost choked on my water at their banter. Tanner talked more the longer we hung out and I could see why Greta liked them. They clearly cared for her.

"Now, let me guess what you are. I've been reading about astrology and shit." Aaron stared at me and went up and down my body, but not in a creepy way.

I stood still with my arms crossed until I'd had enough. "Oh, lord. Come on. You will not guess this."

"I think I can. Give me a minute."

Tanner shook his head and focused on Greta. "You coming by tonight?"

"Depends. What's the occasion?" she answered, her tone rising in interest.

"It can't just be wanting to hang out with us?"

"Eh. You're already here." Greta shrugged at me. "Sometimes they throw awesome parties at their house. Other times it's a slut-infested orgy."

"Gross." I scrunched my nose at the thought. "The picture I have in my head of them now is not a good one."

"It's probably just like that," Tanner admitted.

"Legs and asses everywhere. With beer pouring from the ceiling."

"What the hell? What do you watch, because that sounds like a porn?" Tanner asked.

I laughed and met Greta's eye. We communicated without words — she wanted to go but didn't want to make it easy. "I don't watch porn. At least nothing like that. Legs. Legs and hairy asses everywhere."

"Sagittarius!" Aaron yelled, causing all three of us to jump. "Sorry, but I figured it out. You're a Sagittarius. When is your birthday? Greta, when is her birthday?"

Her eyes widened and she put her hand over her mouth. Hell, if he hadn't gotten it right. He spun to face me, a shit-eating grin on his face. "I fucking knew it. I'm awesome."

"How in the hell?"

"You're a wanderer and I know you like to camp." He paused and pointed at Greta. "She told me. I'm not *that* fucking creepy. You love being outside and you appear to be athletic. You're also straightforward and honest."

I stood with my mouth open at his snap judgment. His correct assessment startled me, what with me never having had anyone read me within minutes before.

"Since I'm clearly right, you both better stop by tonight. It's going to be awesome."

"Sure, sure. Bye, Aaron. Way to freak us both out." Greta indicated the door with narrowed eyes.

Tanner just shook his head and smiled at me as he walked by. "See you around, Callie."

Aaron walked out with a huge, obnoxious grin but then popped his head around the door and indicated the fridge. "Okay, I don't want you thinking I'm super fucking weird. I saw the picture on the fridge from your birthday. I read the date. See you tonight. Bye."

Greta threw the magazine at him and shut the door. "Freaking Aaron. So, you want to go? Hot baseball players and free drinks?"

"I have to run some errands, but after that, why the hell not?"

Chapter Two

Zade

I crumpled the list of the shit I had to get for my sister. Why the hell had she put tampons on there? *Fuck. Me.* Her flu had worsened over the weekend and she needed help but... *Hell.* What a nightmare. I perused the ladypart aisle at Target and sighed into my fist. I had been here ten minutes. I had no idea what 'sport compact' meant. I retrieved my phone, ignoring a couple of texts from a girl who'd gotten my number last weekend. Rookie mistake. I knew better than to let them near my phone.

I pressed my sister's number, praying she picked up first ring. It almost worked — she answered the second.

"Zaria, *tampons*?" I growled.

"Yes, Zade. Open your narrow mind for a second and realize that your sister, the best person you know, is a woman. Man up."

"It's hard to man up while in the lady aisle. Damn. Too many choices." I ran my hand over my face. "I have no fucking idea what to grab."

"Dear god. You are a sad human. Have you never gone on a tampon run for one of your little hussies?" Sickness clogged her voice but the humor shone through. She loved messing with me and I couldn't say she wasn't right.

"FaceTime me then and show me." I held the phone out and tried to hit the right button, but she declined it. I called her back, letting out a string of curse words. "What the hell, Zaria?"

"This is too much. Figure it out." She then hung up the phone. I laughed. My mom liked to tell me that Zaria helped balance my self-esteem, which had apparently been growing inch by inch since I'd been in college. I considered it confidence, while they considered it an ego. I worked out to remain in shape, worked my ass off for a baseball scholarship and had no qualms about what I wanted in the future. Sure, I might have had a reputation for being a womanizer, but eh, I had no regrets.

Last year had been the best year ever. A freshman pitcher with the best stats and a full ride... Life. Was. Fucking. Awesome.

Except, when my sick sister guilted me into helping her...by buying tampons. I had two things left on the list and her torture of me bordered on abusive. Girl products...*fuck you, Zaria.* I read the list again, plotting my revenge on her. *Tampons, sports compact and maximum hold hair shit. Yep, time to man up and read some girlie boxes.*

I walked to the area where I thought it made the most sense to store them. Colorful bottles stared at me from every direction. I bent, reading each box. Nothing matched the name on the list.

"God damn it," I said to no one in particular. Someone snorted and I searched the aisle for whoever had made the sound. "*Woah.*"

"Well, that's the first time I've gotten that reaction." The woman's smile somehow transformed her already beautiful face into one of a model. I loved women, all shapes and sizes, but her... Her beauty stood out above all the other faces I had seen. Her long hair sat on top of her head, a few curls escaping. I had a thing for hair and the guys gave me shit for it, but I had the urge to reach out and yank the ponytail loose. I wanted to see that dark hair spread over a pillow.

"I highly doubt that," I replied to the gorgeous stranger. To top it off, she wore no makeup and she wasn't looking at me with wild eyes. She had no idea who I was.

"Consider me flattered then." She walked closer, her sweet smell penetrating my senses. "I couldn't help but notice you were uh, struggling a little bit."

"Oh really? I think it's perfectly normal for a guy to be hanging out in the lady-product aisle without a care in the world. I pick up my Tinder dates here." I motioned around with my arms and she quirked a lip in amusement.

"Interesting. How's that been working out for ya?" She placed a hand on one of her hips and I glanced down to admire her toned legs. She had to be an athlete, no question about it, and the strength of her body intrigued me no end. Not many girls could look hot as hell in athletic shorts and no makeup, yet *she* caught all my attention.

"I'm about two for four."

"Hitting five hundred ain't too bad." *Oh god. Baseball talk.*

"Baseball fan?" I raised an eyebrow, somehow already knowing her answer.

"It is the greatest sport in America." Her red lips formed a smile that I couldn't help but match with my own. "I take it you are as well? I noticed your Toledo Mud Hens hat. Detroit fan?"

"Marry me. Right now," I demanded and she threw her head back and laughed. Part of me wasn't kidding. She fucking knew the farm team for the Tigers? My *teammates* didn't know that.

"Ah, my dad wouldn't approve of a Tigers fan... meaning I graciously decline your kind offer." She rotated around and pointed to a White Sox logo on the back of her tank top. "We would be doomed to fail."

I nodded, checking out her toned ass. God, her body had me weak. "Sometimes there's a little fun in doing what's wrong."

She pursed her lips and scrunched her nose. "I feel like that could be a line you've used before. Try harder than that."

"You've got me. Most of my Tinder dates like that line." I shrugged, partially kidding.

"Hmm. With a face like yours, I bet you can say just about anything." She eyed me, which I had zero problem with. "Now, let's talk about feminine hygiene products."

"Uh. Must we?" I groaned but decided to do just about anything to continue talking to her.

"We must. Now, what are you looking for?" She stepped closer, into my bubble, and I tensed up. That never happened to me.

"Sport tampons? Does that make sense?" I sounded like a schmuck. I knew it. She knew it. I mentally cursed my sister—again.

"Sure does. It's the blue box right here." She reached up, standing on her tiptoes, and I admired her calf muscles. She handed me the box and I willingly took it.

"Thank you, kind stranger. I swear my sister does stuff to mess with me." I set the box in the cart and she assessed me in disbelief.

"The ever-nagging sister, yes. I've heard of *her* before." She smiled, dimples popping out on either side.

"You don't believe me, do you?"

"I'm not sure. You do seem rather uncomfortable in the girl aisle and you strike me as someone who doesn't do something he doesn't want."

"Good assessment. However, I have another thing I have to get for her and I really don't want to do that. Care to help a guy out?" I tried the line, knowing it sounded ridiculous. She waited three seconds too long before deciding to grab the list from my hand. I took that as a sign of agreement and cheered. "You rock."

"I'm doing my kind deed for the day. The pay-it-forward type of thing. I expect good karma after this." She hurried out of the scary lady aisle. She walked fast, her strong legs carrying her with grace. She had to be a runner and I suddenly wished she ran in front of me every mile I had to run. She ducked down another aisle and I quickened my pace to catch up with her.

"Where are we going?" I frowned at the hair products all around us. Colors were tough for me. Pinks and purples were a little too similar.

"This is the hair aisle. Do you not buy your own shampoo?" She tilted her head and I shrugged.

"Sure I do. But CVS is easier to navigate."

She laughed and picked up two bottles of some purple stuff. "Here you are."

I read the bottles and placed them in the cart. "Thank you. Seriously."

"You're welcome. I hope your sister enjoys it." She said the word *sister* with emphasis and wide eyes.

"You think I made up the sister line, didn't you?" I cringed, imaging Zaria dying laughing about this.

She wet her bottom lip so quickly I almost didn't see it. The motion made me want to beg on my knees to see it again. "I want to say yeah, but I don't want to come across as a tool."

"You'd be honest. But I assure you, my sister is very real and will laugh her ass off when I tell her a woman didn't immediately trust me."

"Hmm, now I'm curious. I'm inferring from that statement that you pick up women frequently."

"As I said, I'm two for four in the Tinder department. As far as Target pickup lines, I'm currently zero for one." I slid that in there, hoping to at least get a smile. It did. *Bam.*

"Cute." She continued to eye me and I let her. She wasn't blatant or intrusive. She weighed her options and I appreciated that in a woman. "Who said you struck out, though?"

My eyes widened at her insinuation. An unfamiliar sensation of joy spread through my chest. "When someone turns down a proposal, it's hard on the ego."

"Not yours. That I am positive of," she teased, her tone matching mine.

"All right then, White Sox, the ball is as we say, on your field." I paused, hoping she enjoyed my baseball banter.

"Grocery shop with me. It tells you a lot about a person. If you pass the test, then we can go to the ball park." She paused and smiled. "Notice that I did not insinuate anything about getting to any bases?"

"Duly noted." I indicated for her to walk down the aisle. I meant it to be the act of a gentleman, but it didn't hurt to get another peek at her perfect ass. "I've never done a grocery shopping date before. How does it work?"

"No idea. Just thought of it." She spun around and caught me staring. "Strike one, player."

"I'm assuming I get three before I'm out?"

"Smart man." She pulled a list out of her bag. "Game on. Now, if you're hosting a party, what snack food do you go for?" she asked a few minutes later as we walked into the chip aisle. I'd passed the first two tests about how I drank my coffee and my favorite flavor of jelly. Strawberry, by the way.

"I feel like every question is a quiz of sorts. I didn't study," I admitted.

"You'll do fine. Take a swing." She reached for some pretzels and salted chips from the shelf and I thought about it. My mom tended to buy Doritos and chips and salsa. Always a safe choice.

"Chips and salsa."

"Okay. What beer matches with chips and salsa?" She side-eyed me and did the quick lip-lick thing. I found her quirk endearing. She wasn't doing it to be sexy, which somehow *made* it sexy.

"Tough one. Two options for me. Modelo or Corona."

"Damn. Good answer. Did you cheat somehow?" She winked at me and continued down the aisle. I was acting like a fool with a dorky grin, but I didn't care. I had never enjoyed grocery shopping before.

"I like your test. I'm passing pretty well."

"Don't get too macho. I've been holding back on you." She took some pasta and stopped in front of the sauces. "This one is major."

"Okay. I'm braced." I held on to the cart and planted my feet. "Give it to me."

"What type of pasta sauce do you normally buy?" She pointed to two options. "Garlic and herb or traditional?"

"Hmm. I have to go with the truth, traditional."

"Ah, we'll call that one a hard foul ball." She held up some garlic and herb spices and threw them into the cart.

"Right side or left side?" I asked, hoping to throw her.

"Right. You swung a little late." She hummed a bit as she continued down the aisle and headed toward the next. The dark-haired woman, whose name I had no idea of, had me wrapped around her finger after knowing her an hour.

"I tend to pull the outside pitches to the left, actually. I'm working on that."

"Are you keeping your shoulder closed? If you open it up too soon, you'll pull every pitch imaginable." She hadn't glanced up at me and I stood baffled. *Who is this mystery woman?*

We approached the frozen products and I knew we were near the end of her list. I desperately wanted the date to continue. "Can I ask you some questions now?"

"That's fair. It has been one-sided and I'm all for equality." She lifted a pint of rocky road ice cream from the shelf, my favorite by the way, and put it in the cart.

"What's your name?" I held my breath.

"Ah, noticed that we skipped that part, huh?" She smiled and walked up to the edge of the cart, only a foot of space between us. "Give me your after-game analysis."

"I want to be clever right now and come up with some baseball talk and wow you with my intelligence, but I'll mess it up. I'm going with honesty."

"As they say, it is the best policy." She twisted a lip, her amusement at my struggle quite apparent. "Carry on."

"You intrigue me. I don't want the grocery shopping date to end and I really hate grocery shopping. You clearly know baseball and even though you declined my proposal, I'm willing to give you another chance." I meant every word and I enjoyed the heat in her eyes. However brief it remained, I cheered inside.

"How kind of you." Her face was unlike anyone's I had ever met. "How about this? I'm all about fate and overcoming challenges. I'll give you my name. But the rest is up to you."

"Fair enough." I loved a challenge.

"Callie."

"Callie? No last name?" I begged. She began walking away and I had no choice but to let her. My dream girl played games and yet she'd somehow caught me.

"I'm a student here. That's all you're getting." She pushed out of the aisle and grinned at me one last time. "As we say, the ball is on your field now."

Chapter Three

Callie

"Have you ever had something like that happen to you?" I asked Greta, explaining to her what had happened at Target. "It felt like a scene from a movie, I tell you."

"I love it. That sounds amazing." She swooned, grabbing a plate of pasta. "We're getting back to that, but have I told you again how much I love you?"

"You're only saying that because I cooked you food." I chuckled, not disliking her open affection *all* the time. "Plus, my dad taught me how to cook well."

"Thank you, Mr. Williams," she moaned after taking a bite and a shiver of pride went through me. "But, our sexy mystery stranger. Describe him again to me."

"Tall, strong as hell, kind hazel eyes." My pulse quickened with just a thought about him. I had never in my life enjoyed a random conversation nor liked grocery shopping like I had earlier. "His jaw line — I tell you, paintings didn't have shit on him."

"His hair? Dark or blond?"

"Dark, messy but styled. He had the scruff going for him, too." I closed my eyes, replaying our conversation. *I haven't had one person affect me that much before. Ever. Why is it terrifying the hell out of me?*

"Dark hair is my jam. And a beard? Butter me up and marry me."

"You're a nut." I released a long, pent-up breath. "He towered over me. I love tall guys for some reason. And I could see the outside of abs from his shirt. Washboard."

"Lady boner city. I hate you for not getting his number. It sounds like he would've gladly given it to you."

"I have zero clue why I did that. But it felt right. If I never see him again, it's a perfectly juicy story I can keep in my spank bank for years." I joined her at the table and ate my portion of the pasta. "He was almost too attractive. Plus, you know how important the year is for me. I can't afford distractions. No matter how damn good-looking they are."

She scoffed. "Please. You're not doubting yourself, are you? You're pretty damn hardworking—I know you'll kick ass. Screw your parents' doubts."

I cringed, unsure at her words. Every time pride filled my chest, insecurities snuck in and I doubted myself. *Why did I think I could do this?* "I don't know."

"You *do* know. I know." She put her arm around me. "Wasn't he interested? Are you trying to play it cool?"

"Nah, the interest went both ways. He hid nothing with his heated looks and accidental touches." I appreciated guys who made it clear and didn't play games, stringing girls along.

"We are going to get hit on infinitely all year. The dynamic duo is back at it." She wiggled her eyebrows at me really fast and I groaned in response.

"Not that again."

"Oh yeah. I'm using you for your looks. I'm not above that."

"I'm positive you're not." I thought about the shenanigans we'd gotten into in high school, and winced. We were quite the pair. My hair dark and curly, hers blonde and straight. My athletic curves, her tall, willowy figure. We had a reputation that some might consider bad, others awesome. I loved her to pieces and had had a dorky countdown until move-in day. Three years living with my best friend...hell yeah.

"You and Chris. The baseball player from our rival school. You were the talk of the town." She just had to bring up the worst dating story of all time and I stuck my tongue out at her. "Even your dad—"

"Threatened to disown me. I know. *I know*. But, I wanted to lick him. Swoon-worthy boys make girls do foolish things. Myself included." I sighed and batted my eyelashes. "Totally remember he had great hands, too."

"Okayyy, weirdo. Did Mr. T have good hands?"

"Mr. T?"

"Mr. Target. Until we find out his name, he's Mr. T."

"I oddly like that." The nickname created an awkward vision in my head. My mysterious stranger and the real Mr. T combining into one superhuman. I shook the thought away before it became more bizarre. "He had great hands and I have a feeling he plays baseball somewhere. He threw in as many baseball zingers as I did."

"If anyone had the ability to slide into home with you, ten bucks it'd be a baseball player." She chuckled. "I hope for both our sakes you see him again."

"Your sake?" I arched an eyebrow. "Explain that."

"I want to see your hunky specimen handmade by god for you. If not, I have no choice but to assume love is dead."

"Dead, eh? What's going on with you and Tanner?" I switched the attention from me to her. It worked like a charm, her face cheeks tinging red.

"Nothing's happening, really. We've been friends for the past year or so, casually, but then all summer we began hanging out every week."

"And?" I egged her on. "Clearly something's there. I sensed it, saw it in action and frankly I'm hurt you didn't tell me about it."

"Callie!" Her face fell and I broke out into a laugh. "You were messing with me, weren't you?"

"Damn straight, woman. I know you wouldn't keep something from me. However, we need to come up with a plan for you and Tanner to get physical. Let's get physical, physical." I continued to sing the old song and Greta joined in with her squeaky voice.

"I do plan on wearing something really body hugging for tonight. Do a little shimmy here, shimmy there. He can't miss it." Greta did a little boob dance at the table and I laughed, loving her even more.

"He'd be stupid or blind if he missed it." I stood and picked up her empty plate. "Cook's rules — cooks don't clean."

"You can cook for me every damn day and I'll clean every inch of the place." Greta hugged me again and I leaned into it. She had been and always would be my rock.

"We've got ourselves a deal."

"Good. You go shower and pick out a girlie outfit. We leave in an hour."

* * * *

"Tanner will flip." Greta pulled down the hem of her summer dress, with pockets again, as I tried to assure her the dress fit her perfectly.

"I think I distance myself because I'm afraid of rejection. He's one of the best ball players here. He could have any girl. Why pick me, ya know? I'd rather stay friends than try and be humiliated."

"That's brave of you to admit. I think half the problem people our age have is fear of rejection." I sighed, thinking of all the bad dates we'd been on and the countless horror stories of dating. "You are amazing and are one of the best damn people I know. Tanner cares about you, friend or more than friends, and you don't have to make any decision right now. Because you promised me these parties were fun. And I want to have some fun." I hooked my arm around her neck, her height even with mine in her heels. "This is my first college party. I'm sweating. I'm nervous."

"I'm a terrible friend. I'm worrying about boy issues when I should be celebrating us being in college together after all these years. Punch my tits."

"I'll wait to cash that in when it's needed. Like, if you're being a twat one day. Right now is not that moment. We are going to walk into that party and have fun, damn it!"

"Yes! C and G are back, baby!" Greta shouted and some girls across the street cheered us. We burst out laughing and took our time on our way to the house. "Now, you've met Tanner and Aaron. Hopefully you'll get to meet the other two guys. They're dreamy as hell."

"Who are you calling dreamy? It better be me, Greta." Aaron poked his head out of the front door with a big-ass grin.

"Of course. You're a gem, Aaron." Greta went to hug him. "You smell nice. I'm proud you showered."

"When you have sex as much as I do, you have to keep it clean." He winked at me and I choked on my laugh.

"God, you're a slut." His face broke into a shit-eating grin and I thought his over the top sex-crazed brain entertaining.

"Self-diagnosed and no sign of rehab. Come on in, ladies. Greta, your dress...damn girl. Damn."

"Thanks. Thought I'd try it out." She blushed.

"Killing it." Aaron held the door open for me and gave me an up and down. "Callie, you slay me."

"How's that?" I winked at him, which he ate up.

"Not many girls choose to wear outfits like yours to our house." I frowned at my black skinny jeans and gray crop top.

"I can't decide if you insulted me or nah." I peered up at him, to see him checking out my ass. "Aaron."

"My bad. You're rocking the jeans. But, no, that wasn't an insult at all. I hate to sound like a tool bag but—"

"If you start a sentence like that, it probably means you are. Just saying." I held up a hand to protect myself and heard laughter behind me. I twirled around to see a pair of long legs and yet another incredibly attractive guy.

"He is a tool. Don't let him fool you." The deep, commanding drew me in and I had a hard time looking away. *Why is their house filled with models? Why am I sweating? Ugh!*

"You must be one of the other roommates. I'm Callie."

I went over to shake his hand, but not before wiping mine on my jeans, and his large grip swallowed mine.

"Hi, Callie. I'm Jeff. Nice to meet you. Don't let Aaron get you all ruffled up. He's like the little kid who always runs around the neighborhood."

"I heard that, asshole." Aaron smacked Jeff on the back of the head. "And I told her most girls wouldn't wear that here."

"Oh, right. Because you guys host *orgy* parties. My mistake. I'll leave the clothing at home next time." I crossed my eyes and both Aaron and Jeff laughed.

"He might be exaggerating a bit." Jeff smiled sheepishly. "But, trust me, you are fine as hell in that outfit."

"Seriously, do all of you guys just ooze sex all the time? All of you could be models." I caught Greta's eye. "Seriously, G. Are they always like this?"

"Pretty much. They're just a bunch of horny guys who are *way* too good-looking for their own good. It doesn't help they're hella good at baseball."

"Are they safe?"

Jeff laughed again. "We are. The red room of pain is downstairs." His reference to *Fifty Shades* made me snort. They had a sense of humor and were attractive enough to be models. The combo made me question Greta's *just friendship* with them.

"Okay, good. For the future, my safe word is 'banana'."

Greta threw back her head and laughed and I joined her on the couch. "What's your safe word?"

"I feel we should stick to a theme. Cucumber."

"Penis-shaped foods. My favorite. My safe word will be...hmm...'sausage'?" Aaron ended it with a question. "Too far?"

"A bit." I took in my surroundings. Jeff sat on the other side of me and handed both me and Greta cans of beer. I wasn't much of a drinker, having only tried it a handful of times in high school. I didn't want to drink if I could help it but didn't want to stick out. I opened it and nodded to him. "Thank you."

"No problem. I'm glad we could meet. This one has been talking about you all summer." He pointed to Greta and she put her arm around me.

"Aww, you're the best, G." I leaned in to her for a second. "I'm glad to meet you guys, too. It's weird—I know you guys from positions you play or your last names. If you don't know, I'm a huge baseball fanatic."

"She's mentioned it, but how huge?" Jeff asked, interest clear as day on his face. I smiled. I was, somehow, in one day having conversations with the two best-looking people I had ever met in my life.

"Pretty big. My dad coaches a local college team back home and I grew up traveling with them every summer. I've followed the White Sox since birth and can name every member on the roster, the farming system and what's currently wrong with management."

"Good God." Jeff put his hand over his heart. "I feel like I've been struck with something."

I fake-gagged at him but also blushed at the mollification. These guys got chicks like Greta and I binged on reality TV—every night. I enjoyed the flirting—who wouldn't?—but I had zero intention to actually follow through with what they insinuated. "How good are you, then?"

"At what?" he answered, wide-eyed.

"Baseball, you fiend. Do you ever stop?"

"Honestly? No." He held up his beer. "To new friends."

"Here, here." I clinked my can to his and some of my anxiety left, the tense butterflies in my stomach flitting away. *I can totally do this. I can make friends and be social...and normal. Yeah. I can.* "I think it's going to be one hell of a night."

"Hells, yeah!" Greta yelled.

"Now, want to visit the red room of pain?" Jeff asked, a smirk forming.

"I think it means something else, but once again, if I say banana, you have to let me go," I flirted back.

"Deal." He motioned for me to head to the basement. "The rest of you coming? If we're gonna do it, let's do it right! I want our reputation to precede us."

Chapter Four

Zade

"You are damn lucky I love you." I cleaned the dishes as my sister rolled around on the couch, moaning in despair. "You take me for granted."

"I don't wanna hear it. You took all the attention away from me when you were born. I want redemption," she wined, sounding pathetic as hell. Maybe I should be nicer — she still appeared to be sick and all. Zaria hated admitting any weakness so it had to be major. Plus, her roommate didn't return for another two weeks, leaving her solo at her place.

"I'm better looking than you. That's why." I said the one thing I knew angered her. She growled into the pillow and I chuckled. "Don't hate, appreciate."

"You're annoying."

"I bought you tampons. You owe me majorly. And I mean *majorly*." I cringed, thinking about the terror again. Except I'd gotten to meet Callie, which had been the highlight of the month.

"I know. You're a real hero." She reached for some tissues and blew her nose. "You mentioned someone helped you pick them out? How in the world does that happen?"

"She offered to help, commented on my Toledo Mud Hens hat and we hung out for an hour or so. She refused to give me more than her name and, this is the best part, she said she goes to the university. She has to know who I am, right?" I could barely walk into a dining hall or lecture without people coming up and talking to me. Professors who I'd never had said hello to me. I know I was dabbling with an ego problem, but I had broken plenty of school records and made a good name for myself on the field. The attention had been well earned, in my opinion.

"You are pretentious as hell, baby brother. Maybe, just *maybe*, the girl knew who you were but didn't want to start anything because you're *you*." Zaria spoke with love, but her words stung a bit. We shared almost everything except my hookups, but she also wasn't stupid. She attended the same school to become a teacher, only a year older than me, and unfortunately she knew about my, uh, fans. Hell, even our mom gave me shit about them every once in a while.

"I never thought of that. Honestly though, her eyes showed no recognition. She never asked my name, which makes me question her. But I judge people pretty quickly and I had no warning signs." I frowned, trying to perceive any hint of fame chaser in her. "She caught my attention for more than an hour. First time it's happened to me."

"Hell. Zade, I find you sad and hilarious." Zaria picked up her cup of tea with a spark in her eyes. She gave me a grin that I knew from experience meant she was enjoying my pain. "Tell me more. No, tell me *everything*."

"Aren't you sick? Wipe that smile off your face and stop being a pain." I took my phone off the charger and replied to the group message sent from my teammates and housemates. They were having another party. I always had a good time at them, but I wanted to sit tonight out. Plus, Zaria and I always hung out once a week. Our mom had instilled the rule without room for negotiation since she'd gone to Europe for the year. She demanded weekly calls with us both present. Finding time in our schedule had been tricky, but somehow Zaria and I had worked out a routine. Our mom had moved away four months ago, thriving in her late career, and we wanted nothing but the best for her.

"You look smitten. How cute. I'm emailing mom in the morning with a page-long summary. She'll love it." She laughed, but then it transformed into a pathetic cough. I cringed. She sounded gross. I regretted coming over.

"I shouldn't have fucking told you."

"Yeah, yeah, yeah. But you need advice and I'm an expert." She had always been a little *too* smug with her counsel.

"It wouldn't be creepy to Google Image Callie and students at the university, right?"

She broke out into laughter.

"Probably, then?"

"Why not? I think it's vague and this girl is way too good for you." She leaned back and closed her eyes. "Obviously I like her. And approve. Callie from Target."

"I'll let you rest. I'm going to read up on some baseball stats."

"You crashing here?"

"Maybe. There's a party at the house. If I head back, I'll have to hang. Not sure if I'm up for it. I have a killer run tomorrow." I'd decided to train for a half marathon, to keep me focused in the off season but also to raise money for a charity. Three of the other guys, none of whom were my roommates, were also doing it. I wanted to be prepared before we began our group runs because, although I worked out a shit ton for baseball, I had zero running endurance. People assumed athletes were able to run or go upstairs without getting winded, but I always got out of breath. I hated it.

"You know where the couch is. Have at it." She stood, sniffed and gave me a sleepy smile. "Thanks for helping me tonight. You're the best, bro."

"You got it, Z." I uncovered her laptop from the excuse she called a desk, helping myself to it. I did my normal routine of checking the baseball highlights. The nerves and anxiety about the future grabbed hold of me every time. I wanted the opportunity to play in the majors more than I could breathe. The dream and desire had burned in me for the past year — well, more like since birth. Every single decision I made followed the path to achieve my dream and it caused me just as much anxiety as it did excitement. I already had the attention of three scouts after a killer Freshman year, had talked with two others and had begun looking for an agent. It was *almost* happening.

My phone went off with a notification from Aaron. I clicked on the Snapchat, assuming he'd sent me a video of chicks making out or dancing. I watched a dumb video taking place in our game room. Greta, a cute girl who'd become a good friend over the past year, stood playing a game of foosball with some other girl. Aaron placed the camera on them, Jeff standing next to them with his arm around... *No. No fucking way.*

Callie. My Callie. Callie from Target! My heart raced, my ego needing to know if she'd played me, but my gut telling me to find her. I fired off a text to Aaron to keep her company and ran out of my sister's townhouse. Adrenaline coursed through me, making me tap my fingers on the wheel of my jeep as I broke every speed limit to reach the house.

Why is she at the house? Does she know who I am and messed with me as a prank? Jeff...he loved pranking me. *Asshole.* The thought of being played pissed me off. I thought we'd clicked and I wanted to spend more time with her. I hadn't been captivated by a girl in...well, forever. *Fuck.*

The music blared as I parked down the street. I had to walk to the house and it annoyed me. *Why live here if I can't park in the driveway?*

"Hey, Zwillow! Lookin' good, baby."

"Z-man. How's the arm doin?"

"Z-money. My main guy, good to see ya."

I waved at the various passersby as I ran up the sidewalk. I appreciated their concern and interest in my pitching career, but I wasn't feeling diplomatic or noble. My mission remained — find Callie. The front door stood wide open and I made a mental note to say something to Aaron and Tanner. They were the party animals, Jeff being the middle child who went along with the flow and I took the cool, older brother persona to heart. I looked out for them but also had a lot of fun. I walked in to the sound of a raging party and had decided to head downstairs when long fingernails clawed my arm. I saw who had touched me and sucked in a breath of dismay.

"Veronica." I jerked at her fingers on me and waited for her to remove them. She took her time, caressing my chest in the process.

"Zade. I came here hoping to run into you." Her high-pitched baby voice made me cringe.

"I live here, so yeah, odds were good," I replied. I had no desire to talk to her now, or ever again. She used men and was toxic to the baseball team. She wanted to fuck a baseball player and I wouldn't have put it past her to film it. *Hell to the no.*

"When are we going to do this? We both want it. Why fight it?" she purred, thrusting her large tits in my chest. "I'm not wearing anything under my dress."

I cringed, desperate to get away from her. I gently pushed her out of my way. "I need to head downstairs."

"Zade. Me and you will happen." She flashed her eyes in warning and a shiver went through me. She defined the word crazy with a capital *C*.

"Whatever." I upped and left her standing with demons in her eyes. *Let her try, but hell no. Never touching her.* I had standards, most of the time.

I stormed down the stairs, heart pounding harder than it should have been. I darted my gaze around the game room, searching for the face I had etched into my mind. "Jeff!"

"Hey, man. I didn't think you'd be here tonight. Good to see ya." He gave me a bro hug and I clapped his back.

"Where's Callie?" I asked, searching the room.

"Callie? You know her? What the hell? I called dibs." He frowned and shook his head.

"*Dibs?* Come on, we don't do that." Anger poured through me and he flinched at my aggression. Hell, it scared me, too.

"Fuck. I met her tonight, bro. I didn't realize you knew her." He held up his hands and shrugged. "I think she left a bit ago."

"Damn it. Do you know her last name?"

"Uh, no." He gave me a weird look. "What's going on?"

"It's hard to explain without making me seem pathetic." I ran my hand through my hair. "Is Greta still here?"

"Probably left with Callie. That's her best friend she talked about all summer who's starting here. She moved here from Chicago yesterday." He tilted his head in confusion. "I don't want to step on your toes here, man, but she's a hell of a girl."

"I met her earlier today. She didn't give me anything but her name. She intrigued the hell out of me. Then I saw Aaron's Snapchat. I rushed over here." I saw no signs of Greta or Callie, but humor danced in Jeff's eyes. "What?"

"I'm enjoying this. You struggling." He attempted to cover his mouth with his hand, but failed.

"Fuck off." I put no heat in the words and sighed in resignation. "I might as well have a beer or two. I guess I won't see her tonight."

"I think we'll be seeing a lot of her. But I have a feeling that Greta will kill you."

"Why are you smiling about it?" Sure, he was my catcher and he had my back both on and off the field, meaning I trusted him to no end, but I didn't like the knowing expression on his face.

"Because if any girl could kick your ass, my money is on Callie."

"You know for sure after hanging out with her for an hour?" I barked at him, realizing the hypocrisy of my words. It all made sense now. She didn't know who I was. She defined my dream woman—baseball talk, naturally beautiful and had a great sense of humor. I'd never pegged myself to have a type, but I wanted her to be it.

"Pretty much. She handled Aaron like she was his babysitter. That takes someone with balls and moxie."

"*Moxie?*"

"My mom sent me a word of the day calendar and that one stuck with me." He peered down, almost embarrassed.

"Own that shit, dude. You're sounding smart as hell. Kind of contradicting the whole 'dark mysterious catcher' thing you normally do."

"Thanks for the pep talk." He lifted his head, an odd look taking over his face. "If I can ask, what would you say to Callie if you saw her here?"

"Hadn't thought that through yet. Probably demand her last name. Ask her out."

"Interesting." He ran his hand over his jaw and winked at someone in the distance. I followed his gaze and thought I'd fallen through cracked ice. Callie stood on the other side of the room, looking over at us. When her eyes met mine, they widened and she broke out into a one of the biggest, best smiles I had ever seen.

"Dude, seems like whatever happened earlier is in your favor. Good luck, bro." Jeff clapped my back and left me on my own.

I stayed put as she walked toward me. She wore a shirt that showed off two inches of her toned stomach and I inwardly groaned. How no one else in the room was begging at her feet beat me. She owned the room with her walk. She stopped in front of me, shaking her head.

"What are the odds, eh?" Her eyes danced with a joy that matched mine. "Part of me should feel worried that you stalked me."

"I'm the one who should be worried." My voice came out gruff and hoarse, the exact opposite of how I felt inside.

"Why's that?" She moved her weight to one of her hips, the shift causing her head to tilt a little to the side. Her dimples came out again and I fought the urge to kiss them.

"I live here."

Chapter Five

Callie

"I can see how you'd be concerned then," I replied, shocked at the coincidence. I swore he could hear my heart, the beat echoing throughout my chest. "I assure you I did not stalk you."

"I wouldn't have minded." He bent lower, his presence intoxicating and overwhelming. I wanted to wrap his scent around me at the same time as I wanted to run for the hills. The draw to him was too much, too strong and too everything I avoided. I refused to let him be a distraction and consume me because I knew that story already. He struggled to talk. I knew the feeling. He grinned and shrugged. "I tried to find you online."

"How'd that work out for you?" I asked, curious and appreciative of his bluntness. It wasn't every day a guy who had *his* face and *his* body admitted to chasing a girl.

"Not well. I regretted the second we parted not getting your number." He smiled down at me and that made my toes curl. All the attention made me feel like the only person in the room.

"It's best to live life without regrets. Regrets are just moments you learn from." I cringed at my incessant need to use cheesy sayings when my emotions overwhelmed me. "Like, I'm going to learn from the fact that I use dorky quotes multiple times a day."

He laughed, the crooked smile causing all sorts of feelings to rush through me. "Then I'm going to demand I get your number. I hate regrets, and I regret not asking earlier."

"Hot damn. You charmed me." I gave him my number and heard the notification of a text from him.

"I texted you. Now you have my number. Please, feel free to use it anytime, all the time. I feel like this opportunity is too good to pass up." I held up my hand to slow him down.

"While I agree with you, I have some more tests for you to pass." He smiled, revealing he'd enjoyed my challenge earlier.

"Bring it on." His eyes crinkled at the sides, a gesture that came from smiling a lot. His wrinkles made me inexplicably happy.

"They might be tough, kind of difficult to get through." I lowered my voice and leaned in closer. "Are you sure?"

"Let's start now. Follow me." He held out his hand and waited for me to take it. I paused, debating my inner turmoil. *Is it moving too fast? Do I trust myself? Do I care?*

I'd moved here to follow a dream and take chances...and he might be worth the risk. I took his hand and he rubbed his thumb over mine as he led me out of the basement.

I noticed the glares and odd looks I received, but I didn't think anything of it. They had no idea who I was or why I was leaving the room in an oh-so suggestive way, but they weren't my friends and I didn't care. *I* knew I wasn't going to sleep with him. Fuck the rest of the noise. As they say, *Haters gonna hate.* He pulled me to a second set of stairs but stopped, causing me to run straight into his back. His incredibly hard back.

"Ouch!" I rubbed my nose and he spun around with an apology already forming on his lips. I waved him off, but he bent his face to almost touch mine. His eyes were out of this world, blue and yellow rings making an oddly hazel color. They *glowed.* I loved that about some people. Their joy shone from them. Joy easily spread to others and I hoped I projected that for people, too.

"Let me see. Are you okay?" He took my face in his large hands. He searched deep into my eyes and I held my breath. His lips were close to mine. *Inches away.* "Callie?"

"Physically, yeah." My voice came out in a pathetic whisper.

"What's wrong, then?" he asked, concern pouring out of those eyes. They were going to be a problem.

"I'm having a hard time thinking when your mouth is that close to me. You have a really nice mouth." I felt the color drain from my face. *Not* smooth. *Not smooth at all.*

He licked his bottom lip and bit down on it, not hiding the fact that he found me funny. "You have a nice mouth, too."

"It sounds worse when you say it back." I closed my eyes and shook my head as though it had the power to rewind the past minute. "I'm learning I shouldn't talk when my head is all fuzzy."

He laughed and ran his thumb over my bottom lip before standing again. "I like your 'no regrets' mantra."

"What can I say? I'm pretty wise." My normal wit came back after he stood up. I'd *never* reacted to anyone like I did to him. It unnerved and exhilarated me.

He opened a door to a room and paused before meeting my eyes. "I know it looks like I'm inviting you into my room, but trust me, we aren't going there."

"Hmm. You have one shot to not mess it up." I meant the words as a half-joke, but he nodded. "I think you have two strikes from earlier, still."

"Fair enough. I'm pretty good at staying alive with the count full." He winked, which only some people could pull off. He *definitely* pulled it off.

He motioned for me to follow him and led me to a window. "Let me open it really quick and I'll help you get up."

"Take your time. I'm being nosy." I inspected the pictures on the built-in desk in front of the window. "Is she your sister who you were shopping for?"

"Yes. I wasn't lying." He pushed the panes open, the fresh air smelling fantastic. "I told her all about you."

"Yeah?" I blushed and grinned at his comment. "And?"

"She already likes you for not giving me your number." He hopped up onto the desk and held out his hand for me to join him. I took it and he pulled me up with little effort. We sat side by side, our legs pressed together. I froze, the attraction drowning me.

"Is this the place you usually take your conquests? Your desk?" I tried joking, but it came out like an awkward grunt. "I mean, it's nice and all, but..."

"Yes. My desk usually seals the deal." He laughed and scooted back farther and now sat on the roof. "However, the roof is actually the spot I wanted. Come on."

He held out his hand, crouching on all fours, and I took it. The moon shone in the background, the music pounded from the basement and yet time seemed to freeze like a Hallmark movie. I must've stopped moving because his eyes narrowed in concern. "Callie? It's pretty level out here. You won't fall. I promise."

I gave him a shaky smile, letting him believe the height had trigged my mental freak-out. I crawled out of the window and sighed as we sat on the roof of an old house. It leveled out and although my heart raced like a clown was chasing me, a sense of ease surrounded me. Comfort with him and his words, his kind eyes and the way his body pressed against mine.

"I love a challenge, so, quiz me, woman." He sat with his arms around his knees, his large frame looking childish. The gesture warmed my heart and I mirrored his stance, our shoulders touching in the process. He shifted his weight to glance at me, those eyes doing things to me, and I gave him a shy smile.

"What's your name?" I asked.

"Zade Willows." He leaned closer, his ear inches from my neck. His heart beat against my back and I broke out in goosebumps despite the humidity. "What's your last name, Callie?"

"Williams." His name rang bells, sounding familiar, but I had no idea how. I frowned, thinking as hard as I could where I might have heard that name.

"Callie Williams. I like your name. Is that an odd thing to say to a girl?" he asked.

"I don't think it is. I'll take the compliment. I went to high school with a girl named Afreeka. I've been blessed with a simple name." I enjoyed how his body shook with light laughter. "I know your name somehow and it's frustrating as hell because I can't think of how. Did we secretly know each other already?"

"Hell, no. I wouldn't have stayed away if I knew you before." He spoke with such unabashed certainty that I blushed. I didn't blush easily.

"I oddly believe you with that statement. You seem to be someone who goes after what they want." I played with a loose hem on my jeans and thought about my next question. "What's the story about being a Detroit fan?"

"Ah, yes. I'll explain, but then I need to hear your White Sox story. It's only fair. Also, I've been dying to know how you clearly know a lot about baseball." He shifted. Now he sat in front of me. We weren't touching, but we had nowhere to look but at each other.

"Of course." I waited, desperate to learn anything and everything about him.

"My family is my mom, sister and me. It isn't some sad struggle story, but my dad left us when we were kids and the three of us grew closer. We lived outside Detroit and my mom always got free tickets to Tigers games from her work and we went to them every summer as a family. It's nostalgic and built the first blocks of my love of the game." He took my hand in his. A tremor went all the way through my body as he intertwined our fingers. Butterflies broke out…no, more like a damn zoo stampede. "I promise this isn't a trick or some line I use, but my sister is honestly one of my best friends. Our family is close and baseball is a shared love."

"No, I believe you." *Swoon. Everything is almost too easy, too coincidental, and I should be freaking out.* But I'd promised myself I wasn't playing those mind games. I needed to take chances and live. I worked hard enough to find some enjoyment. "Zade, baseball is romantic. The history, the fans, the players, traditions, the camaraderie…everything is romantic from the first pitch to the last out. I get it. I'd hate for you to think this is a line I use on guys a lot, but my family lives for baseball."

He chuckled and squeezed my hand tighter. "Oh, yeah? How's that?"

"My dad is a college coach and every summer we traveled with his team. I always kept score in the dugout and my mom pretty much became the mother hen of the team. Snacks and towels and water and all that. We've had players live with us in the summer and off months and we've been to five weddings. Baseball is a way of life. It takes Dedication and hard work to be a fan of the sport."

"God, that is probably the sexiest thing you could say to me." He bit his lower lip in a seductive grin, one I'd never get out of my mind. "How do you know about the Mud Hens, though?"

"One of my dad's players and my friends, Bryce, plays for them right now. My parents went to one of his games earlier in the summer, but I couldn't make it. He has a lot of potential throwing, but he still has some kinks to work out before they call him up." I sighed, momentarily thinking about Bryce and his arm. I should call my dad the next day to catch them up on my weekend thus far. The thought of my dad made my stomach tighten — we were not on the best of terms. My departure for a school hours away had not sat well with him. But I pushed it to the back of my mind and focused on the handsome guy in front of me.

"That is fucking awesome. I'm glad you decided to move here." He did his half-smile at me, but I frowned.

"How did you know that?" I never remembered Greta mentioning him as one of her friends and the wheels started turning. I was in a romantic daze where my brain acted slower than normal, but I had a feeling I knew who he was. And it wasn't a good feeling.

"Jeff told me." He looked self-conscious but met my eyes. "I was at my sister's tonight helping her. She really is sick." He winked again, his magical eyes toying with me. "But I saw a video from Aaron and you were in it. I rushed over here."

"I'm flattered, but should I be concerned about that?" I teased, knowing I would've done the same thing.

"Nah, I'm not creepy. I prefer the word 'dedicated'. I haven't smiled that much with someone I just met, ever."

"I have to agree with you on that one. It is overwhelming, though, don't you think?" I waited for his answer. *Our chemistry is crazy, intense and most definitely two-sided.*

"I've never met anyone like you before." His eye pierced mine. "It is a lot to deal with, but I like high-pressure situations. I can handle it."

"I'm assuming you mean on the field? You have baseball player written all over you." I scooted over and pulled my hand out of his grasp. "Let's see here. Hmm." I ran my fingers down his forearm, a bold and foreign move on my part, and caressed his muscles.

"Strong forearm, left slightly larger than the right." He sucked in a breath and kept his eyes on mine. My presence affected him and the notion empowered me. I traced the vein that bulged out. "My bet is left-handed pitcher, definitely a starter. You have the confidence and swagger needed."

"You're killing me right now, by the way." His eyes heated over in the sexiest way. "You're spot-on."

"Not my intention, but I'm enjoying it. No bases will be met tonight, Zade Willows." The name. *Zade Willows. Zwillows.* I knew him. I'd heard of him. Greta had told me *all* about him. I released my hand and jumped back. The recognition and awareness threw a bucket of cold water over me.

"What's wrong? Are you all right?" The heat lingered in his eyes but now worry had taken over. I blinked a couple of times, wishing I hadn't figured it out. He had a reputation. A womanizing one. *What a deal-breaker.*

"I'm okay." I sighed, squeezing my eyes shut as an unwelcome pain went through my chest. "I should go, Zade." I said his name with a hint of regret and his face fell. I felt bad, but I knew I could never get involved with him. I knew the type and it always led to heartbreak.

"What happened? I thought I read the signs like we were really hitting it off? Did I say something?"

I shook my head. "I'm sorry if I led you to believe...I don't know. We were flirting. But I just, hell, I need to head out right now. I'm sorry. Nothing can happen. *We* can't happen." I crawled to the window and slid down the desk. I paused, fighting the urge to cry. My eyes stung as I ran into Greta on the stairs. She didn't even ask why when we walked out of the party two minutes later. *God, what did I do to deserve her as my BFF?*

"Care to share or want to wait?" Her calm voice and her arm around me grounded me.

"Mr. T is Zade Willows."

She hissed and let out a string of cuss words. "I did not see that coming."

Chapter Six

Zade

I woke up feeling hungover, although I wasn't at all. The clock read six and I groaned as I got ready for a seven-mile run. Fuck if I wanted to forget the whole half marathon and play video games all day. *Am I depressed?* The feeling was unnerving and unfamiliar. I thought about asking my friends, but I already knew their reactions. Zaria always blamed me for doing something wrong, Jeff and Aaron laughed at me and my mom, well, she rationalized and picked the best solution.

I had no idea what had happened with Callie, but it had fucking sucked. Something had changed for the worse and I needed to find out what it was. A long run always cleared my head, or at least burned a couple hundred calories. I snatched my phone and headphones, needing a hell of a playlist to get me pumped. Before running, though, I needed food. The kitchen had every shelf filled, thanks to my roommates' moms. Some might call it cheesy, but we appreciated our moms. They were the backbone of baseball players. When we needed encouragement, they were there. When we needed advice, a reality check or food, they were there. I sent a quick text to my mom to talk later.

"Morning." A voice purred at me from the hallway. I recognized her as one of Veronica's friends, Lilly or Laurie or something. Another cleat chaser and nothing but trouble. I refused to acknowledge her. "Grumpy today? Did you not get a happy ending with the new girl last night? Shame, shame. I can give you a quickie right now if you want."

"Do you even have dignity left? No. I'm more than okay," I barked at her. I hated girls who reeked of desperation. "Get the hell out of here."

"Mm. You are cranky. Let me help you." She walked up and put her hands on my shoulders, the contact making me cringe. I had no idea what she carried or who she'd slept with. I needed trust and my mom had warned me about the types of girls who wanted a guy for one reason alone—popularity. She stank of one of those girls and I needed to warn the other guys about her.

"Please don't touch me." I stood, causing her hands to drop and her face to sour into a godawful expression. "I'm heading out."

I slammed the door, opting out of eating anything more than fruit. I'd luckily put my wallet in my pocket because I would need food after the run. I preferred to not dodge the crazy slut all morning, actually. Thank god I'd bought a lock for my bedroom door. I knew I sounded whiney about girls chasing us because we were baseball players about to go into the majors, but sometimes it sucked. *Like right now.*

I blasted some punk rock and took off running down the trail by our house. No one else was out, it being an early Sunday morning. I welcomed the peace. Three miles in, my lungs got used to the movement. I powered through the first cramp when it settled into a rhythm for the last four miles. I thought about the future, what I wanted and of course Callie. I hadn't had a relationship since high school. And, honestly, that really hadn't been a relationship — more a continuous hookup for a couple of weeks. I wasn't a relationship type of guy. I didn't do flowers or dates or romantic dinners. But Callie could have dragged me anywhere and I'd probably have gone. I needed to talk to her and demand answers.

The world enjoyed playing with me sometimes and this had to be one of those times, because, farther up the trail, I saw a long dark ponytail bouncing in a run and tan, athletic legs. I grinned, sped up and, by god, Callie had chosen to run the same time I did. She had headphones in and wore tiny running shorts. *Fuck me.* Every step she took, I fell harder. I didn't want to scare her so I sent a quick text, hoping she'd read it.

I paced myself behind her and she turned back, recognition on her face. I waved at her. She didn't stop running but pulled out her headphones. I took that as an invitation and ran up next to her. "Hey." *God, I sound lame.*

"Morning." She kept her pace and continued running straight ahead. "If you weren't sweating like you've been running for a while, I might accuse you of stalking me."

"I can see how that it looks that way. But no, I've already run three miles. Four more to go."

"Training for anything or off-season workouts?" She spoke in a friendly tone, but she didn't meet my eyes. Unlike me, she didn't gasp for each breath.

"Both. What about you?"

"Eh. Nothing in particular. I like running 5Ks. I like the free shirts."

I laughed and changed my pace to be a little slower and match hers. "You run every day?"

"Almost every day, yeah."

"Alone?" I frowned, not liking that idea. It was a semi-safe neighborhood, but some muggings and assaults had been reported in the past couple of months. Plus, when all the college kids came back, the numbers increased because of all the intoxicated dumbasses.

"Yeah. I thought it was safe. Why?"

"It is, but, a couple of incidents occurred last year. Nothing major." Did I want to scare her? No. Did I want to convince her to run with me? *Yes. Hell yes.* "I'm actually looking for someone to train with for the half marathon coming up in November. Any interest?"

"Damn it." She shook her head, not breaking stride. "That sounds like a good deal, but I don't want you to get the wrong idea."

"It's just running." My stomach dropped, though, because that wasn't a good sign. "It helps us both out. We get along—well, I thought so at least, and you shouldn't run alone. Plus, I need a partner."

"Let me think about it. Sometimes I like to run in silence."

"Me too." I did, but I'd have agreed to about anything to get her run with me. "How about this? We finish the run today then I buy you breakfast and we discuss the terms."

"That sounds like a date."

"I don't do dates, Callie. It's breakfast. Order a waffle or an eggo. I don't care."

She frowned for a second then broke out into a smile. *Thank god.* "I can do that. I love me some eggos."

"There ya go. That wasn't bad, eh?"

"Shut up. We have over three miles left and you're exhausting my thinking power right now."

"Is it because of my good looks?"

"I regret my decision already." She bit back a smile and we continued to run in a comfortable silence.

* * * *

"God, I didn't stretch enough. I hate myself." I lay on the grass on my back, pulling my legs to my chest. I waited for a group of kids to pass near us before continuing. "I feel way older than I should right now."

"You're an athlete. You should be in better shape." She had one leg spread out, stretching her hamstrings, and I had a hard time focusing on anything else. Why had I never noticed how sexy girls were when they stretched? *Am I being a total perv?* "You don't need me to tell you about the importance of a pre-run routine."

"Yeah, yeah. You sound like Nicole. Our team trainer. She terrifies me." I wasn't lying. She really did. She was smart as a whip, knew everything but had no filter and had no problem telling is if we were being fucking dumb. Sometimes, I was *fucking dumb.*

"Sounds like a smart lady." She gave me a small smile, a shared moment between us, and I grinned back at her. "Did you bring a water?"

"No, I forget. I rushed to leave the house."

"Here, have some of mine. Why rush out?" I avoided her glance. I didn't know why I didn't want to tell her, but I refused to lie to her. It served no purpose. I took a swig of her water, grateful because my throat was burning.

Shading my eyes with a hand to look at over the park, I collected my thoughts and how to best express them. "Girls stay at the house sometimes. I hate it." I met her eyes, seeing a flicker of recognition and it pissed me off. "Explain the look, Callie."

"Oh, nothing." She darted her gaze away, clearly caught.

"I knew something happened last night, but I couldn't figure it out. We clicked, Callie. You know we did, yet here you are distancing yourself and judging me. I don't think it's fair. I want to know why."

She sighed, meeting my eyes. "I told you I've been around baseball my entire life. I know a lot about the game, and with that, about the egos and types of leaders each team needs. Our attraction distracted me, and I realized I'd already heard of you before. You were only referred to as Zwillow and your reputation is not one I wanted to be a part of."

Anger seethed through me but I kept my composure. "What reputation is that?"

She pulled her legs to sit criss-cross and tangled her fingers together in clear discomfort. "Zade, you mean to tell me that you have no idea of the womanizing reputation you have?"

"I'm curious to hear it from you. I think I need to hear it. Then maybe the spell will be broken." I let my hurt shine through. She wasn't saying anything rude, but it still pissed me off. *The one girl who fascinates me is the one to be put off by my past.*

"You're known for your wicked arm on the field and wicked ways in the bedroom. Girls want to be a notch on your bedpost and you're notorious for 'not doing relationships'. If you can sit here and tell me none of that's true and that you aren't a playboy, then I'll listen." She waited, holding my gaze, but I couldn't deny what she'd said.

"I don't do relationships. That part is true." Disappointment flickered on her face and felt like scum. For someone who avoided feelings, she fucking confused me. "I want to defend myself, but I have a feeling it won't matter."

"I don't bullshit, Zade. I won't be a girl who sleeps with you before you make it to the majors. That isn't who I am. I don't use anyone because of fame or talent. But I also protect myself from people who will hurt me." She released a long, pent-up breath and slowly met my eyes. "But, regardless, I can't afford any distractions. I need to get straight As."

"You think I'd hurt you?" I ignored her grades comment—I'd ask her about it later. I held eye contact, hoping to convey my thoughts. I refused to hurt her, ever.

"If I let you in too far, and you're already further than people I've dated for months, yeah. Yeah, you would. Whether you meant to or not, it's inevitable." She avoided my eyes, choosing to pull up strands of grass instead.

"How so?"

"I know your type. There'll be cleat chasers every step of the way and for someone who says they don't do relationships, it wouldn't work with someone who only sleeps with someone they're committed to." She shrugged, like it made perfect sense. "We get along—

Challenge Accepted

that's clear as day. I don't want it to be awkward. Plus, I'll be studying a lot. I can't have a relationship my first year."

"So what are we going to do then?" I asked, stunned and confused.

"Nothing. We can be friends if you want. I'm almost positive we'll run into each other with Greta being such good friends with your housemates. I enjoy your company, Zade, I really do."

"What about our insane chemistry?" I knew she sensed it. I'd seen it last night, felt it even now, sitting close to her. I affected her as much as she affected me.

"I do not base my decisions off that." She laughed and took a sip of water. "Maybe something'll happen in the future, maybe not. But I'm choosing to not let what we started go further right now."

"I can't say I'm not disappointed."

"I am, too, and I'm sorry. This is like the wrong place, wrong time sort of thing. I wish we met in five years or something." Her head on her hand, she watched me. "I'm not judging you for your past, Zade. I don't judge anyone for past mistakes. But, based on my experiences living the baseball life and even dating some players in the past, I don't want to get hurt. I have to put myself first." Her brown eyes went fiery, passionate. Something else hid behind those eyes and I was dying to figure it out.

"I can't fault you for your honesty." I tried to give her a small smile, but it came out like a grimace. "I've never been in a situation like ours before."

"Being turned down?" Her mouth lifted on one side, a dimple popping out.

"Pretty much," I admitted. "Which I know makes me sound like a tool."

62

"Kind of. But you're not a bad guy."

"But I'm not good enough for you." Any one of my teammates should be nut punching me for sounding like a bitch. But they hadn't met anyone like Callie before.

"I wouldn't say that. Let's just say you aren't throwing what I want to hit. I need a fastball high and outside, but you're throwing change ups and curves."

"I can change my pitches," I begged, not recognizing myself.

"Nah, you can't do that. The curves and change ups are what make you, you." She gave me a small smile and put her hand on my shoulder. "I understand if you don't want to run with me anymore."

"What? I didn't say that." I frowned, pulling her up to stand face-to-face with her. "We're still training together."

"Ar-are you sure?" she stuttered. *Is my proximity getting to her?* I found a small silver lining in my playbook. She used her head too much and I needed to convince her to use her body. I had to win her over somehow.

"Absolutely. I'm not a complete dick. We can be friends, right?" I held out my hand and she glanced at me suspiciously. She should, because she had no idea what I had planned. "Plus, regardless of my reputation, I earned all As last year. I could help you, you know, if you needed it."

"I don't like the mischief in your eyes right now, but sure. We can be friends." She put her hand in mine. We shook and I let go, begrudgingly. "And, I want to earn those grades myself."

"A determined woman is someone I can appreciate. Now how about the eggos? I promised I'd buy."

Chapter Seven

Callie

"Guys, calm down. I'll go get her." I smiled tight-lipped at my parents, because they didn't quite deserve the full one yet. Their faces on the screen wore tentative smiles, too. I loved FaceTime. Greta and I had remained best friends living miles apart for the last year because of it and I'd convinced my parents we'd talk as often as they wanted. It had helped seal the deal with me going here. Well, that and the bargain we'd made prior to my year off. I smoothed out a frown, remembering the contract they'd made me type out. I'd gone a step beyond and gotten it notarized to be a smart-ass. *Of course.* "Greta, get in here!"

"Coming!" She waltzed through my bedroom door and waved to my laptop. "Hi, Mr. and Mrs. Williams!"

"Greta, good lord. We've known you for years. Call us Glenn and Emily," my mom replied, waving back at her. Where my dad could be intense, my mom could be sweet. Right now, she was being sweet.

"It feels too weird. But I can try...Glenn and Emily. Nope, can't do it." She frowned, muttering "nope" over and over. We all chuckled and she joined me on my bed. "How's Chicago?"

"Beautiful right now. Weather has been perfect, not too hot and not too humid. But enough about us — how is it going? Are you going to take care of our girl, Greta?" My dad. *Of course.* I stuck my tongue out at them because I was *that* mature. My maturity had always been an issue, especially with me being an only child. *'You won't survive on your own, Callie. You've never even held down a job, Callie. You can't just move away for school, Callie. You need to earn the right, Callie.'*

Greta's voice brought me back to the present, the awkwardness of the call with my parents hitting me hard. "I mean, I won't leave her in dark alleys every night." she replied without missing a beat.

"Oh good. Once or twice is good for her, but any more than that..." my mom joked, perhaps sensing my tension. She'd always had a sixth sense when it came to my emotions.

"You assholes. I'm right here. I make good decisions." I gritted my teeth, knowing damn well I'd worked hard to save for the year.

"Of course you do, honey," my mom cooed, always the cheerleader and motivator in the family. I could be anything in the world and she would support me. Well, except the career path I wanted, because it wasn't consistent enough. It was a 'gamble' to get into sports medicine. *Ugh, hypocrite.* "Do you like the new apartment?"

"It's super nice. I can't believe Greta managed to get such a hell of a deal." I nudged her with my shoulder. "It's close to campus, has a pool and has parking."

"We like it thus far. She cooks, I clean. We're a nice couple," Greta joked and my parents laughed on cue. I knew how lucky I was, having such an amazing best friend. I don't think I would've worked as extremely hard as I had to go to my dream college if it wasn't for her. My parents had wanted me to attend a community college, get a job to prove I could be responsible and save enough for my first year. After having met all their requirements, I would have a trial shot at the university. *My damn trial year is going to be the death of me.*

"Perfect. I'm glad you called. We wanted to check in with you before school starts." My dad's authoritative voice carried through the speakers.

"Wait, Mr. Williams —"

"Glenn," my dad interrupted her.

"Glenn. Guess who Callie ran into and is now friends with?"

I glared at her. My dad knew everything about Zade Williams. "It's no one, ignore her. I try to." I moved to end the call, but my dad didn't back down.

"Who, Callie?" His sharp eyes met mine.

"Zade Williams," I said the name, Greta grinning like a fool.

"Holy shit. *The* Zade Williams? Z-man? Left-handed pitching, up-and-coming hotshot? No way." My dad's face lit up and my mom lifted her cup of coffee, knowing the conversation was far from over.

"Yes, father. Him." I elbowed Greta. Hard. She knew my parents and I were not on the best terms and yet she still smiled as though everything was rainbows and shit.

"Tell me everything." He crossed his arms and settled into the chair. Knowing him, I had no choice. Baseball was his life.

* * * *

"I'm going to get you back for that." I yelled at Greta, *hours* later after I finally got off the phone with my parents. *Damn her and her sneak attacks.*

"I'm sure you will, but I'll be ready. Your dad already in love with him?" She raised an eyebrow, a smirk on her face.

"Head over heels," I snorted and opened the fridge. "What you feeling?"

"Options, please," she teased her own personal chef.

"Beer-battered chicken, cashew chicken, or the classic tacos."

"Tacos are for Tuesdays. Tequila Taco Tuesdays." She gave me a stare that made me feel stupid for not knowing. I pulled out the chicken and showed her my middle finger.

"You're crazy. I love crazy, but you are a whole different type."

"Just remember that."

She bit her lip, giving me a sheepish look.

"What else did you do?" I knew that tone. That tone *never* meant anything good for me.

"Well, you know how we were going to watch the Sox at our place tonight?" She held up her hands in surrender and I readied the spatula to hit her if needed.

"Yes. Yes, we are."

"I invited people over."

"*People.* I have a feeling not just random people. People that include baseball people, right?"

"Yup. You're quick." She hopped onto the stool and held her head in her hands. "I asked Tanner and Aaron to come over to which they replied, 'We'll all be there.'"

"I can't fault you for inviting them. They are tons of fun. However…Zade."

Her eyes clouded. "I hate that your dream guy is Zade Willows. I fucking hate it because the guy you described is not the one that I know or I've heard about. But you can still be friends with him, yeah?"

I regretted the worry on her face. She loved her friendship with Aaron and Tanner and she worried about *me*. "Greta Michele. I can handle myself. Zade is…I don't know. We're going to be friends." My heart ached, disagreeing with my brain, but my brain knew better.

"I don't want him messing with you. I saw your reaction to him and I know his reputation. I've seen it in action. I hate it." She bit her lip. "Are you positive you're good?"

"I agreed to run with him every morning. I'm going to have to get used to seeing him. I love living with you and I want to experience everything. I'm fine. I promise I'll tell you if I'm not."

"I can't believe you agreed to run with him. He's hot as hell. I want to rip off my shirt every time I see him sweat. How can you handle it?"

"It's hard." I pointed to my head. "But I'm using *this* to think, not my lonely, overactive lady bits."

"Part of me finds it admirable that he'll run with you. It makes me feel more comfortable that you aren't running alone."

"Thanks, mom." I dodged her swat and opened a couple of beers the guys had brought over the last time they'd been here. "I need to prep the chicken. Will you put the game on?"

"You got it, girl. Put on an apron or something. You'll drive him crazy."

"That's not my plan, G. I don't want the attention, because I know I'll cave. I want him to not look at me with those sexy eyes." I shivered, imaging it. "This isn't some rom-com where we play cat and mouse. I don't want that. You know how hard I worked to get here. Even if he is a damn saint, which we know damn well he's not, I can't lose focus."

"Sure, sure." She gave me a small smile, her eyes telling me she really did understand. "You're going to kill it this year, kiddo. Trust me." After giving my arm a pat, she left the room to put on the game. By the time I had the chicken ready to cook, the front door burst open and if testosterone had a smell, it was them. Cologne and soap and leather all mixed together as the four of them walked in.

"Hey, guys!" Greta walked up and yanked the beer from Aaron's hands. She'd changed into jeans and a cute striped low-cut shirt. I'd never changed from my shower, still wearing my old Sox long-sleeved shirt on with running shorts. As I'd said, I wasn't trying to catch Zade's attention. I wasn't trying *anything*.

"Greta, looking good." Aaron patted her head and veered toward me. "What the hell smells good?"

"Beer-battered chicken." I pushed myself up on the counter, ignoring Zade's stare. I sensed it everywhere but I chose to not accept it. "I didn't realize all of you were stopping by. I'll have to make more."

"No worries. We had food earlier." Jeff joined us and rammed more beer into the fridge. I'd always known college students drank, but I had no idea where they all got it. Their parents? Siblings? Older students? *What if they have fake IDs? Am I lame that I have no idea how to get one? Ugh, stupid year off is screwing me over socially already.*

"Speak for yourself. I want to eat that." Aaron pouted and opened a beer to hand to me. "Want one?"

"Hells, yeah." I thanked him and set the timer on for an hour. "We probably have more in the fridge. I'll cook more. Owe us next time."

"You sure?" Jeff asked, closer to me now. I glanced at Zade, who leaned against the counter with a bottle to his mouth. His eyes were dancing with humor, that jerk. He loved every second of this.

"Yeah. Go enjoy the game and banter. Greta has been dying to play Cards Against Humanity all day. Shoo." I hit Jeff with the spatula I'd threatened Greta with earlier. He smiled at me and left the kitchen, and Greta laughed at something Aaron said.

"Need help?"

"Nah, I got it." I knew Zade would offer, just as I knew I'd say no. I went to the fridge and searched for an extra pack of chicken. I heard him behind me but misjudged my step, causing me to run into his chest. "Damn!"

"Sorry. I thought you heard me." He placed his hands on my shoulders, making me feel small and protected and *ugh!* "Let me help. Tell me what to do."

"I have a feeling you'll insist. I might as well let you help. It would be more work to get you to leave, I'm sure." He laughed as I distanced myself and poured out an extra can of Heineken. I'd learned what beer worked best with the chicken, and I always chose Heineken. My dad argued, but no one could tell me differently.

"Yeah, pretty much." He leaned with his back against the opposite counter from where I worked. Thankfully, our bodies didn't touch. "So, boss me around, kitchen lady."

"Hmm. I need the flour again. Could you grab it? It's on the fridge." He set it down on the counter and I placed garlic and pepper in front of him. "Mix the spices in the flour for me."

"How much flour and spices?" he asked, his brow drawn in concentration. I hated how cute he looked. He put one hundred percent effort into the smallest thing. I could only imagine seeing him on the mound.

"Wing it. The amount of flour doesn't matter." I placed the mixing bowl in front of him, but he ran his hand over his jaw, a line appearing between his dark eyebrows.

"Uh, I need directions that are more specific."

I laughed. I couldn't help it. "I get it. I needed that too when I was learning. Here. Watch." I put the flour in the bowl. "This doesn't matter—you have to have enough spices in it to make it proportional."

"That makes sense." He grinned at me and held my gaze for two seconds too long. He looked at me as if we were more than friends even though we'd only known each other for a couple of days. I broke his gaze, snagged the pepper and garlic and handed them to him.

"Pour them in, maybe a spoonful or two, and mix it." He did and I watched him. The expression on his face was perfect. It was a mixture of concentration and something I couldn't tell…but he clearly enjoyed learning.

"Have you made anything like it before?" I poured the beer into a bowl, the chicken breasts open and raw next to it. I pressed them into the beer and snuck a glance at him.

"I'm not the best with cooking. I'm good with boxed instructions." He shrugged and a small smile formed. "How did you learn to cook?"

"My dad." *Part of his teaching-me-to-support-myself obsession.* I'd hated the weekly lessons, but cooking had slowly grown into a passion. I'd never admit it to him, though, because he'd brag. I grasped my beer and took a swig. The burn of the liquid calmed my nerves, which were going haywire around him. "Now, after it soaks for a little bit in the beer, you are going to grab one of the pieces, dip it in the flour until it's covered and place it in the pan."

"*Me?*" His hazel eyes widened.

"Yeah, you. You wanted to help. I'm going to boss you around." He nodded and focused on the task. His large frame became adorable in the small kitchen, the bowl almost as big as his hands, and yet he held it all so delicately.

He began the process and I nodded. "Good, keep going. Now, try not to spill flour everywhere. If it gets wet, it's a bitch to clean up."

"Good to know." He did a fairly good job of dispersing the spices onto the chicken and I went to find the butter. We were going to cut it into small pieces to put on top of the chicken so they'd melt into it. It made it a tad bit tastier. *Plus, I love me some butter.*

"Done. What's next?" He turned to me with the biggest smile on his face, I warmed, all the way down to my toes. *Damn that smile.*

"Butter." My voice cracked, but I spun around hoping he wouldn't notice. I held a knife and went up next to him. "Watch." I cut a small square and placed it on one of the breasts. "You got the rest?"

"Yup." He took it from me, our fingers touching. I sucked in a breath at the contact and quickly took a drink of my beer. He gave me a knowing smile. He'd seen my reaction. *Damn it.*

"Game started!" Greta's voice broke our trance and I retreated into the back of the kitchen.

"Go watch the first inning. How long must I put it in for?"

"Hmm. It needs to be an hour. You can time it on your phone. The first batch will be done soon." I checked the clock and saw it was seven. We would eat late, but oh well. Good company for the most part.

"I'll finish this. Go." He winked at me and I stormed out of the room. Greta and Aaron shared the couch while Tanner chilled on the floor. Jeff sprawled out on the recliner, which left the sofa. A sofa built for two people.

"Let's goooo," I chanted and heard chuckles around me. "I know you guys play and all that, but they are *my* team. My house, my team, my rules." I glared at all of them, even Greta.

"What kind of house rules?" Aaron asked.

"We drink when we throw strikes, we double clap when we get a hit and make the motion for riding a horse when there's a homerun." I went through the motions and Zade walked in, almost crying with laughter. "All of you have to follow."

"I'm a Tigers fan, though, so ain't going to happen. It goes against who I am." He plopped right down next to me, our arms inches apart. I retracted mine and held them across my body instead. It was safer.

"Fine. That's fair. But unless anyone else is…house rules." I saw the strike out and held my beer high. "Drink up!"

Hours later, I waved off the compliments Aaron and Jeff threw at me for my cooking. They insisted on cleaning up since I'd cooked, and I wasn't going to fight them on that. "Technically, everyone should help clean up since Zade and I cooked."

"Damn. She's right. Let's go, Tanner. We'll let them relax." Greta stood up and threw me a saucy look. I had no idea what that meant. *She pushed me away from Zade and now she's pushing me toward him? She makes no sense.*

"Is it hot in here?" he asked, pulling my focus back to him. He had his arm along the back of the couch and appeared completely at home.

"Really? Going with that one? That's a strike." I laughed and swatted his arm. He'd used such a ridiculous line and yet I laughed.

"Back to that? I like our little game." He leaned in closer and I waited on his every word. He roamed his stare across my face, each second feeling like a slow caress. I bit my lip, anticipating the kiss I had dreamed about for days. His breath hit my face. "Callie…you have flour on your face."

"Huh?" I sat back, unsure I'd heard him right. "I-I do not."

"Sure do. Right here." He dragged his large finger down my cheek and held up white powder. "Thought you'd want to know."

"You dick." I picked up a pillow and hit him square in the chest with it. "I thought, hell, I don't know what I thought, but damn you."

"We're *just* friends, Callie." He lowered his voice, enjoying using my words against me a little bit too much. "Did you think I leaned in to kiss you?"

"It's time for you to go." I stood, pointing at the door. "Get out." I blushed. He was right on all counts and he'd played me like a fiddle. And I'd let him.

"Ah, don't be mad. I was having fun." He walked toward me and I held up a hand.

"No, no you don't." A smile broke out on its own and I laughed, despite the embarrassment.

"Just admit I win the round. I'll head out but the score is 1-0."

"It's only the first inning, though. I have time." I jutted out my chin in challenge.

"The thing is, though, Callie, I want us both to win the game."

Chapter Eight

Zade

Christopher Fitzpatrick paced the office in front of me, coffee in hand and a flat expression on his face. I sat straight up, still as a board, and waited. He only spoke when he was damn well ready. I'd waited for him, like, countless times before. I had no choice, really. I respected the hell out of him and he had my back no matter what. He was a player's coach. He protected his players and went to the ends of the earth for them. I'd told him my Freshman year that I'd chosen this school because of him. His response had been a gruff clap on the back and that had been that.

"We need to discuss your future." He continued to pace, still holding his black coffee in his hand. "You have options, son, but I want you to take the best route."

I nodded. I didn't want to fuck it up any more than he wanted me to. "Coach, I want the same thing."

"Good. Good. I'll admit that after your success last season, I became worried. You never know. Success can get into your head." He sat down, set the mug on the desk and studied me with his laser-sharp stare. "What's your plan? Are you trying to get drafted after your junior year? It's never too early to talk about this."

"Coach, I made a promise to my mom to get a degree. My plan hasn't changed." I meant it. I had three years left until I graduated, yet the taste of the majors tempted me. I questioned my plan every other day and I understood his trepidation. "I'll put off the draft until my senior year."

"I can't tell you what to do, but I hope you stick to your plan. I got a call that your name is being tossed around and while that makes me happy, you're still young. I've seen it happen enough where the thrill is too much, too exciting, and players have left. They left without a backup plan and end up screwing themselves over."

"I want it more than my next breath. But I need a degree. I know pitching is a long shot and I know that I need a backup plan if something happens. I've experienced what it's like, sir, to be hungry. I never want that to happen, ever, and having a degree is one step in that direction." I thought about the years we'd struggled as a family, right after my dad had left. It was a bitter taste because while that time had helped form who I was, it still infuriated me because it had hurt my mom and sister. I didn't have any father issues, surprisingly, but that was because the two women in my life were strong as hell.

"Good. Now, we need to plan your training when classes start. I gave you the summer off. You and Jeff need to throw twice a week and you need to start Pilates."

"Pilates?" I asked, not certain what the hell that was. "Yoga shit or something?"

"It's a new thing some major athletes are doing. I met with Nicole and she's on board. We have enough funds to hire a full-time Pilates instructor or some shit like that to work with you on individual goals. You need to stop in Monday sometime to meet with the new instructor and Nicole. It will build arm strength and ideally get you a couple notches higher on the gun."

"Damn, really?" *Is that possible?* My goal was to reach ninety-five miles an hour, but I'd been stuck at ninety-three the past two years.

"That is the plan. I read up on that shit and the bands and weights work muscles that normal training can't get to."

"I'm in."

"I knew it. Now, how are your classes?"

"Uh, okay. I'm booked with classes all day Monday, Tuesday and Wednesday. On Thursdays, I have two discussions and Friday is one morning class." I wished had no classes on Friday, but the schedule didn't work out that way. I wanted to major in sports management, the thrill of working with athletes and helping them find their future sounding way too good a backup plan. I wanted to knock out the gen eds the first two years and I was also able to take two classes that interested me. Classes were hard for me, specifically math and sciences. I'd worked my ass off to get straight As and I planned on continuing just that.

"Thursday and Saturday you are throwing. I'll call Jeff." He glanced at his calendar and clicked his tongue in thought. "We'll aim for Monday or Tuesday to throw battle practice and build in some workouts between that. Sound good?"

"Yes, sir. We'll make it work." I clapped my hands, pumped to get back into the swing of things. I didn't like being bored and not active. "Oh, I'm running a half marathon in November."

"Good but don't break a damn ankle. Now get out." He smiled at me briefly before looking at the door. Christopher Fitzpatrick didn't express any emotion besides intensity and that was okay with me.

"Have a good day, sir."

I'd expected something worse or an ass ripping with the pacing he'd been doing. I had zero complaints about the encounter. I sent a quick text to Zaria explaining the early meeting because it had worried her, too. It sucked I'd had to cancel my run with Callie, which had become my favorite part of the morning. We'd gotten into a nice rhythm of banter during the time and we had exercised together for a week straight. I knew it was crazy that I'd only known her a week and yet she'd snuck her way into my close circle.

I drove home and stumbled upon Jeff and Aaron playing a videogame with bags under their eyes. They were wearing the same things from the day before. "Assholes, did you sleep at all last night?"

"No way, bro. We have a bet going on." Aaron didn't even take his eyes off the screen. "Loser has cleaning duties for two weeks and has to be DD. This is too good to give up."

"So, you're going to play until one of you passes out?" I asked, more than amused. They were dipshits and my best friends. I took the free spot on the couch and watched them battle. Jeff fired insult after insult at

Aaron, yet it made no difference. Tanner joined me shortly after with a handful of bread.

I pointed to it. "Where'd you get that?"

"Callie," he said with his mouth full.

"What? I want to try it."

"Hell no." He held it out of reach. "It's for helping move something for her." He snarled at me and I backed off. Tanner went bat-shit crazy when it came to eating, as in, he never stopped. We were a rag-tag crew. Jeff and I were the pressure guys, built for our roles on the team. Aaron played the cocky-as-hell short stop who flirted with anything and everything. Tanner had different roles. His body rivaled a tank—huge, massive, solid. People assumed he played football rather than centerfield.

"Fuck you and your mother!" Aaron stood up and threw the controller across the room, knocking over a stack of plates they'd collected throughout the night. He marched down the hall to his room and slammed the door shut. I guess he'd lost.

"Sucks to suck." Jeff stood up, yawned and fell face-first onto the blanket on the floor.

"Damn. Sucks for Aaron. He challenged Jeff, too. Dumbass. Jeff is undefeated in this game." Tanner shook his head in disbelief and raised his eyebrows. "How was meeting with coach?"

"Not bad. Talked about this year and the draft." As sophomores, we all had the potential to be drafted in the next two years, and although we were all competitive among ourselves, we all wanted us to make it. Like really fucking make it big. We were teammates for life and I had no qualms about discussing the future with them. Anyone else, hell no.

"I know you were torn. You make up your mind yet?" Tanner wanted to stay for a degree, too, which puzzled us, because with his hitting average, he very well might be drafted the first round.

"I'm staying until I graduate. I need to. I'd regret it if I didn't and I want to win a pitching award the next three years. Get more experience down here."

"Good for you, man." He shoved the rest of the bread into his mouth and moaned a bit. I ignored the twinge of annoyance running through me. Fucking made no sense.

"Plans today?" I asked, hoping for something to do.

"Football game. Greta and Callie are stopping by. Aaron and I were planning to go with them." He peeked at the clock. "Shit, they'll be here soon. I need to shower." He left the room and I went to Aaron's with a sudden idea. I knocked three times, with no answer.

I tried the door, but he'd locked it. I knew Aaron pretty well and he couldn't handle losing at all. He'd probably put on his noise-blasting headphones and passed out. Could I have tried harder to wake him up? Sure. But I didn't. I saw an opportunity and ran upstairs to quickly throw on a jersey. Tanner walked out of his room and gave me an incredulous look.

"Dude, Aaron is not going. I tried getting him up but nothing." I hoped that sounded truthful and not instead a ploy for Callie.

"Sure, sure." He checked his phone. "They'll be here soon and we're going to head to my parents' tailgate."

"Thanks for the invite, asshole." I ran downstairs and double-checked my reflection in the mirror to make sure I didn't look like a total clown.

"You had a meeting. Plus, Aaron and I go all the time. It made more sense." Tanner replied to a text and ran his hand over his jaw, pretending to stroke a nonexistent beard. "Greta seems to think you're only coming because of Callie."

"It's a part of the reason. And I like supporting our school's other sports."

"Sure, sure." He grinned again and I wanted to punch his face. "Let's go."

I followed him outside, nervous to see Callie. When we ran together, conversation came easily and I knew what to expect. This felt different and Greta's suspicions were spot-on. Tanner waved at the two of them walking down the road and I sheepishly copied him. "Do I look like a damn fool, Tanner?"

"Not a total fool, but a little off your normal swagger, yeah. It's fun, though. I'm glad you're joining us today. Normally, it's me and dumbass Aaron. It'll be a good time." He clapped my back and I appreciated the action.

"Hey, guys!" Greta smiled at Tanner and it faltered a bit at me, but she smiled all the same. "Good to see you again, Zade."

"You too, Greta." I met Callie's eyes and smiled. "Hey there."

She huffed at me. "Hey there? You crash our tailgate and we get a *hey there*?"

"Ah, well, only thing I could come up with. I feel like a schmuck for tagging along, but Aaron is out of commission and who doesn't love a good day of football?"

"Hmm. Not sure I believe you, friend, but I'll take it, I guess. You said you had a meeting today—how did it go?"

We fell into two lines as we walked toward the stadium. Greta and Tanner were in an animated conversation about something and I trusted Callie, even in the short time I'd known her. "It went well. I met with my coach and talked about next couple of years, the draft and the next steps."

"I bet that's frightening as hell." She reached around to put her long hair up, the motion causing her already too-small jersey to rise. I admired her toned body and a pit formed in my stomach. *Why am I crushing so damn hard when she laid down the line?* She cleared her throat, drawing my attention back to her face. "I know from talking with my dad that too many of the young players leave with the excitement of the majors without the experience of the next level. Often times, they don't make it. It's a hell of a transition from high school to the farm system. Not anyone can do that."

"It is scary as fuck, actually," I admitted and she laughed, putting her hand on my arm. She did that a lot when she laughed or thought something someone said important. It wasn't anything special, but her touch did things to me.

"What direction are you leaning toward?"

"Finishing up my degree." Any lingering doubts I had about it left when I told her. She nodded vigorously and did the arm thing again.

"I know it probably doesn't matter, but I'm glad you said that. Education is important. I'm interested to hear all about what you want to study, but I'm also really excited for tailgating. I hear it's awesome." She grinned, excitement pouring out of her.

"You ever been to one?"

"Nope. First time." She clapped and pointed to a group of people dressed as mascots. "Look at them!"

"You have no idea what's to come. You're going to love it." I felt insanely happy that the day's events had turned to this. "You've played bags before, right?"

"Bags? What in the world?" She looked around, openmouthed, and Greta shot me a doubtful look.

"You throw a bag of corn into a hole." I laughed at her expression. "Really. If it lands on the board, you get a point. If you get it in the hole, you get three points. The goal is to get to twenty-one points first."

"This game seems super freaking weird. Greta, you've played before?" She shared a look with her friend that I couldn't decipher.

"Are you fucking with me?" I studied the two of them, searching for clues. "You are, aren't you?"

"I guess we'll have to find out." She ran her tongue over her bottom lip and walked ahead of me. *Damn woman's driving me crazy.*

Chapter Nine

Callie

I'd never had a problem getting up early to run before, but now I walked with an extra *oompf* in my step. I snagged my headphones, water and keys to go meet Zade at the trailhead. The five-minute walk gave me enough time to wake up and mentally prepare for the run.

He bent down to tie his shoe and I enjoyed the curve of his arm. He took care of his body and I found that trait admirable beyond reason. We were only given one body to live in and it made sense to cherish it, but he took it to the next level. I wanted to ask his body mass index, but that might have crossed a line or two. I used the lame attempt at flirting he'd tried the day before on him. "Hey, there."

"You." He stood and glared at me. "I'm not happy with you."

"You'll get over it," I teased, enjoying the easy smile. "It was too easy, come on. I'm from Chicago. I know what 'bags' is."

"I wouldn't have taken you for a player." He crossed his arms, the muscles bulging, and I forced my eyes to stay on his face. "You cost me twenty bucks."

"I'll buy ya something pretty with it. Come on, let's run." I took off down the path and heard him catch up to me. "Plus, your face was priceless."

"I taught you the rules *and* tricks. He pouted, his bottom lip protruding out a little bit. "I feel used."

"Aw, Zade, it happens to the best of us. How about I buy us breakfast?" I'd remembered to grab the twenty and put it in my pocket. I shot him a side glance — he was fighting a smile. If I'd been concerned about offending him, it would've been wasted because he was playing me right back.

"I guess it's settled."

"Glad we're friends again. Now, more running, less talking."

* * * *

"I have to say, besides your little game yesterday, I really enjoy hanging out with you." Zade held up his coffee and clinked my mug. "You make me laugh."

"Oddly, that was cute. Thanks, Zade. I don't want to boost your ego, but I generally enjoy your company." I observed him over the mug and swooned. His hair curled from sweat and he hadn't shaved for the past week. The combination of the shaggy hair and hazel eyes was enough to make a nun question her decisions. "You are a pleasant surprise."

"How so?"

"Moving here, hours away from my parents and hometown and only knowing Greta is scary. Knowing I'm putting all my eggs into one basket is even more so. I don't have a backup plan. Do or die." I sighed, running my hands through my hair at his rapt attention. "I consider myself bold and hardworking, but I'm still a lonely small fish at a huge place. I'm a year behind all of you. I hate it. But meeting you, and your roommates too, made it a little less scary."

"Glad to be of service. You know I'm not complaining you're here, but what made you come here now as opposed to last year?" he asked and the familiar sinking of my stomach returned.

"Personnel training, actually. I want to work with athletes and rehabilitation." I realized again that our lives were intertwined. He smiled and I didn't have to ask to know what he thought. I forced myself to ignore our compatibility—again. "I told you my dad is a coach. He wanted me to get a steady, consistent profession. When I told him I wanted to come here, as opposed to the community college he coached at, he said no. Him and my mom…they didn't want me to fail. I didn't have a good track record. It's hard to blame them."

"What… Why do they think that?" His brows drew together.

"I wasn't the best in school. I got average grades. I hated the bullshit classes." I played with the napkin instead of his meeting his eyes. It made admitting my shortcomings a little easier. "I had to work twice as hard to be average and we don't come from money…and I had to get a job and save up for a year to come here. If I do well this year, I can come back."

There. I'd said it. I clenched my fist, digging my nails into my palms. I hated admitting my weakness. I *hated* it. I wasn't the smartest. I knew that, but I worked hard. I dared to open my eyes, as Zade had yet to respond. I saw him staring right through me, as though he saw into my damn soul. I shivered. "Zade?"

"I had no idea. I just… I can help you study. If you want."

My heart skipped a beat at his offer but I shrugged it off. "Enough about me. What about you? We never got around to discussing your major."

"Sports management." Smiling, he leaned back in his chair. He softened his tone, his voice sounding like honey and lust. "I have more questions for you and answer them honestly."

"Hmm. I'm nervous, but I'm in. I've asked you enough questions during our runs."

"That you have." He grinned, the lines reaching his eyes. "Okay, favorite sport besides baseball."

"Hockey," I answered without thinking about it.

"Team?"

"Black Hawks." I showed him the logo on the back of my phone and he chuckled. "I'm a bit of a tomboy, if you haven't noticed. I'm an only child and took on the role of both kids. I played football and hockey, took dance classes and played the guitar. I have subscriptions to all sporting channels."

"Fuck." He ran his hands over his face, sighing into them. "I asked you that day in Target and I'm close to asking you to marry me again."

"Nah, I'm good. Plus nineteen is a bit too young for that, don't ya think?"

"Sure, but damn, woman, you're killing me. Okay, next question. Rock or rap?"

"Rock, no question asked. The more classic the better."

"Give or receive."

"Wow…that sounded sexual." I searched around us, making sure no one heard him ask. He blushed, the lightest tint of red appearing slowly at the top of his cheeks. It damn near made me want to grab his face and kiss it. "*Zade*," I scolded him.

"Uh, damn. I meant, like presents." He shook his head, closing his eyes. "Do you prefer to give someone a gift or receive one?"

"Now I feel like a schmuck." I used his word and it got a small smile out of him. "I think I enjoy giving presents and seeing the joy on people's faces, but I wouldn't say no to a present. I don't think anyone would, really. Well done with a tricky question."

"You answered it well enough. Next one, this one is a make or break one." He leaned closer and I met his eyes. "Dogs or cats?"

"Dogs. Forever."

"Good. Favorite movie?"

"*Remember the Titans*."

"You're killing me. Favorite book?"

"*Game of Thrones*."

"You read all of them? Damn." He laughed and attempted a terrible British accent. "'You know nothing, Jon Snow'."

"I read a lot last year. All my friends went away and I stayed behind, alone." I frowned, hating how miserable I sounded. "It got boring." I'd read more in last year than I had ever had. Although it had sucked, all the work had helped me get here. "I take it you watched the show?"

"The first season. I never had time and with classes starting…I'm going to be swamped. Wait, I remembered something you said. You play the guitar?" His eyes widened and I grinned with the confidence I grew into.

"Yeah. Greta and I used to be in a band in high school. We sang at events in town. I still play every once in a while." His mouth dropped open for a second and quickly closed. Guys had told me in the past it was sexy when I played, but I'd never played for anyone besides myself. It was an escape and a passion. That was all.

"Do the other guys know this?"

"I think she told them, but I'm not sure."

"They are going to die. Seriously, you guys are cool as hell."

"Says the potential pitcher who could get drafted. But thank you." I warmed at his compliment and the heat I'd seen on our first day together came back. *Uh-oh.*

"Okay, you need to tell me something awful about you. Please." He gave me a tortured look. "I'm not kidding. What's one of your flaws?"

"I'm terrible at cleaning. I ask questions constantly during movies. I chew gum really loudly. I like to think I know a lot about politics, but really I know nothing. I'm not a quick learner." I thought about something else, but his frown grew deeper.

"What about your flaws?" I tried to keep the conversation light, because the heat building in those eyes startled and captivated me.

"My foolish past of sleeping around." He mumbled the words so fast I barely caught them. *His past?* What did he mean?

He stood up and frowned at me. "I'm trying really hard, Callie, but pretty soon we are going to have to talk about this. This," he motioned between the two of us, "is going to be something great."

"Zade, I—"

"I know. You don't have to explain it again. I'll head out." He turned to leave but then gave me a partial smile. "Thanks for breakfast."

* * * *

I picked up my guitar and tuned it to the key I wanted. I needed the musical therapy, each note more beautiful than the last. Clouds shaded the campus and although the summer heat remained, I welcomed the slight chill. I began with a cover of an old Stones song. I hummed to it and closed my eyes, losing myself in the music. I wanted to escape the paranoia about not making it this year. *What if I don't get the grades? What if I love it here, but my parents make me go back home? What if Zade breaks my heart?*

Another guitar joined mine and Greta sat up the couch with her hot pink guitar and our voices harmonized. We sang a song or two, our old covers from high school weaving in and out. We played for a couple hours, the joy indescribable to anyone who didn't know music.

"Damn, girl. I missed this shit." She set her guitar on the table and fell to the couch with her legs and arms failing everywhere. "We still got it."

"Agreed." I carefully placed the guitar in my old case and smiled at the university logo.

"Is that smile because of Zade?"

"Not at all. I saw the sticker you gave me and realized I feel at home here. I didn't know how I'd feel, but it wasn't this." I joined her on the couch and she laid her head on my shoulder. "Thank you for helping this happen."

"Anytime, sister. I'm glad you said that. I worried and second-guessed my roommate abilities."

"Shut your mouth. We've been friends for ten years. Living together, no matter how crazy you can be and messy I can be, won't change that." I patted her arm and she snuggled into me. Best friends were weird. They were pillows, secret keepers, advice givers, ass kickers and motivators. I would never find another Greta in three lifetimes.

"I'm feeling insecure lately and I hate it," she whined. "I want you to love it here. I'm crushing on Tanner, but I should be focused on school. I can't decide on a major. My brother is back at home, again. Zade Willows is after my best friend and I don't know what to root for."

"That is a lot of feelings. Let's start with the easiest. I. Love. It. Here. You are supportive as hell and oddly, I like the rag-tag baseball crew of friends you came with. I told Zade that today actually, before shit got weird. I'll fill you in later about that. But you can totally crush on a guy and focus on school. Just get your homework done first before doing him."

She burst out laughing and I felt proud of my use of words. "I like that. I don't know if it's two ways, though. We haven't exchanged heated touches or sexy stares."

"Real life is not like the movies or romance books you read," I told her in a pointed tone. "He clearly likes you. He's protective of you and always watches for where you are."

"He might, but he doesn't look at me like Zade looks at you." She sat up and eyed me. "I'm not kidding, Cal. I know he's been a womanizer in the past, but he's never acted this way with a girl before. Daily running dates? Breakfasts? He's barely acknowledged girls he's hooked up with. You're different."

"I present a challenge to him and that hunk of a man likes a challenge. I can tell whenever we play a game or joke around. I'm something he can't have, thus, I'm desirable. That isn't a firm ground for a relationship. And you know my grades have to come first. No matter how tempting Zade is. Now, Tanner comes over almost every day. He brings you food. That is one fine trait for a guy to have. But, G, you can always make a move."

"I don't want to ruin the friendship, though." She sighed and fell back to the pillow. "I don't want to make a fool of myself and end it all. I'd rather have him as a friend than try and fail."

"Never let the fear of striking out keep you from playing the game." I smirked, knowing Zade might appreciate the quote.

"You're a dork. I want to veg out. Movie night?" She got up and I nodded. I took out my phone, typing the text without thinking too much about it. Friends texted each other, right?

Callie: I just used the quote, never let the fear of striking out keep you from playing the game. In real life. I have a problem.

Zade: You do. Did it help, though?

Callie: Not at all. The comment was entirely ignored. Hmm. Now that I think about it, I'm pissed. It was really good advice.

Zade: What's your advice for someone then who keeps striking out? Do you tell them to stop trying and quit or what?

Callie: Good question. Approach it differently. They don't have the fear, but the approach isn't working. I'd have them try something different. Switch it up. When it doubt, shake it out.

Zade: Maybe you're not too shabby with these quotes.

Callie: Are we cool…about earlier?

I typed out the text, my finger hovering on adding more. I saw the gray dot that showed him typing come up then disappear four times.

Zade: Yes, Callie. Regardless of what happens, I'll be a friend to you.

Chapter Ten

Zade

"Get your head out of your ass. Let's go!" Jeff yelled at me through his mask. "You're throwing shit right now. You're better than this." His dark eyes bored into mine, a little anger and disappointment in them. It made me feel lower. I *was* better than this.

"Fuck. I know." He threw the ball back at me, hard, and I took a moment to collect myself. I stood on the mound, my second home. I should be flying high, not pissed off and tight. I'd stretched for an hour with Nicole. I was loose as hell and yet the muscles pinched and I held back. "Let me go back to the slider."

"Give me ten." He bent low and signaled for the pitch with three fingers. I counted to four, brought the ball into my glove, counted to four again and did my wind-up. My mind cleared, the only thing in focus Jeff's glove and the sound of my pitch. I went through every routine I had and the ball missed the target by a foot.

"Fuck!" I yelled, kicking the dirt around me, and I flinched at my coach's twisted expression. This was going to be *the* season. I wanted it enough, worked hard enough for it and I needed do whatever it took to make it happen. Jeff threw me the ball with a blank face. I went through the motions again. This one went better. The third and fourth and fifth were okay. We moved on to the change and hitting spots with the fastball. Instead of the adrenaline I normally had, I felt like the insecure high schooler who struggled with finding a position. We moved to the curve, but after two or three, we both knew it wasn't going to go well. "Jeff, let's stop."

He gave me a curt nod and jogged toward me. "Z, clear your mind, man. You aren't throwing your normal shit. What's going on?"

"Honestly, nothing. That's what I don't get. I'm tight as fuck despite warming up all morning." I fisted the ball in my hand, the pressure pinching at my shoulder. "What are you seeing?"

"Wind-up is the same, the release is a little off. You don't have your normal movement or consistency, but don't worry, man. It's the first run through since summer. You'll get the fire back. You wouldn't want to be throwing fire in August... Hell, that'd be a false sense of security." He patted my back, the support helping me. Jeff didn't bullshit and always told me if I needed to be worried. I trusted him with my arm and calling the game. The trust had to be two ways or the flow would be off and I chose to believe him.

"I wanted to leave feeling more confident. Instead, I want to go listen to Adele and pump weights in the gym." I laughed, although I wasn't in a great mood.

"If you do that, let me know. I could do with some simpin' now that you mention it." He inspected the ground a little too long and I inwardly groaned. He had something going on too and I was only concerned about my own pitching issues. *Way to be an ass.*

"What's up?" We continued to stand on the mound, but our coach had left already. I expected to hear from him the next day about my mediocre performance. "I was sucked up in my own world, but you seem down."

"It ain't anything big. Money issues." He shrugged, avoiding eye contact. "It's not me. My mom and dad. I'm on a scholarship, but they're struggling and I'm torn between trying to get drafted for the signing bonus or staying here and not being able to help them out. If I chose the stay, it's for me and only me. If I signed, then I could help them."

"Shit." I felt for him. "I wish I could do more for ya, man, but that is a tough call. Have you talked to them about it?"

"That's the thing — they won't admit it to me. I heard about it by accident and now that I know, I haven't told them. I'm morally torn and coach wants to help, but it's ultimately up to me." He wiped sweat off his forehead. "They won't ask, but they're my *parents*, man. I need to help them if I can. They've traveled all over the state with me since I was six, helping me follow my dream of baseball. I owe it to them."

"I would do the same thing, honestly. But, if you want advice or not, you need to talk to them. If they're anything like my mom, they'll be fucking pissed as hell if they knew you were contemplating giving up something for them. Talk to them. Worst-case scenario, nothing changes. Ya know?"

"We'll see. I wish I had a sibling or another family member to discuss shit with, but it's only us three." He frowned and kicked the dirt. "Let's throw more. I need the distraction. Your arm good?"

"I can do another thirty or so. Let's go." With a new mission in mind, I went back to the mound and lost myself in the process.

* * * *

"You threw better the second time around. What did you change?" Jeff asked me, walking back to the training room to get me some ice. "Seriously, you threw like two different people."

"I don't know... I focused less on my own issues and threw. I left my head for a while and now that I'm back in there, I'm questioning everything." He nodded in understanding. "People don't realize the game is much more mental than physical. It takes a lot of strength."

"That's why you're the pitcher. You have the ego and confidence for us all." He patted my back. "Go get your ice. I'm hitting the showers."

I waved at him as he headed farther into the locker room. I needed ice and to zone out with some hardcore music. Some guys preferred country or rap to pump them up. I always chose some Van Halen and Stones. I walked into the empty training room and anticipated the cooldown. I hooked my phone up to the aux cord and took a bag of ice. I'd done it enough times in the past to know how to use the wrap and keep it on my throwing arm. It looked sloppy, but at least I knew my muscles were relaxing.

My phone went off with some texts, but I ignored them and lay down on the stretching mat. Four songs went by and I heard some voices in the distance, but I didn't care. They'd seen me do it before and coach was fucking great at having people leave me alone. We all had our odd little tricks and needs to prepare for the mental part of the game and mine happened to be pre- and post-workout reflection. I thought about what had gone well, what had gone poorly and how I envisioned myself throwing the next time. I was thinking about all the things I needed to do when I heard a familiar voice. I raised my head, shielding my eyes from the bright light, and saw Callie through the window talking animatedly with Nicole. Callie hadn't seen me yet, but I gasped at Nicole's smile. She *never* smiled.

I pushed myself to sit and studied Callie. Perfect, beautiful, off-limits Callie. *Damn that woman.* She spied me through the window and her eyes widened for a split second. I winked at her and gave her a cheesy smile. She returned it and disappeared from view. Oh well. I'd see her the following day for our run. Coach might be proud as hell because I now craved running. He didn't need to know it revolved around Callie. I stood and stretched my arms above my head when I flinched. "Fucking hell." The pain in my left arm frightened me. It had come out of nowhere and bit unlike anything I'd experienced before.

"Hey, Zade. What's with the face of pain?" Fucking Callie waltzed over wearing skin-tight yoga pants and a workout tank top. How she managed to look that fucking good after a full day of classes shocked me. I wanted to pout and have a beer.

"Beside the fact you always turn me down? Why are you here? Stalking me?" I meant it as a joke, but the tone of my voice made me sound like an asshole. I didn't correct it, either.

"Ah, as much as you wish I was, I'm not. I have a clinical class and I wanted to explore the stadium. I planned to walk around with Nicole, maybe send some pictures to my dad, but then I saw you in here. Thought I'd say hi. But now you're acting mental so maybe I'll head back." Her mouth turned down, making me feel like a dick. I needed to remedy that because Callie's smile was one of the top things in the world.

"Don't leave," I demanded instead of asking. "I didn't throw as well as I should have today and I'm not handling it well."

"Is that why you're acting like a kid whose daddy benched him?" She leaned against the counter near the door and I wanted to pick her up and lay her on the table. God, I wanted to spend hours exploring her. I'd taken too long to answer her question. I cleared my throat and went with the truth.

"I threw like shit. My catcher is going through shit. My arm feels like shit." I sounded like a bitch, but my mouth continued, "I have too much fucking pressure on me to play well that I can't have days like this. Word spreads. I don't want people saying that I lost the momentum I got last year. People told me it wouldn't last." As soon as I said them, I realized the root of my problem. The pressure of the year before held a dark cloud over me, suffocating me and preventing me from succeeding before I'd even tried. I didn't want to be the kid who was a star Freshman year and slowly slid into being a nobody.

"You don't strike me as a guy who lets others affect him." She walked toward me, eyes blazing with something. She stopped a foot in front of me. "Why do you pitch?"

"It's what I've always done?"

"No, that isn't what I asked. Why do you continue to do it?"

"I…like the control. I love the game. I love being able to strike the guy out in the bottom of the ninth. I love the sounds, the smells, the atmosphere and the mental toughness I need. It's all I've ever known and I need it like I need air." I sat down on the bench and put my head between my hands. "Does that make me sound like a sap?"

"Nah, you sound like someone who loves the sport. You're letting the mental part of the game affect you physically. That is error number one. You are Zade fucking Willows. Your opponents fear you. Your teammates respect the hell out of you. People like my dad watch you and follow your stats every game. You could get any girl on campus with the flick of your throwing hand. Own that shit, man." She joined me on the bench and knocked her shoulder into mine. "Why the doubt?"

"I wish I knew. You can continue telling me how awesome I am, though. That helps."

"I'm sure you don't need it." She touched the skin around the bag of ice and frowned. "How long have you had it on?"

"Eh, five songs' worth." I shrugged. "I usually keep it on for about five or six."

"*Boys*," she scoffed and unwound the wrap. "Thirty minutes, max. Check out your skin. It's all red."

"I can handle it." I sucked in a breath when her fingers grazed my bare chest. She pulled the ice off and clucked her little mouth at the redness there. When she dragged her finger over my body, I lost all feeling anywhere else. She stood over me, practically straddling me. "Uh, whatcha doing there?"

"I'm looking at your arm. You said it hurt. I'm finding out why." She bent, her face inches from mine, and my body tightened. My dick twitched but I put my best game face on.

"Uh, okay." I sounded barbaric, like a caveman trying to talk to someone in the present day. She did that to me though, made me lose all sense of confidence and swagger. *Damn her, again.*

"Do you mind?" she asked, placing her hands on my left shoulder. "I thought Nicole stretched you before you threw. You're really inflamed right here and swollen." She pressed her fingers on the part of my arm that pinched and hurt. I jumped up, causing her to lose her balance and fall into me.

"Shit. I'm sorry." I caught her, her tiny waist in my hands, and she swallowed. Her eyes were on my mouth, her teeth pressing down on her bottom lip, and it took every ounce of self-restraint not to kiss her. "Here." I picked her up without effort and helped her find her footing again. "If you couldn't tell, that hurt."

"I got that, yeah. You stretched before, though. Did you after?"

"Yeah, of course. I need to take care of my body."

"I can see that." She ran her tongue over her bottom lip again, so fast my stomach clenched. I needed to get my shit together.

"I'm going to do that again. Can you handle it?"

"Fine. Do it." I covered my face with my arm and she gently pressed the inside of my throwing arm. I recoiled from her touch and hissed.

"Don't be a baby. Whatever hurts is right here. Were you extending too much during your release?" She took my fingers into hers, working them through her hand. I enjoyed the touch way too damn much. She became a little light in the dark storm in my head. "Answer me, Zade."

"I don't know. Probably," I sulked. I had the ego of a pitcher and when I melted down, I was chaotic. A small hand smacked my face. It wasn't gentle or hard, but it got my attention. "What the hell did you do that for?

"You are being a tool right now. Stand up." She stood back and crossed her arms over her chest. "Show me the motion."

"Motion?" I sounded like a dumbass, but her cleavage was on display and that sort of took up all the concentration I had left.

"Yes, like when you pitch." She rolled her eyes. "I want to see the motion."

"You think *you* can help me?"

"Yeah. I know I can."

Chapter Eleven

Callie

Dad: You helped Zwillows throw?

Callie: Sort of, in a way. His release was off. I suggested it. He changed it.

Dad: My daughter helped Zwillows. This is every dad's dream come true.

Mom: You're both being dramatic. How are your classes, sweetie?

Callie: Fine, Mom. I'm going to love the clinical portion of the class. I can move ahead and do a special project seeing as I worked at the Sports Enhancement center all last year. So, the job is totally paying off. I get to shadow the athletic trainer!

Mom: Wow! See, honey, everything happens for a reason. You should trust us more.

Callie: Ugh, maybe you and Dad were a little right.

Mom: I know we were. But it pleases me to see you understand, even if it is a little bit.

Dad: We can bond later. Tell me about Zwillows.

Callie: But yes, Dad. It's surreal. He's a huge well-known talented pitcher but has mental issues and I've seen enough of those guys on the field growing up with you. I talked him through it.

Dad: I can't say I've ever been prouder.

My dad saying he was proud of me stopped time. My chest swelled and I vowed to continue working my ass off in any way I could.

Excitement pounded in my blood as I snatched my bag and weaved my way through the old college campus, one of the first in the country. I loved the ivy and colors of the trees. I sighed, an annoyingly large smile on my face, and navigated my way to where my second course of the day, sports nutrition, met. The building's small, familiar classroom welcomed me. I didn't feel like I attended a school with forty-thousand-plus students — it was the same size as my high school classes. I smiled at the guy next to me before sitting down.

"Hi. How's it going?" I pulled out my laptop and prepared to take notes. The polite guy smiled a little too big and a little too long at me before he sat up straighter. I was not a stranger to being hit on, but, it wasn't something I aimed to happen or particularly liked. My smile faded a bit.

"Are you new here?" the guy asked. "I'm sorry to stare, but you sort of seem familiar."

"I am new here, yeah. It's my first year. My name is Callie. Are you a townie?" I held out my hand and he took it with a shy smile. I regretted judging him before knowing him. He had a good smile and aura. My mom always went on about getting a feel for someone at first meeting. Some people had good auras, while some people had red and yellow neon lights to avoid. The guy who wore an old band T-shirt and had shaggy blond hair seemed like a good one.

"I'm Radcliffe, the college townie. Born and raised here." He cringed a little at my shocked expression. "I know, I know my name is out there. My friends call me Rad."

"Super interesting name. Can't say I've met a Radcliffe before. Are you one of those people who has two last names?" I asked.

"Like, Jones Fred or an Eric Steven or something?" He laughed and I joined in.

"Exactly. I feel like I need to know your last name before this goes further. I mean, you seem nice, but I have high standards with friends." The professor swaggered in and the class fell silent. I caught Radcliffe's gaze and we shared a small smile. I guessed I needed to wait to find out his surname. The professor wore an all-matching Adidas sweat suit and I couldn't decide if I liked it, wanted one for myself or judged him. He rambled on about course expectations and our first assignment. It intrigued me. I'd lucked out having zero homework yet. However, Nicole's program already had my mind spinning.

"You are going to pair up and create a diet based on the team I assign you. You must cite all sources and provide details as to the hows and whys. If you've heard about me, you know that I'm tough. I'm adding more to your assignment than the other courses. You need to prepare an exercise plan, diet, weight loss snacks and muscle gaining meals within a week. Pair up—I don't care with who—and make plans. If you want to be a trainer then you're going to have to work with coaches who are assholes and demanding with no people skills. I am the least of your problems, unless you suck. Then I can't help you. Now, go." He plopped onto the desk and put headphones in, watching something on his phone. My mouth dropped open. I sat there, shocked at the behavior of our teacher.

"Don't be worried. That's Patz for you." Radcliffe shrugged and pulled out his laptop. His shaggy hair covered most of his face, the curls blocking his dull brown eyes. "He's one of the best, actually. He played professional hockey for ten years, injured his shoulder and ended up here. He'll tell it like it is. My sister had him years ago and he still uses the same syllabus and all."

"I had no idea. Who did he play for?" I frowned. I should know this.

"Boston, I think. It was a long time ago. Want to partner up?" He gave me a cheesy grin and added, "My last name is Rutger."

"Radcliffe Rutger." I closed my eyes and bit back a laugh. "You sound like a...prince or duke or something."

"I know. It scares away the ladies." He said it without a hint of sadness. "But when I become famous, I'll sound awesome as hell."

"Yes, you will, Rad Rutger." I laughed and scooted my desk closer to him. "I'm down to work together, but

I should warn you, I'm a workaholic and really need to do well here."

"Don't judge me, lady. I'm also a book-loving dork. I'll put the effort in. Now, I'll go get the assignment. Start a document and share it with me. Email's the same as my name."

"You got it." I began the process and we got a good hour of work in before Patz told us to get out for his next class. We'd barely touched the assignment, for which we'd been given a young hockey team. Despite being a former hockey player, Radcliffe showed no worry or anxiety over it, unlike me. I swallowed down the pressure to succeed. His easy-going attitude helped my anxiety. "There's no way we can finish this at the discussion Thursday. Are you able to meet sometime over the weekend?"

"Oh yeah. What works best for you? Friday, Saturday, Sunday?" He closed his laptop and held out his phone. "Give me your number and we can figure it out, if you're not sure."

"Probably best. My roommate and I might have plans. She's needy like that. So, I'll let you know tomorrow?" He put my number into his phone and my phone went off.

"Sounds good. Nice to meet you, Callie." He smiled and took off in the other direction. I waved and headed to my next class. *Something* about this university fit me, the hard journey to get here worth it. I grinned a little too wide, drawing some stares as I headed across the quad to psychology in the sporting context. None of my classes were boring and I had no qualms about studying. My future career meant everything to me. I got to class early and chose a seat at the back of the room. I wasn't a fan of lectures with hundreds of people because the teachers were too impersonal. My pulse raced as small beads of sweat dripped down my lower back. My nerves were shot to hell.

I stood out as a newbie, with the school experience being the secret online classes I'd taken that summer. They never required face-to-face interaction, but classes here were *so* different. Putting in the work had allowed me to be in a second-year class for psychology, but then I stood out as the awkward new girl. *You can do this, Callie. Man up.* My neck tightened in tension, the sound from the front distracting me. A door slammed open, all eyes darting to the entrance to the lecture and I saw none other than Zade stroll in with nothing but a laptop and a gaggle of girls trailing him.

He smiled, putting his arms around two of the girls, and chose a seat in the front. The professor walked up to him and shook his hand. He oozed charm and grace, which made me gag. He showboated and seeing him with his fans reaffirmed my decision to remain only friends with him. Sure, the attraction went both ways and the past two weeks had been more fun than I'd imagined, but Zade Williams was a heartbreaking distraction I refused to gamble with. I put one headphone in and pulled out a pad of paper. I tried to focus on taking dubious notes, but my gaze pulled to Zade's head. He sat in the middle of a row of girls, beautifully tall and built girls, and seemed to be the king of the world. I pulled out my phone and sent a picture to Greta. It didn't help that the professor droned on about the syllabus when I'd already found it word for word online.

Callie: He's like a king around here. What the hell.

Greta: Yeah, he kind of is. Zwillows Pillows is a real club. They follow him around.

Callie: He's great and all, but...damn. That's a real name?

Greta: Yup. They have a Twitter and track his movements around campus. Jealous?

Callie: I wouldn't say that. Disappointed that it seems he is who I thought he might be. He seemed different.

Greta: Aw, my girl Cal had a crush.

Callie: Nah, not crush. Hope. This lecture sucks. I want chocolate.

I didn't hesitate before pulling up Zade's number and giving him shit. My personality was too bold to let something like *Zwillows Pillows* go. I laughed at the ridiculousness of the situation. I got the fact that people were fans of athletes, I really did, but following their movements? Stalking them for real? Maybe my dad coaching had numbed me to the celebrity treatment some athletes got, or maybe I was normal. They were regular people with cool talents.

Callie: Zwillows Pillows. Are you effing kidding me?

He pulled out his phone and leaned away from the girl hanging on to him. The motion was small and insignificant. I shouldn't have enjoyed it. But I did.

Zade: I know the president. I can get you VIP membership.

Callie: Nah, I'm good.

Zade: Say the word and I'll get you a sticker. There are perks of the club...pictures of me, signed shit, you name it.

Callie: Glad to see you got your swagger back. Douchebag swagger, but you're back to your normal self. I wouldn't be surprised to find girls trailing you.

I baited him to see his response. I never played games and yet I just had. I hated people who did that, but my fingers had a mind of their own. It was a hard battle to fight when my heart, head, lady parts and now hands were all on different paths. And each one thought they were in control.

Zade: Want to be one to follow me around? I'll put you first.

Callie: Hard pass. Hard pass, man.

Zade: One day, Callie, one day.

I grinned and caught myself. I needed to stop this shit. I was flirting and I liked the attention. I put my phone back on music and began making to-do lists of everything I needed to get finished by the weekend. I only checked my phone three times to see if I had a text, which I didn't, before class finished. I snuck out before the crowd and headed toward the favorite campus restaurant, Cam's. It smelled like shit, had beer stains on the floor and had been notorious for frats and bros to hang out. I'd heard about this place all last year. I couldn't wait.

I walked into the place shortly after and saw Greta and Aaron sitting toward the back. Tanner's large frame almost blocked Greta's bright blonde hair. I smiled a little too wide, drawing some unwarranted stares from a small circle of women. I avoided their hostile stares and walked over to the dingy booth. "Hey, guys!"

"Callie, girl." Aaron scooted over and I took the spot next to him. "We ordered three pitchers and are about to play quarters. You in?"

"Hmm. Beer and games? Hells yeah." Greta and I high fived and Tanner and Jeff joined us, Tanner pulling out a small ping pong ball. How he always came prepared for drinking games beat me. "Everyone here?"

"Yup. Z might join us, but you never know. He has to weigh his options. Tits and ass, or us. I wouldn't blame him." Aaron shrugged and Greta caught my eye. An unwelcome lead pit formed in my stomach. I'd made my stance clear to him and he had every right.

"His loss then. Let's do this!" I found a clean glass and filled it up from the pitcher in the center of the table. Jeff and Tanner squeezed next to Greta. She seemed tiny between them, all squished and shit. I took a picture, her smile contagious. As the drinks continued, I took more pictures and laughed so hard I almost peed. Aaron spilled beer on his shorts and it gave the impression he'd pissed himself, and Jeff told us a story about his brother shitting himself on a train. I held on to my stomach, my laughter out of control. Greta and I stumbled to the bathroom.

"Oh, my god. I need to go. Now!" Greta yelled, yanking my hand. "This way."

I followed her to a piss-smelling hallway. "Are you taking me back here to kill me? It looks creepy as hell."

"It's Cam's. You get used to it." We marched into the small room and smiled at the girls primping in the mirror. "I'm glad we did this. I know it's Thursday, but damn."

"I agree. This should be a weekly thing." We went to do our business and came back out to see three girls glaring. I gave them a weird look and one approached me. Greta stepped to stand next to me. I didn't think she needed to protect me or hold me back, but my nerves went on edge.

"How did you two end up sitting with *them*?" The blonde twisted her made-up mouth at us and I recoiled. *Who speaks to strangers like that?* "What did you do?"

"Excuse me?" I stood tall, looking down at the nasty stranger. "Who're you to be rude to someone you don't know?" Greta sucked in a breath but kept her arm on my shoulder. For whatever reason, the blonde had her hatred directed at me.

"You come here and slide right into the group. What did you do to get them to notice you? Sleep with them? All of them? I don't get it. You don't even wear makeup. Are you fifteen? Gross." She sneered at me, looking me up and down. Pure disgust crossed her face and made her appear ugly. Not only in personality, but in jealousy.

"Listen here." I stepped toward her, my lack of height not really an issue. My temper made me taller. "First off, these people you are referring to are *people*. They have normal lives and friends. They make up their own damn minds and clearly, if they gave you the curb, it was for a reason. Secondly, come at me again and you won't win." I stepped closer to her, her eyes

113

widening in fear when I looked her up and down in the meanest way I could. "Cleat chasers never get far. You're ten a penny."

I yanked Greta's hand and dragged her out of the bathroom, her mouth hanging open. I didn't stop until we reached the main area. Music drowned out our conversations from others and we blended in. After that altercation, I wanted just that—to not stand out. "What the hell? Who are these girls?"

"Callie. That was amazing and awesome and terrifying at the same time. I'm kind of turned on and scared." She put her hand on my arm and shook her head. "God, you are awesome. I got nervous. I hate girl fights and intimidation. You handled that…easily."

"Nah, it's easy to stand up to spiteful people. I have a harder time standing up to people I love or care about. That's really hard." I waved off her compliment. "I've seen enough of people like her to know they're after one thing and that's to use potential players for fame. They try to ruin the players' lives or trap them and they think the world owes them something."

"Damn. I need to learn how to do what you just did."

"Anytime. So let's head back—I want to beat their asses." I wiped my hands on the back of my pants, the sweat collecting the more I thought about how angry I felt. "For real though, I'm going to need you to hold me back if they come at me like that again."

"I'm not sure… I think it might be more entertaining to watch. Plus, they say a *best* friend ends up in jail with you while a friend only bails you out." She paused, running her tongue to the side of her mouth. "Actually, I want to be a part of it. I need more adventure in my life. Oh! We need to watch those cool fighting movies to learn—"

"No, stop." I yanked on her arm to pull her in the right direction. "Settle down, psycho."

Chapter Twelve

Zade

I avoided the grasps of Carly and Jen, and excused myself by saying I had to go throw, but really I needed to escape them. I tried not to think about how Callie probably thought I was even more of a dick after she'd heard about the damn Zwillows Pillows. I cringed. God, I hated that name. I despised the club, hating the entire premise of it. But I loathed it more knowing it proved Callie's claims right. *Should I text her again? Nah. God, when did I lose my ability to convince girls to be with me?*

My phone went off in my hand. *Mom.* I answered it on the second ring. "What's up, Mom? This is unexpected."

"Hi, Zade. You don't know the effort it took to call you. Appreciate me." She sighed into the phone, but I'd bet a million bucks she had a smile on her face. "Tell me everything. Classes. Workouts. The girl your sister mentioned."

"Aw, hell. I'm going to kill Zaria. No girl yet." I put headphones in and decided to stroll home. It had been a while since my mom and I talked. "Classes are interesting. I'm only taking five to balance the workouts."

"I'm debating what I want to know more about. Start with throwing. You started last week, right?" She yelled at someone in the background and I chuckled. She was a boss, in all senses of the term. She was strong and independent as hell, found comfort in telling others what to do and she was right almost every time. "Well?"

"Geez, Mom. You called me, remember?" I laughed and decided to answer with the truth. "I'm tight. It's been pinching a bit, but I'm starting a new workout that focuses on body strength. Nicole is kicking my ass and her new Pilates instructor is her on steroids."

"Pinching? Have you talked to Christopher? You should bring that up to him."

"I follow Nicole's orders. She says I'm fine, I'm fine. That's what I'm going with." Some girls grouped up and all pointed and smiled at me. I waved at them, causing them to squeal. I bit back a smile. They were insane. *Fucking Zwillows Pillows.*

"She is a tough cookie, that Nicole. I love her. I'll need to have my assistant send her a fruit basket. Does she like fruit? A trainer wouldn't want a thing of chocolate. Probably a sin or something. Hmm. What do you think?" She spoke without breathing in between her sentences.

"Mom, you're a nut. I miss you." I was a full-fledged momma's boy and had no problem admitting it. I loved my mom. "I think she'll love a fruit basket."

"Good. I already put it in my to-do list. Now, dish it on the girl."

"Don't you want to hear about my classes? I'm a student first, athlete second."

"Yeah, fine. Sure. You're going to be fine. You work hard, study hard and I'll ground you if you don't remain a good student. Enough about that."

"How will you ground me? You live an ocean away!"

"Uh, I have my ways. No more phone bill paid. I'll plant spies in your life you won't know who're real or fake."

"You're terrifying."

"You're avoiding the topic."

"Damn. Okay. She intrigued me but she wants nothing to do with me besides being friends. That's really it." I sighed. "Also, it's weird talking to you about this."

"I love it. Finally, a girl who isn't jumping to jump into your bed."

"Mom. Awkward." I blushed, like crazy. "Ew."

"I am a very forward-minded person. I can handle it. You better be being safe or I'm going to send you STD pamphlets in the mail. Every week. To the house. You hear that?"

"Good lord, mom. Super glad we had such a happy talk."

"We aren't done, son."

"Yes. I'm done. We'll talk this weekend with Zaria. Love you." I didn't wait to hear her response and hung up. I shook my head. My mom had to be the best and craziest person I knew. She texted me, as I knew she would, and I laughed.

Mom: Love you too. Be safe. I can still ruin your life.

The uneventful and silent walk back irked me. Everyone should have been home. *Where are they?* I checked my phone and saw a text that I'd overlooked from Aaron. They were at Cam's. Callie and Greta were there. That answered my next question of what I was going to do. I threw my laptop onto the table and headed straight there.

* * * *

"Z-man, good to see ya? How's your summer going?" Jake, the long-time bouncer at Cam's, shook my hand. He'd always been a good dude and I liked him. His neck tattoo might be too intense with the skulls, but I wasn't one to judge.

"Real nice, yours?" I cared to know but also tried to spot my friends and Callie in the distance. It was more crowded than normal, the excitement of the new year bringing out everyone and their mother. I saw no signs of my overbearing friends or Callie's long dark hair. Her hair stood out anywhere, the brunette waves a goddamn weakness of mine. He spoke about his trip and I said the appropriate things. I excused myself to go search for my friends and spied them in one of the back booths with two or three empty pitchers and a wild game of quarters going on.

Instead of approaching them right away, I watched them. Callie and Greta were cheering, their lazy smiles probably fueled by the beer. Aaron laughed and jealousy coursed through me. They rarely got that animated around me unless we were on the field. Once again, I questioned myself and I hated it. Jeff saw me and motioned for me to join them. I waved like a fucking dork and strode over. Callie met my eyes and bit her lip. That was new.

"Look who it is! Z-man, Zwillows!" Jeff yelled, a little too loudly, and a couple of others around us clapped. I shook them off, not wanting the attention right then. "Join us, bro. I thought you'd be hooking up with some girl with nice knockers."

"Not today, no. I got home to an empty house. It sucked," I admitted and stood at the end of the table. It smelled like beer and although I didn't drink a lot, I wanted to. I saw Callie's twitch of her face at Jeff's words and I wanted to erase that. "My mom called me. Nothing too exciting."

"Sure, sure," Jeff said. All of us used Tanner's catchphrases, to some degree or other. Aaron had his arm around the back of the booth, his fingers dangling close to Callie's shoulder. *Fucking hell. If he makes a move on her…well, I can't do a damn thing about it.* Her hair had been twisted into braids, something I hadn't seen her do before. It made her more girly than athletic. Just another reason why I was caught up in her I stared a little too long and Aaron cleared his throat.

"We were telling Callie about the club that opened downtown and we're thinking about heading to it next weekend. Whatcha think?" He narrowed his eyes at me and I had no idea what the fuck that meant. His playboy status beat mine…meaning he stood no chance. Yet he tugged the end of Callie's braid and she laughed. She fucking leaned into it and laughed.

"Yeah. I'm in. Should be fun." My voice sounded off. I needed a drink. Jeff seemed to sense my discomfort and tried to fix it.

"We'll order another pitcher and you can join next round. Now you're here, we can have teams of three. Way easier than having a sub for each team."

"Yeah, Jeff isn't the best at this," Greta claimed, Tanner nodding. "You guys get him."

"Hells no. We get Zade." *Callie.* I smiled as my name left her mouth. I liked it. I liked it a lot.

"Girl, please. You and Aaron are kicking our asses. We get the guns." Greta pursed her lips and did the strange girl thing where they had a conversation with their eyes. I watched back and forth between them, smiling. They were always entertaining.

"Fine. You get him this time." Callie pouted. Aaron leaned in to say something in her ear and I clenched my fist.

"I'll go grab a couple more." I headed to the bar and some pretty bartender immediately served me. One thing about the bar—they didn't care we weren't twenty-one. No one did. Her coy smile distracted me. Irrational anger at Callie and Aaron took over and without realizing what I was doing, I upped the charm. "Hi, there."

"Zade Willows. What can I get ya?" She leaned over the bar, putting her tits on full display, and of course I noticed. I wasn't dead. Her name tag read *Ellen* and I gave her the full Zade show. Compliment them, flirt with them and leave with them. I had mastered it my freshman year, sleeping with girls way older than me. It wasn't something I bragged about and it certainly explained why Callie wanted nothing to do with me.

"How about a pitcher of beer, Ellen? Anything on tap. Surprise me. You strike me as a girl who's good at surprises." I lowered my voice and winked. She ate it up, spilling a little beer on the counter. I pretended not to notice and watched her walk away.

"You never stop surprising me." Callie's voice broke into my thoughts and my stomach clenched in remorse. Her face crumpled for a second.

"Saw that, did you?" I leaned on the bar to face her. Her braids complemented her tight black tank top and equally tight jeans. Her legs were fucking amazing and I realized I loved seeing her in denim. Or workout clothes. Anything, really.

"The whole shebang. You confuse me, Zade. You really do."

"Right back at ya, babe." I smiled and a small red flush tinged her cheeks. Good. I wanted to tear down the wall she'd built between us and caveman her back to my house. But I wouldn't until she gave in or I got over my unnatural attraction.

"I actually came over to tell you that Aaron put his arm around me to send a message to the creepy guy who hit on me earlier." She bit her lip, looking down at the ground before meeting my eyes. "I realize it looked like flirting, but it's harmless and not going anywhere."

"Okay, then." My words sounded harsh but my stomach relaxed. Her face fell and once again I'd behaved like an asshole. Ellen chose that moment to bring the pitchers with even more cleavage showing. She smiled sweetly at me and didn't even glance at Callie.

"It's on the house. Here, call me any time." She handed me a card with a number on it and I gave her an awkward smile.

"Thank you so much." Callie clapped. "I love when my boyfriend gets free drinks because he plays with balls. You're the best, Ellen!" Ellen stared at her, mouth agape in horror. Of all things I could've done in that moment, I threw my head back and laughed. Ellen stormed off, probably crying, and I should've apologized. But I didn't.

"Holy shit, Callie." I put my hand on her shoulder and she fought a smile, too. "That was...something else."

"I meant it to annoy you, not make you laugh like a goon." She sucked in her cheeks and a full smile broke out. "But I'm glad I amuse you."

"I don't know why that cracked me up. I get a lot of shit like that sometimes and I've been known to play into it," I admitted with a shrug. I let go of her shoulder and itched to touch her more.

"No, really? With Zwillows Pillows in full swing...it had to be tough to not get an ego. I bet you *hate* the attention."

"At times, yeah. At times, no." I handed her a pitcher and took the other. Whatever had happened between us left and our normal banter came back. We walked to the booth the guys had taken over in the back corner, away from the bar area and enough out of sight to relax without attention. It was the charm of Cam's—no one bothered anyone. Callie headed into the booth first, squeezing her tiny body next to Aaron and Jeff. "Scoot over, ladies. I'm on your team."

Tanner rolled his eyes and Aaron made a scene as he moved over. I joined on the opposite side, directly across from Callie, my legs too long to fit comfortably. I stretched them out. She raised her eyebrows at me and I shrugged. "Not enough room."

"Uh-huh."

"Did you hear what Callie did, Z?" Tanner sniggered as we all poured a glass. "It was bad-ass."

"Fuck yeah, it was. I'm team Callie forever." Aaron put his arm around her and squeezed. "Tell him."

"Eh, it's not that big of a deal." She shrugged his arm off, making me happier than I had been seconds ago. "Anyone would've done the same thing."

"Uh, no. That's false," Greta added and I got impatient. "She is the definition of goals."

"Tell me." My voice commanded Callie's attention and she took a large sip of beer.

"Some bitch in the bathroom came up to us and talked shit about us hanging out with you guys. It was ridiculous and rude as hell." She shrugged and made an amused face. "I happened to walk right up to her and threaten her."

"Bro, she's on Snapchat. Some girl filmed it in the bathroom. It's Veronica!" Jeff handed me the phone and I watched the encounter with a surge of pride and a whole unfamiliar feeling floating through my chest.

"Fuck. This is awesome." I grinned. "You are one bad-ass chick, Callie. I'm glad you're with us." I refrained from saying *elated, ecstatic, overjoyed* because I wasn't a damn chick, plus my teammates didn't need more fuel to make fun of me. But damn, Callie changed the game.

"Here, here." Aaron held up his beer and I followed suit. "Cheers!"

"I told you guys that you'd love her. Cheers to me, too!" Greta yelled and we did. These two crazy girls somehow fit into our odd team.

Chapter Thirteen

Callie

Callie: I can't run today. Beer. Beer is the devil.

Zade: Beer is the devil but don't let it win!

Callie: No. I'm canceling. My head is a pile of hammers. An entire team of hammers.

Zade: I promise you'll feel better if you come.

Callie: Darkness. That makes me feel better.

Zade: Don't crap out on me. I'll bring coffee.

Callie: I like that word. Keep going.

Zade: We'll walk. It's okay to have an off day.

Callie: Cinnamon rolls.

Zade: You got it. Thirty minutes?

Callie: I'm wearing my Crocs. You can't force me to run.

Zade: If anyone can pull off those monstrosities, it's you.

Callie: One point for big word. Nice.

I rolled over in my bed and chugged the glass of water on my nightstand. I wasn't one to feel ashamed of drinking the night before, because I knew I'd done it to myself. It had been a great night, full of laughter and jokes. I popped two aspirin to stop the storm in my head before grudgingly putting on some loose shorts and a baggy Sox shirt. I tied it on the side, pausing to help the pounding stop, and threw on my Crocs. I didn't care how fashionable they were. They were comfortable as hell.

The Midwest weather hadn't broken yet and the humidity still suffocated my lungs on the walk to the meeting spot. And I moved at a slower pace than normal due to the damn hangover. I took my time getting to the bench and Zade watched me with a shit-eating grin on his face. He wore an old baseball shirt and black shorts. It was simple yet he pulled it off pretty damn well. I shielded my eyes and groaned.

"Hi there, champ. Looking great today. Ready to go?" He patted my knee as I sat down. Unlike our normal runs, no people were out this beautiful morning. Birds chirped, trees rustled and my heart beat way too fast with just the two of us on a deserted trail. *Yikes.*

"Ugh. Your energy is obnoxious." My knee tingled at the touch.

"I get called a lot of things but obnoxious, no way. I'm happy. Perky. Flirty. Bossy." He paused and handed me a cup of coffee. "I can keep going."

"Shh. Coffee. Now."

"I got it black with peppermint flavoring." He grinned his half-smile and I groaned into the container. "That's how you like it, right?"

"Exactly." I took a sip and leaned against the bench. "Thank you."

"You got it. We've got a good streak going and we couldn't have a mere hangover ruin it." He pulled out a small bag and handed it to me. "Cinnamon rolls, as promised."

"You're amazing." I took a bite, moaning. "Never let me insult you again."

"I like hungover Callie. She's full of compliments and is nice to me." He leaned his shoulder into mine. We did that a lot. Touch. I was getting used to it.

"I'm weak. Not myself." I hid my face behind the takeout cup, knowing I was close to cracking. I'd lasted barely three weeks, fighting it. "Did you have to go far for these? I haven't been able to find a decent coffee shop near our place."

"Eh, a block or two. I was wide awake earlier. I drank one too many last night and I burned through it around five."

"I bet with your body you don't get hungover."

"Not really. I get groggy and that's about it."

"Lucky. I can't say I'm surprised, though. You're solid muscle. With that body, you need a lot of alcohol to mess with you." I hoped he didn't read into those words, but I blushed all the same. "You know, because you're an athlete and shit."

"Nice save." The laugh lines appeared around his eyes again. "Don't worry. I won't assume your compliments are you hitting on me. You've made that pretty clear."

I nodded instead of responding. He smirked and took a sip of his coffee. I remembered our conversation from Target. "You like the peppermint, too, right?"

"Yup. One of many things we have in common." He noticed my Crocs. "Damn."

"They look good, don't they?" I stretched out my legs, unintentionally bringing attention to them. His eyes heated over and I brought my legs back to my chest. My stomach filled with butterflies and I didn't like it one bit.

"Mm-hmm."

I studied his profile. God, he was good-looking. He was kind, ambitious, and…hell. Maybe my weak state made me super complimentary. His deep voice broke me from the derailment of my sanity. "I meant to ask you something last night, but I forgot."

"Go ahead." I sat, curious. Our questions usually became a game of sorts, but I always had fun.

"The way you verbally laid a smack-down on Veronica—"

"I'm sorry about that, by the way. If she belonged to one of your gaggle, I don't want to start any trouble. I hate when people talk about athletes or stars like they owe them something."

"One of my gaggle. You say the weirdest things. But no, she is not one of the gaggle. I don't have a gaggle."

"You totally have a gaggle."

"No, absolutely not." He waved his hand with a dramatic flair that made me snort. He stared at me, his hazel eyes swirling with humor. "Now, before you rudely interrupted me."

"I'm an ass. I know," I interrupted him again. "My bad."

"Should I raise my hand? Or should we have a talking stick?"

"I might have been a hell-raiser in high school. I talked too much and got into trouble," I admitted without shame. "My teachers either hated or loved me. I spent some time in detention. Nothing like the *Breakfast Club*, though."

"Well, there goes that fantasy of you I had built up. You dressed as Molly Ringwald."

"I was more of the dorky chatterbox kid."

He gave me a look of disbelief and ran his hand over his jaw. I watched the motion, transfixed by the strength in his arm.

"I happen to enjoy your chatter, even when you interrupt. But if you do it again, I'm going to shush you with the finger."

"Oh, like when you put it on my mouth?"

"Yup. Now, shush."

I nodded vigorously and groaned, grabbing my head. "Hammer. Damn it."

"You drink water and take aspirin?" He set his coffee on the ground and walked toward me. Concern took over his face and it made him even more endearing. "Dehydration is the real reason for the pain, and well, you know, the alcohol, too. But the lack of water is the painful part."

"I know, and I shouldn't complain because I chose to drink. It annoys me when people complain about things they can change or self-induced. If I sound whiney, smack me."

"You aren't whiney." He held out his hands. "Turn around."

"Why?"

"I'll show you what I learned once when I had a migraine. You can use this trick for headaches, hangovers, migraines or stress. I use it for all three." He clapped his hands. "Come on, turn around."

"Uh, okay." I obeyed. My heart beat fast and I was sure he heard it. But he said nothing. "What are you doing?"

"Applying pressure." He smoothed my hair off my neck, the movement sending goosebumps down my body. I shivered. He pressed two fingers onto the two pressure points behind my ears — hard. "It's going to hurt but relieve the pain."

"Uh-huh." I managed to get out two syllables, somehow. His hand gently applied pressure, rubbing out the muscles. I closed my eyes, moaning into my fist. *Shit, he has good hands.*

"How does it feel?"

"Uhh." I closed my eyes. "Yes."

He laughed softly and continued the movements. "Good. Did you know about the one in your hand? Here, give me your coffee." I held out the coffee and he set it on the ground. "Right between your thumb and pointer finger is another pressure point."

He kept one hand on my neck, pressing down, and had my other hand on his leg. He pinched the skin between my fingers and although it hurt, the pressure in my head disappeared. I met his gaze and nerves took over. His eyes burned into mine. His jaw was tight, pained, and I knew how he felt — I felt it, too.

We stayed like that, him touching me and me fighting every urge to climb onto him. He pressed harder and a small moan escaped my mouth. He let go and jerked back. The loss of his touch made me feel cold. "Better?"

"Yeah. Thanks." I avoided looking at him as he avoided me. This had gotten awkward and I needed to get it under control. "Your question?"

He cleared his throat. "Right. It was about your anger at Veronica. I thought about it once I got home, but I feel there's a story I'm missing."

"Not sure what your question is exactly. I'd never met her before and didn't appreciate her sick plan."

He gave a strained laugh. "I know that. I feel like you have a history or something with people like her. Maybe I'm crazy. I'm curious, that's all."

"You're sort of right." I guessed the time had arrived to tell him about my hang-up with him. *You can do it.* "I told you I grew up around baseball players and I've seen the likes of the good, the bad and the ugly of the sport."

"Of course. You're also a baseball nerd, which is super-hot." He winked, his normal flirtatious self coming back to life. I preferred *this* Zade. He was easy to get along with and fun. Serious Zade? A danger to my heart.

"Anyways, I'm not commenting on that one. There are two parts to the story, so bear with me. The first time I saw a cleat chaser try and ruin someone's life I was sixteen. His name was Carter. He had all the talent in the world for a small-town kid with a dream. Long story short, she wore him down. He cheated on his longtime girlfriend and I know it takes two, but I still swear the bitch drugged him."

He recoiled, angry as hell. "Who the fuck does that?"

"I know. It makes my blood boil." I clenched my fists. "She took him to court for childcare payments and dragged his name through the mud. The child wasn't his in the end, but he lost focus on the game and his stats struggled. He still plays in the minors, but the future he had at that time was bright. She dimmed it."

"And the second part?"

"Seventeen-year-old Callie had a crush on an All-Star catcher. Shocking, right?" I laughed without any humor in it. His eyes had filled with pity. I glanced away. "You know how the story ends. Girl likes boy, boy likes girl, girl chases boy, and boy suddenly breaks up with girl because of naked women in his bed."

"That's not a story I like or have heard. You're skipping on the details, Callie. Tell me what happened." His eyes now held a tinge of anger.

"It was my first love or boyfriend or crush, whatever. We never made it official, apparently, well that's what he said. We were together the entire summer before my senior year, or I thought so at least. But these cleat chasers were relentless. He was in college, dating a high schooler. They played every trick and won the game."

"The asshole cheated on you?"

"Since we weren't technically together, I guess not. But to me, it appeared he did. It was hell. He stood me up at homecoming and those cleat chasers posted tons of pictures of them online. It was...shitty." I had no lingering feelings for Gage, none whatsoever, but the memory still burned with shame. "When I see those types of girls who don't care about anything but their own agenda, I get pissed as hell."

"Rightfully so." He twisted his face but then changed to his easygoing smile. "I for one am glad you're on our side of the field, though. I wouldn't want to face your wrath."

"You should be." The intensity of the moment lessened. Zade had the unique talent of making me feel turned on, worried, comfortable and joyous all with a smile. *Damn him.* I took the last sip of my coffee and got some energy. "You were right."

"Of course I was, but about what exactly?"

"I do feel better now."

"I have a way with people." He stood up, stretched and I ogled the hell out of his abs. "I can pose for you if you want a picture."

"Shit. I got caught." I shrugged and heat rushed to my face. "I'll join Zwillows Pillows and get a pillow case or something."

"Fuck. That's embarrassing." He clapped his hands and pointed to the trail. "Now, we are walking five miles. No complaining."

"In Crocs? No way."

"Stop your excuses. They say excuses are like assholes—everyone has one." He puffed out his chest and I snorted.

"Classy guy. You're a real prize." I stood up and threw the empty cup in the trash. "Fine. Let's walk.

"Go ahead of me. I can't trust you to not look at my ass."

All I could do was flip him the bird.

Chapter Fourteen

Zade

A week later, Jeff and I walked into the store, bearing a list that consisted of meat with a side of meat. Our diets demanded protein and vegetables, but none of us cooked worth shit. We've heard of some guys having their parents send them meals, but most of ours were out of state and by now we'd gotten through the food they'd packed us off to college with. It was up to us to cook and we sucked. No other explanation.

"Ay, hamburger helper is total shit, right?" Jeff threw a box of it at me. I caught it and read the back. Generally, fake ingredients were the worst.

"Yeah. Probably shouldn't." I set it back and searched for mashed potatoes. I couldn't make them from scratch but boxed ones were fine. "Has Nicole sent you a meal plan yet?"

"Yup. Pretended I didn't get it, though. I want to enjoy August this year. I'll focus more in September."

He found a pack of Oreos and threw them into the cart. "Yolo."

"You're a tool." I didn't put them back. I loved me some Oreos. "If Nicole knew we were drinking tonight..."

"Who the hell cares? We're young. We're in college. I love the sport and have dedicated my life to it. We can kick it back sometime." He picked out some other boxes of shit and we made our way to the liquor and beer aisle. "We haven't had a party since before school started. We're due."

"You right, you right." I saw the case of beer I wanted, damn well knowing we couldn't actually buy it. One of the older guys on the team had already dropped the alcohol off. Having good teammates was fucking great. "You invite some of the Kappas?"

"Hell yeah. Kappas, Thetas and Omegas. They are the best sororities." He clapped his hands together, tilting his head to the side. "Oh, and Callie and Greta? Yeah, they're coming, too."

"Yeah, she told me this morning." Tonight would be hard as hell. We were pre-gaming and all going out to the new club. I'd let what Callie had told me about her high school boyfriend sink in all week and it made sense. She didn't quite put me in the same category as that asshole, but she was hesitant before getting involved with someone. I understood it, but I couldn't be her boyfriend. What a stupid thought...right?

"You guys good? You have a weird relationship. She's hung around us as much as Greta, who we see as a little sister. But Callie is not...sisterly."

I stopped the cart and waited, praying he wasn't interested. I had no claim on her, not anymore, and yet contemplated telling him to back the hell off. "We're fine. We're friends." I shrugged. "Not that I haven't tried for more."

"I think it's hilarious. All the women whose hearts you broke—this is payback for that. Callie and Greta are way too cool for the likes of us. That's why our friendship is awesome. They keep us on our toes and call us out on our shit. I like to think of them as our life coaches."

He pulled out his phone, seemingly unaware that his words bothered me. "Sweet, Kelly and her twin sister are coming. They are my goal for the night. Want me to see if they can bring more friends?"

Kelly was hot. Like, cover-of-a-magazine hot, but she was also fake as hell. I hadn't been with her but had always wanted to, until now. The thought scared me. Jeff stared at me, waiting for my answer. "Sure, the more the merrier."

"That's my boy." He kept walking down the aisle and I followed, worried about my sex drive. It had been a month. The longest dry spell I'd had since coming to college. I owed nothing to anyone and something needed to be done. I was cranky and uptight. "Hook up with someone tonight, Z. With the stick in your ass, you need it. Callie ain't going to happen."

"Thanks man. Appreciate it," I replied. Even my friends knew my swagger was off.

"Looking out for you. It's what I do."

We bought everything on our list, but my mood worsened. I liked challenges. I never gave up, but what Jeff had said rang true. The world had served me up a good side of karma.

* * * *

The music pumped through the walls of the house. The bass shook the chair I sat in and I relished the feeling. The only time I loved rap music was when the atmosphere called for it. This called for it. I surveyed our basement, currently filled with people in various states of dress. Girls danced with red cups in their hands, guys played beer pong and cheered like idiots, Jeff and Tanner stood at the table playing DJ for the night and Aaron had last been seen leaving the room with a pretty brunette all over him. I smiled, content sitting on the chair with my third drink in my hand.

"Can I join you?" Frankie, one of my on-and-off hookups, who I hadn't seen in a couple months, sat on the arm of my chair. "You seem lonely."

"By all means." I scooted over, causing her to fall into my lap. I wasn't unaffected by her body. My dry spell messed with my head while her short dress left nothing to the imagination and distracted me. She used to be one of my favorites, if I had them. She knew what I wanted and expected and she never nagged.

"It's been a while. I've missed you." She crossed her legs over me, my hand having no place to go except her thigh. I ran my finger down her soft, smooth leg. I preferred strong legs but hers were nice. "How have you been?"

"Nothing new, really. What about you?" I small-talked her, already bored. She was a perfectly decent person, but all we had in common was sex. Great sex, but I wasn't sure if I was up for it. I hated myself for the doubt, but Jeff's words crept back up again. *She's too good for you.*

"School is going really well. I love my classes." She frowned a little bit. "You seem tense. Want to go upstairs real quick?"

We both knew what she meant. Her eyes flared with heat. I needed to get off and release the crazy amount of tension I had been carrying around. I had nothing to lose. I hadn't seen Callie here yet and if I did…nothing, nothing would happen. She'd friend-zoned me to the max and I hated it. I took Frankie's hand in mine and smiled at her. "I'd like that."

"Perfect." She dragged her finger down my chest and pulled me in for a kiss. It was quick, her fruity lips not unpleasant on mine. I matched her kiss and broke it apart. "You have a great mouth."

I didn't respond and headed upstairs. I weaved through a couple of people and stopped when I saw Callie walking down the stairs. She wore the black jeans she'd had on the first time I'd seen her here. Her hair hung in loose waves down her shoulders. She spoke with some guy on the stairs and laughed. Her whole body went into her laugh and she met my eyes. Her face lit up like I was the fucking best thing in the world and it wasn't fair. Her perfect, makeup-free mouth opened to say something but then she stopped.

Frankie poked her head around me, giggling. "Why'd you stop, Z?"

Callie's smile faded.

My heart sank and remorse filled my body. The sinking pit I'd only had twice in my life grew in my stomach and I dropped Frankie's hand. "I'm sorry, I uh, I can't do this."

"What?" Her face fell in hurt and I took off toward Callie. She hadn't waited a beat before heading back up the stairs. My heart raced. No way we ended before we gave it a try. I craved a chance with her. I needed it and we both deserved it.

"Callie!" She walked out of the front door, but the command in my voice stopped her. The entire room hushed, the scene unfolding in front of everyone. I strode over to her and saw pain in her eyes. I fought the urge to grab her and instead ran my hand down her arm. She shivered at my touch and I lowered my voice, preventing the whole damn room from hearing. "Can we talk?"

"We probably should at this point." She focused on the floor instead of my face and a muscle in her jaw twitched. *Not a good sign, asshole.* "Want to head up to the roof?"

"Yeah. I'd like that a lot." I held out my hand, not unlike what I'd done with Frankie, and guilt washed over me again. She took it and I led her to my room. "Thank you for coming with me. I thought you were going to run out."

"I thought about it, but I'm not a coward. We need to do this. It's been building for a while." She nibbled at her lip as I opened the windows and hopped up onto the desk. I scooted out first, waiting for her to do the same. It was so much like that first night a month ago when I'd thought I'd found the perfect girl in the world. Now, our pasts kept us apart and I wanted to punch the wall at how much it sucked.

We sat side by side, not saying anything. Despite the party raging below, it seemed as though we were the only two there. She had her longs legs stretched out and chucks on her feet. The bass continued to boom, but I waited her out. She deserved to speak first. She finally looked me the eye and I held my breath. Regardless of what she said, it was final. We couldn't keep torturing each other.

"Zade…" She stopped and gave an exasperated laugh. "I don't know where to start."

"Me neither." I pulled her to me, tucking her into the side of my body. She fit there, perfectly. Her head on my shoulder, our breathing matching, had to be one of the best moments ever. She didn't fight it and, for the first time ever, I knew she was meant to fit me. She smelled like vanilla and cucumber, a combination I never would've liked, but on her, it tortured me. "I have mad feelings for you."

"Yeah, I've come to accept I have them, too."

Fuck. Yes. She acknowledged them! I felt weightless at that moment. "You sound pissed off about that."

"I am. I tried to fight it. I really did."

"I'm glad you gave up the fight. I almost lost it."

"Yeah…we need to talk some things out, though." She sat up and a look of concern crossed her face. "If I hadn't run into you, you would've slept with that girl."

I joined her, sitting up, and I continued touching her. I pulled her until she sat between my legs, her back to my chest. I enveloped her in my arms and tried to say without words that no one else mattered now. "I won't lie to you, I probably would've."

"Don't hurt me, Zade." She spoke, resignation in her words. It sounded so unlike her, who was bold and brave and colorful. I pressed a kiss to her temple.

"Challenge accepted, baby." She leaned farther back into me. "I can explain the girl."

"Nah, you don't have to. We were friends, are friends? I don't know. Are we the same as ten minutes ago? I don't freaking know. This is hard." Uncertainty and fear laced every word. I was unsure, too, but I had no choice anymore. Not when her face fell and I saw every feeling I had reflected back to me.

"First off, we are not the same. We'll get to that. But, the girl... You know I've had a past. You've made that the number-one reason you never gave me a chance. Am I right?"

"Yeah."

"Well, she is someone I used to hook up with. I was in a mood this morning and Jeff called me out on some shit with you. Pretty much told me you were way too good for me and that it wasn't going to happen. I wanted to try and forget about you. That's what I thought I wanted to do."

"I can't say that doesn't feel shitty. But I have no right. I appreciate the honesty though." She relaxed into my arms again and I couldn't hide my smile. I felt like a million bucks. "We have a ways to go before I fully trust you with whatever this is—are you positive you're up for that?"

"Fuck, yeah. You run the show, Callie." I kissed her head again and my heart clenched when she sighed. "Whatever you want. I want a chance with you."

"Ugh. When you say things like that, you make my life confusing."

"You've made my life confusing as hell since that day in Target. You think you have it bad...my mom and sister have been giving me shit since they heard all about you."

"Oh, god. They probably think I'm crazy."

"The opposite. They dig you already. As you said, I had a bit of a reputation before and you've kind of blown that all to hell."

"Can I ask you about it?"

"Anything. I will never lie to you. Ever." I meant the words more than I ever had before. "I ask that you do the same."

"I promise." She whispered the words and tensed up at whatever crossed her mind. "I'm wondering, I guess... Well, shit. I don't know if I want to know."

My stomach dropped. I hated her hesitation, but I knew I had to tell her the truth, regardless of her question. I hoped she believed enough in us now to overlook my past mistakes. "Go ahead. I'll answer you."

"How many? A hundred?" She cringed, turning around. I didn't answer right away and her face paled. "Oh, my god. More than that?"

"Stop. Your imagination is worse than the truth. Definitely less than fifty. It's not like I slept with a different girl every weekend. I had arrangements of sorts."

"Repetitive booty calls?" Her nose scrunched in disgust. If I hadn't felt like a schmuck, I would've told her how cute I found the gesture. "I thought you didn't do relationships."

"I didn't. That's the thing. I slept with the same girls more than once." I enjoyed her blatant display of jealousy, but not her discomfort. "I was always safe, no matter what. I never promised them anything and as soon as they showed any sign of relationship-y shit, I walked."

"I won't throw your past in your face. It wouldn't be fair, but I'm going to go slow. I can't get hurt and you, Zade, have the power to break me into a thousand pieces."

"What makes you think you're the only one capable of getting hurt? You've thrown my life into a shit storm with your toned body and smart mouth. It goes two ways, babe."

"Then we take it slow."

"How slow? Because I've been dreaming about your mouth and things I want to do to it for weeks."

"You were going to sleep with another girl tonight. When we kiss, it's going to be because I'm the only girl you've been thinking about for days." She got up and went toward the window. "Let's go play some beer pong. I want the full college experience, Zade."

I shook my head and laughed. She had no fucking idea that she was the only girl I'd been thinking about, but if she preferred to go slow, then slow it was. But I sure as hell wasn't going to make it easy on her.

Chapter Fifteen

Callie

"You cannot stop smiling and I think I know why." Greta wiggled her eyebrows at me over breakfast the following morning. "I know I flirted on the side of drunk last night, but you and Zade... Dish it, sister."

"Even though I told you about it last night and your drunk ass forgot? Fine. I'll tell you again." I poured us cups of coffee and got comfortable on the couch. "We're...doing this thing."

"What thing?"

"No idea. The *thing*." I wish I knew, but nothing was clarified. I supposed admitting we had something going on was the first step.

"Come on, I wanted the dirty details. I wanted something better than *thing*. I'm disappointed." She sipped the drip coffee I'd started making. "This is the best coffee I've ever had. So that makes up for the lack of entertainment. Damn, Cal, I thought you'd have at

144

least attacked him or something. You have the hots for him."

"Yeah. I do. It sucks. I tried not to catch feelings, but I didn't stand a chance." She nodded at me. "I'm still worried, though. He's a known womanizer. I'm a challenge to him and as soon as the newness wears off... I don't know."

"First off, yes, he is a womanizer. And I know we mourned the loss of Mr. T when we found out Target guy was him, but I think he's different with you. I've seen him around for over a year. He watches you like he's into you."

"That sounds creepy."

"Borderline, but I think it is intrigue. You captivate him. Think of this as a real-life version of *John Tucker Must Die*."

"Great movie. God, Jesse is fucking hot." We laughed. "I told him we were taking it super slow and we didn't discuss anything. All I know is we are a thing. How lame is that? I don't know what *thing* means."

"Who cares? Enjoy the ride. And, Cal, he's not Gage. I know that was part of your hold-up." She frowned, biting her lip in thought.

"I told him about Gage. Well, most of it." I left out the moment when he'd stolen my virginity, left me and made a fool out of me for thinking I was different. Never again would I lose myself in a guy. *Ever.* Light and casual were the way to go. "I gave him the basic parts of it. I didn't want to rehash the traumatizing event."

"Probably for the best. I still *hate* him. Have you cyber-stalked him lately?" Greta and I had a problem of sometimes looking up people from our past. It wasn't bad...unless one of us accidentally hit Like on an old picture from three years ago. "Last I checked, he'd moved to St. Louis. That asshole. St Louis is that armpit of the United States. He'd better feel at home there." She ground her teeth and made the face of a warrior going into battle. "If I ever run into him...I swear."

I cackled. "I'm glad you're on Team Callie. You're scary sometimes."

"I don't want your past to mess up your future. That's the bottom line. I know you haven't had a serious boyfriend since him."

"I've had boyfriends." I shrugged. I hadn't been lying when I'd told Zade that I'd only slept with people I was in a committed relationship with. It had been...hmm...two years since I'd slept with Gage and that was the last time.

"No. You've gone on dates with the same guy maybe three times before calling it off. I ain't judging you, but it seems that Gage is still winning." She made a duck face and I scowled at her.

"He isn't winning. I haven't been interested in anyone, really."

"Until Zade." She finished my sentence for me. "Then see how it pans out. I never would've believed it last year, but I'm telling you, my gut feels good about him."

"Well, you and your gut are something else."

"Yup. Remember the time I saved your life because my gut had a sixth sense?" She got up, smug. "It never fails."

"Nah, you prevented an old man from stealing my chicken nuggets." I laughed, thinking about that treacherous stroll home through an old parking lot at four in the morning. It had been our senior year and our first time really drinking. We'd snuck out and stumbled home to find our parents both waiting for us with disappointed faces. We'd thought we'd been pretty damn sneaky…propping open a ground floor window with old shoes. We should've known better. Greta's parents had found the shoe first, then called mine. I shuddered at the memory…the kitchen table set up as though in a court room and us interrogated as if we'd committed a crime. We'd been grounded for a month, but it'd totally been worth it. "Freckled Joe was a local favorite. He was harmless."

"No, he was a crazy person and would've done unimaginable things to us. So, you're welcome by the way." She made a self-righteous face and marched into her room. "I have to go take online quizzes all day and I don't want you to think I'm storming out dramatically."

"Uh-huh. Sure. You are *never* dramatic." I opened my email. Radcliffe and I made plans to meet at nine in the library to knock out the entire diet plan. We planned on working four hours, and I thought out my snacks. I packed a lunch and spare water. The sooner we got it done, the sooner I could watch the Sox game and veg for the rest of the day. "I'm heading to the library. See you later, G."

The walk held the first sign of the changing seasons. Summer was bleeding into fall, with warm temperatures, but the slight breeze cooled the evenings. I ate it up. Fall had always been my favorite time of the year. Warm coffee, cold nights and playoff baseball. Nothing beat fall.

I found Radcliffe sitting with a scowl at a large table. The library was partially underground while still containing windows. The lack of natural light on the lowest floor gave it a creepy, dungeon feel. It had apparently always been part of the charm of the place. I couldn't contain my excitement at having my first study session there. Radcliffe's scowl broke into a smile when I waved. "Radcliffe Rutger, Prince of Scandinavia, heir to the purple ruby throne. Feared by many, afraid of no one."

"Ha. Ha. Ha." He mocked me, but his eyes were warm. "I must say that was one of the more creative ones I've heard."

"I've got a quick mind." I sat down and pulled out my laptop. "Let's get this done."

"Plans later?" His tone was light, but I knew my answer mattered to him for some odd reason.

"Baseball, baby. Always baseball." I showed him my Sox planner, pencil and old logo on my hat. "You a fan?"

"Damn. I'm more into football. Baseball is too boring for me." He appeared ashamed and I'm sure my glare didn't help. I needed to not care so much when people expressed their right to not like the best freaking sport in the world.

"I guess that's allowed. Sorry, I'm intense about it sometimes. Ignore me."

"No, no. You're okay. You make me wish I followed the sport more."

"It's never too late to start. Might I suggest the White Sox?" I winked at him. He blushed and I sat back, questioning myself. I wasn't flirting, was I? I normally acted like this... God. I hated the unclear expectations and decided to say to hell with it. I wasn't changing who I was. "I mean, pick your own team, I guess."

"I'd be afraid to say any other name. But I am a fan of the Bears. The team my family watched our whole lives."

"Damn, then that sucks. I follow a bit, but I'm more into hockey. That's why this project is fantastic and exciting. Did you do the research?"

"You got it. Let's compare."

We broke the project into two parts and knocked out the first one in an hour and a half. To say I was impressed was being modest. I'd always ended up doing all the work and this rocked. "High five, Radcliffe. We killed that first part."

He smiled shyly and raised his hand. "Yeah. Yeah we did."

I hit his hand with mine and pulled back quickly. "Short break before we start the second? I'm going to go grab a small coffee."

"I'll wait here. Go ahead."

I headed over to the small coffee shop with my phone and cash. I needed a little more boost to get through the day. I had been up pretty late the night before. The thought brought a smile to my face and with his freaky superpowers, Zade must've known I was thinking about him.

Zade: God. I'm not a stalker, but you look amazing.

I searched the area around me, nerves fluttering through me. He must be somewhere in the library, but I couldn't find him.

Callie: Interesting that you followed me to the library. Been following me anywhere else?

Zade: I plead the fifth. Tell your drycleaners hello for me.

Callie: Good one.

Zade: My open mic slot starts in thirty.

I laughed, warmed by the easy flirting. We'd chosen to cancel our run, the party never making it to the club. Instead, the party had lasted until the early hours of the morning at the house. I'd left with a slightly drunk Greta around three. Sometimes she needed a chaperone and, as her best friend, that meant me.

Callie: Can I make a stereotypical jock joke? How did you know we had a library?

Zade: I asked Siri. She's my number 1.

Callie: Are you going to hide behind your phone or actually come talk to me?

Zade: I think I'll continue to hide.

Callie: You have a problem. But suit yourself.

I pocketed my phone, but I stood a little straighter knowing he watched me from somewhere. I had seen him every day since moving here. Literally every day and I didn't want to break the streak. I ordered a small black coffee with a little mint flavoring and had headed back to the table when a large chest blocked me.

"Uh, excuse me." I tried to be polite but then heard a familiar voice. "Oh, hey."

Zade studied me with so much emotion my breath caught in my throat. *Slow down*, my brain told my heart, but my heart was a strong independent woman who took no directions from anyone. He put his hand on my shoulder, squeezing it. "How's the homework coming, nerd?"

I ignored his comment, his fingers dragging down my arm consuming every feeling I had. It was a possessive move, but not unromantic. It was as if he needed to touch me and that was the only place I would let him. I continued to stare at him and he cleared his throat. "Shit, sorry. You distracted me."

"I wish we would've had this talk earlier. You can check me out all you want. Name the place and time."

"Calm down, psycho. Homework is going well. Actually got paired with someone who does their share. I love it when that happens."

"Good for you." His smile held back something and I wanted to figure out what.

"Have you ever had to do partner work?" I asked, curious. Professors raved about how collaboration helped in the real world because we were forced to work with people all the time. I called bullshit. They wanted to grade fewer assignments and make our college experience even more awkward.

"Here and there, sure." He didn't meet my eyes and I put it together.

"Oh, my god. You dog. You made your partner do everything and you probably blew them a kiss or winked or something." I hit him in the chest. "Am I right?"

"You aren't entirely wrong. I'll admit that." He looked ashamed and proud of his little antics. "I do get good grades, though. My mom threatened to send me STD pamphlets in the mail if my GPA goes below a three."

"Wait, what?" I paused. "Your mom said that?"

"Yup. She's hilarious and has a distinct way of parenting. Her threats are often inappropriate and borderline worrisome, but Zaria and I know she means them."

"What else has she said?" I asked. That was good shit.

"How about this…you promise to grab dinner with me tonight and I can tell you more."

"Smooth." I gazed at him, our eyes playing a dangerous game of who broke contact first. I lost, again. I seemed to be doing a lot of that around him lately. "The Sox play tonight. Come over. I'll cook."

"I'll be there. I like watching you cook. It's hot as hell." His hazel eyes went dark, almost green now. "I'll help you."

I blushed from head to toe and walked away from him. "I guess I'll see you later."

"You're running away now, but that's okay. Later, I won't let you." He walked out of the coffee shop and took my breath with him. I took a second to calm my breathing and forced my brain to focus on the assignment. Apparently Zade had been holding back the sexiness, because hot damn, that intense stare was killer.

I headed back to the table to see Radcliffe looking pissed off. I hoped I hadn't been away too long, but time did seem to stop when I was with Zade. "Man, did I take a while? I got to talking with someone. My bad."

"*You* know Zade Willows?"

"Yeah. We're friends." My face heated up and I fought a smile. Radcliffe's normal friendly expression transformed into one of disbelief. "My roommate and I hang out with a couple of the baseball guys quite a bit."

"Hmm." His tone became clipped and icy.

"Why the tone, Radcliffe?"

"I thought you were better than that." He pulled another textbook out of his bag and huffed. "Look, I like you. You're cool. But Zade—he's known for playing girls like decks of cards. One of my good friends…let's say he broke her apart. He's not a good guy. Be careful, I guess that's all I'm saying."

"Thanks for the advice, Radcliffe, but I've known him longer than I've known you." I put my walls up, not liking the way he spoke about Zade. "I think I'm a pretty good judge of character, unless you disagree?"

"Fair enough." He tapped his pen on the table and his once friendly eyes narrowed. "Ready for the second part?"

"Sure, let's go." I swallowed down the doubt and threw myself into the assignment. Whatever the hell had happened was his issue, not mine.

Chapter Sixteen

Zade

I refused to be nervous. Nope. Not even one bit. There was no reason to be because it was just dinner. Callie and I were going to cook and watch baseball. Totally normal. It wasn't a date. I fixed my hair in the bathroom and adjusted the shirt I wore.

"Holy. Fucking. Shit." Zaria barged into the bathroom with wide eyes that matched mine. Eyes are like books to the soul or some shit like that, they say. Right now, I agreed, because hers were laughing at me. "You are all sorts of fucked up over her."

"No, I'm not," I retorted in a mature fashion. Zaria had beaten me in every single verbal spat we'd had since childhood. I stuck my tongue out at her to really finish the argument off.

"You've checked yourself out in the mirror at least ten times. Normally, I'd say you look around eight times, so this is big."

"Fuck off. I do not check myself out in the mirror. Aaron does. Not me."

"Um, sorry, bro. You are a tad narcissistic." She held up her fingers to form a small space between her thumb and pointer.

"Well, you are a tad meddlesome pain in my ass."

"That's my job to be. Mom isn't here and you're one draft away from getting a big head. I'm here to make sure your ego doesn't inflate to the size of your fan club."

I laughed at that one. "Well said."

"Thank you. But you must admit, you do take a lot of time with your appearance."

"I like to dress nice. Ain't nothing wrong with that." I tucked my new shirt into my dark pants and shrugged. "Do I look okay?"

"I might cry. Hold on." She ran out of the bathroom and came back two minutes later with her phone. "Mom, he has a date. He's dressed up."

"Fucking hell, you didn't call Mom? Really, Zar?" I sighed in the way younger brothers did. The wrath of older sisters plagued everyone. "God, let's get it over with. I need to leave soon."

Zaria held up the FaceTime call with our mom, who held her hand up to her mouth and fake cried, "This is a dream."

"The women in my life are loons." I walked out to the dining room holding the phone.

"Is she the same girl you were all torn up about?"

"Yes. That's the one."

"Her name?"

"I am not telling either of you. Next thing I'll know you'll show up at her place with a photo album or something. I literally got her to agree to a date this morning."

"How did you see her this morning? I swear if you say she spent the night—"

"At the damn library, Mom." I pinched the bridge of my nose and sighed. "I ran into her at the library. But I also told you we run together almost every day, right?"

"She's smart? Oh, wow. She studies. Zar! You hear that!" my mom yelled into the phone, her action pointless. Zaria was behind me, hanging on to every word.

"I heard it. Our little Zadey is in love."

"I'm out. You two carry on without me. Since *The Bachelor* doesn't start for another month, don't use me to entertain yourselves!"

"I knew you watched it!" Zaria yelled at me. "How else would you know that?"

"Bye!" I ran like a cat out of water. In the safety of my car, I let out a laugh of relief. I loved the hell out of them, but damn, they annoyed me. But as Zaria said, it was her mission and she did a hell of a good job of it.

With sweaty palms and a racing heart, I drove back to campus. Two things bothered me about the date. The first—I didn't really know if it was a date. I assumed the rest of the guys and Greta might be there, but Jeff had told me they were all going to the driving range. He'd said Greta had suggested it.

I didn't speak girl code, but I translated that as her leaving me and Callie alone for the night. The second thing…was that I hadn't been on a date, if this was one, in years. *Fuck.* I wiped my palms on my pants and pulled into their guest parking lot. I'd bought her a White Sox running bottle instead of flowers. That was stupid. I regretted it as I held it in my hand while I walked up to their door. I knocked with my free hand and tried not to freak the hell out until she answered. I failed.

"Wow." She eyed me up and down, a red tint appearing on her cheeks. "You look nice."

"I feel stupid now." She wore jeans and a vintage Nirvana shirt. She made anything look good and my nerves went into double time.

"Why? I think it's sweet." She smirked and her dimples popped out. That was a real smile. "Come on in. It's us tonight."

That answered that question. Didn't help my nerves but...the two of us being alone in the apartment left a lot of things open for possibility. "I brought you this." I held it out to her to take. *Fuck*. I sounded like a caveman. I spoke in short words, my voice monotone. She had to think I was a fucking loser.

"Is that a hydro bottle? No way!" She took it from my hands and grinned like a kid at Christmas. "These are the coolest things ever. I cannot believe you bought me something. You rock!" She threw her arms around me in a hug and I caught her just in time. Her toned body pressed against mine and I suddenly came back to the present.

"You bet. I saw it and figured it would be a way to repay you for dinner. Despite the fact it had the wrong team on it." I let my hands fall, keeping them on her lower back when we split apart. "I have to admit something."

"Okay."

"I'm nervous as fuck." I said it. I waited. She bit her bottom lip and smiled. God damn, her smile would kill me.

"You seemed a little off when I opened the door, but there's nothing to be nervous about. You know we get along fine." She broke apart from my grasp and led me into the kitchen. "Why are you nervous?"

"I haven't been on a date where it mattered before." I knew I'd said the right thing when her face softened and she walked back up to me. She took my face in her small hands. I held my breath, jaw tense, waiting for her to make a move.

"Damn you, Zade Willows. You say the perfect things sometimes and I can't compete with that." She stood on her tiptoes and I prayed she connected our mouths, but she didn't. She pressed a light kiss on my cheek and sashayed away. I calmed my heart rate down and followed her into the kitchen. I'd told her she ran the show and I would abide by that as long as I could.

She went to the fridge and pulled out two beers, handing me one. "I need one with all the sexual tension in here."

I snorted and agreed. "True that."

"Well, here's to a semi-first date?" She tilted her head and waited for my answer.

"Yup. The next one I'm taking you out, though."

"Let's see how this one goes first. You're a little too eager at the plate. Be patient. Watch a couple pitches."

"I take back every compliment I said about you and baseball. Your perfectly timed metaphors are hindering what I want to do."

"Don't get yourself benched." She oozed smugness with that one and I mimicked her by crossing my eyes.

"Watch yourself, Callie. That mouth of yours is going to get you into trouble." I took another sip of beer but held her gaze. It was sensual as fuck. She ran her finger down the side of the bottle and nibbled on her lip. I needed to gain control or the night would be the death of me.

"Really, now? What are you going to do about it?" As soon as she said the words, her eyes widened. I saw my chance and she knew it. I set my beer on down and cornered her against the counter. Her pulse raced in her neck. I took the bottle from her hands and put it behind her. I still hadn't touched her. I placed my hands on either side of her, trapping her, and ran my nose down her neck. She shook, which matched my own nerves. *Fuck yeah.*

"You smell fucking amazing." I pressed a light kiss on the spot between her neck and shoulder, somehow wanting to mark her as mine. She made the smallest noise when I did that. Her eyes were squeezed closed. "Callie. Open your eyes."

"Mmm. I'd rather not."

I traced her face. My thumbs went to the spots where her dimples were and over her bottom lip. It trembled at my touch and I knew we were close.

"Open them." I bent lower, pressing a light kiss to her jaw line. I kneaded the back of her neck where I knew she loved it. "I need to see your eyes."

"W-why?" She kept them closed. I tilted her head back, my hand covering her entire neck. The sight of her petite neck against my skin made me hard as fuck. But I no longer thought using my little guy. I ran my tongue down her neck, stopping when I got to her jaw.

"Because, Callie, I want you to see what happens when we have our first kiss. I've had a lot of firsts, but I have a feeling this one is going to change things for good."

She opened them slowly and I kissed her. It was unlike any kiss I had ever had. She tasted like beer and mint and I knew I would crave that flavor for the rest of my life. I pulled her hips to mine, her hands pulling on the back of my shirt. I started it gently, enjoying the taste of her. I would've spent hours teasing her, but she deepened the kiss by sliding her tongue inside mine. I groaned.

"Fucking hell, Callie." I pulled back, panting. I kept my hand in her wild hair but put distance between our faces. I couldn't trust my mouth not to be on hers if they were near each other. My world was rocked. Nothing was the same. "That was…"

"Yeah. Yeah. Damn." She ran her fingers over her lips. I smiled. I couldn't help it and she gave me a weird look. "Why are you smiling like that?"

"I know it makes me sound like a sap, but that was a million times better than I imagined it would be." I scooted closer and pressed a quick peck on her. "Seriously, best fucking first kiss ever."

She grinned bashfully and nodded. "I'll give you that. My knees are shaking."

"You should've said something." I picked her up and set her on the counter. "Better?"

"Show off. Hmm. I should be worried about how you kissed that well, but I'm not. I won't be able to think about much else the rest of the night."

"Hmm. How about the rest of the week?" I stood against her and couldn't stop touching her. I ran my hands down her hips, her legs, her arms, and bent low again, stopping right in front of her mouth. "And, Callie?"

"Hmm?" She had her eyes closed again and lips parted for me.

"Believe me on this, no one has ever affected me like you do. This is new for me."

"God, you're good with words. Has anyone ever told you that?"

"Nope. You're the first." And the compliment made me feel like a million bucks.

"I like that. Being one of your firsts." She leaned in to my palm, pressing a light kiss on it. "Now, let me teach you how to cook."

"I'm all in."

* * * *

"This wasn't that hard to make. Why is it always so expensive at restaurants?" I asked her an hour later as we ate beef Wellington. It melted in my mouth and I wanted to cry a little bit. It was *that* good.

"The selection of steak is what is pricey. I mean, these two fillets were like twenty bucks. It's misleading about how easy it is, though. Do you think you'd try to make it yourself sometime?"

"Probably. But I know a person who would help me, so why bother?" I blinked innocently at her and got the reaction I wanted. She laughed and rolled her eyes.

"Awful lot of assuming going on in that big head of yours." She took a bite of her steak. "I must admit, I can't stop staring at your mouth now that I know how good it works."

"Babe, you have no idea what else I can do with it." I said that without thinking and her eyes widened in shock. "But it might be too soon. Forget I said anything. It slipped out."

"How long has it been since you've had sex?"

I dropped my silverware, not having expected that question. Her original shock was gone and a heated look of curiosity replaced it. "Uh, why?"

"Call me incredibly curious. As long as it wasn't the past week, your answer would be acceptable."

"It feels like a trick question, but I'll answer it." I took a sip of my beer and met her eyes. "Before I met you."

She threw her head back and laughed. "No, really. When?"

"Before. I. Met. You." My words heated over, the stakes raising around us at my admittance.

"Oh, well, fuck." She paled and blinked a couple of times. "That was not the answer I expected."

"You've already been a first for me, Callie. You made me question why I didn't date. You changed the game."

"Jesus. It's already intense." She put her head in her hands and sighed. "You say these things and I feel... overwhelmed. Our flirty friendship was fun and easy. This... I don't know."

"I'm an intense guy and give my all to everything. We'll take it slowly, but now that I've had a taste of you, I'm not going anywhere."

Chapter Seventeen

Callie

After hours of kissing and flirting, I walked Zade to the front door. If I'd had to rate the night on a scale of one to ten...it was at least a twenty. He held my hand and kissed it before releasing it. He gave me a sheepish smile and asked the same thing I was thinking. "Is it weird I'm already excited about running tomorrow?"

"Nah, I'm there, too." I grinned to myself, giddy as hell. "Thanks for tonight."

"Literally, any time. Any day." He walked out of the door and pulled me in for another heart-pounding, knee-weakening kiss. "Your mouth made my top ten favorite things."

"What's the rest of the list?"

"I'll tell you tomorrow. Have a good night."

I closed the door to the apartment and slid to the floor. *Am I starring in a damn romantic comedy?* I giggled and flirted. These were actions I tried to avoid with guys, but fuck it. Zade broke down any rule I'd ever had.

Too restless to try and lie down, I picked up my guitar and played some classic tunes for an hour to relax before Greta burst through the door.

"Holy. Shit. You broke him," she squealed and ran into the living room.

"Broke who? What?" She tended to exaggerate and dramatize normal occurrences and I couldn't be sure what or who she was speaking about. And she would only get to the point of the story when she wanted to.

"Please, like you don't know. I need to pee and you need to tell me everything. *Everything.* I will cut you if you don't." She sprinted into her room and I sat there, still unsure what she had referred to. Not a minute later, she came back and practically sat on me. "I can tell by your wild eyes and stupid smile that you had as good a night as Zade had."

I narrowed my eyes in question and she kept talking, hopefully getting to the point of her odd outburst. "So, you know how I went golfing with my old roommate from last year and the guys, right? Well, we ended back at their place about an hour ago." She paused, waiting for some reaction from me. I nodded for her to go on. "We were all sitting around talking smack and Zade strolls in, whistling like he'd won a million bucks. The guys gave him so much shit, Cal, I swear. It was brutal and he took it. He took it and stood with his hands in his pockets and the same stupid grin you have on your face right now. You broke him."

The butterflies were back in full force and I shrugged. "At least it was mutual."

"But, but, but, you don't know the *old* Zade. He would threaten people when they made fun of him or talked shit. He would *never* let a girl get into his head. He sat on the couch and joined us for about an hour and he literally stared right at me and asked if it would be too needy to text you already."

"Oh, hell." New crushes were exciting and the thrill enough to light a fire. "What did you say?"

"I told him to calm his ass down if he didn't want to scare you away." She punched my arm. "This is *awesome*."

"Why are you excited about this? I love you, you know that, but I don't understand."

"Two reasons. One, everyone should know what it's like having that crazy rollercoaster ride of love. The two of you are like a stinkin' movie and I can't get enough. But secondly, you deserve to try again. I know Gage messed with you for a while."

"Two years, but who's counting?" I added to get a laugh.

"Right. You're both suited for each other—it makes perfect sense."

"I'm not going to lose myself in this, though. That's what I fear and he's so intense. The way he looks at me…" I shivered and Greta grinned like a Cheshire cat.

"I need the details. He didn't spill a word to the group. And they share almost everything."

"I'm sure he will when you're not there."

"No, trust me. I know almost everything they do. They don't see me as a girl. I'm like their little sister or something. I know about all of their latest hookups and they don't hold back. They really are players to the core. But, before you ask, Zade hasn't talked about a hookup in weeks."

"He told me that the last time was before meeting me."

"Ah, this is the real shit. I love it. Now, tell me or I'm getting the knife. Did you do it on the table? The couch? Did you make out?"

"I'm gonna need a beer for this."

* * * *

I showed up ten minutes early to run. The anticipation of seeing Zade again was too strong. I was going through an extra set of stretches when he strolled up, looking good as hell. His hair looked ruffled, as though he'd just run his hands through it, and his old shirt fit him like a glove. His face lit up when he saw me. I stood still, unsure if it would be acceptable to jump him.

He made the decision easy when he walked straight up to me and grabbed my face. He lowered his mouth to mine and he tasted of toothpaste and sunshine. I wasn't sure what sunshine tasted like, but he defined it. He kept it toned down from the night before, but I still stood breathless when we parted.

"M-morning," I stammered. "To think I worried about how the morning would go."

"You were worried? I woke up ready to get out here." He tugged the end of my braid. "I like your hair like this, by the way."

"Thanks. And I wasn't worried, per se, but nervous, unsure, you know? The usual after you see a guy you made out with the night before."

"Do you find yourself in these situations a lot, Callie?" He crossed his arms with a small frown.

"Fishing for information, Zade?" I mirrored his position. "But to answer your question, no. No, this is not a normal occurrence."

"Good." He bent to do some stretches and I chose to admire the view since I'd already stretched twice. "Enjoying the show?"

"Yeah, I like it when you bend over." He bent lower and did a booty-pop dance move that had me rolling with laughter. "Oh, my god."

"Yeah, bet you didn't know I can dance. Check me out."

He twerked on me, moving around in a circle so I had no choice but to allow it. I laughed so hard I fell to the ground. "Oh, my god."

"Shit. I didn't mean for my moves to knock you down. I figured you were sturdier than that." He bent onto one knee and held out a hand. "Let me help you up."

"I need more time." I rolled around, tears of laughter falling down my face. "You are…something else. If only your fan club knew."

"All for you, baby." His laughed at himself, which I found attractive. Life was too short to be serious all the time. "I aim to amuse."

"You succeeded." I let him help me up and he kept his hands on me. I made a face at the contact and he gave me a devilish smile. "Zade Willows. We'll never get our run in if you keep it up."

"Fine by me." He tugged the ends of my braids and pulled me toward him. "I can't help myself. Seriously. You do something to me."

I felt like the only person in the world at that moment. His intense gaze, the truth I saw in his words—a small bit of my heart fell to the ground. I didn't expect to ever get that piece back and the thought was terrifying. But, *Do or do not, there is no try.*

I closed the gap and *I* initiated the kiss. He gasped, which pleased me. It was quick, but we both knew it meant more coming from me. "Since we took care of the kissing situation…ready to run six miles?"

"Breakfast after?"

"No promises, Casanova."

We ran in our typical comfortable silence for the first three miles. but around the fourth, my leg started to get a cramp. I voiced my discomfort, but he refused to let me stop.

"Power through it. If it's not shin splits, it'll pass. I promise." He slowed his pace a little as a kindness to me, which I appreciated.

"Distract me through it, please," I grunted. The feeling in my leg took all my energy. No peace, no calm, only pain. I gritted my teeth. "Talk or something."

"Hmm. What do you want me to talk about?"

"What's the best baseball memory you have?" *First question to pop into my head.*

"Oh, man. That's a fucking good one. Probably my Freshman year in high school. I made the varsity team, which was a huge deal as a Freshman. My mom was always working, making sure we would eat, and my sister was a senior. She was one of the popular kids and she could've given me such hell, but she didn't."

"Damn her."

"Yeah, I know. Missed opportunity. But my mom surprised me and came to one of our games and my sister came with her friends. I hit my first homerun that game and the magic that day changed me."

"Yeah? Sounds nice." My smile came out feeling like a grimace.

"There's a magic to baseball. You know what it's like. But now I think about it, my best memory might be playing baseball in the backyard. I told you my mom took the role as mom and dad, so we'd play whiffle ball for hours and hours. Between that and the Tigers games, I fell in love with the sport."

"Your mom is amazing." I focused on everything except my leg. The trees, the insects flying around, the group of students who had early as hell classes, but the pain kept going.

"Callie, let's stop. Come on."

"Fuck." I slowed to a walk and grasped my thigh. "I stretched it out. I don't understand."

"Can you walk?" He kept his arm around me, regardless of how much I was sweating. "There's a bench. Let's sit."

He helped me hobble over to the bench and I gritted my teeth. I stretched out my leg full force and bent low, hoping to find the cause of the pinch. "I'm messing up your routine. Go ahead. I can get home by myself."

"No need to be a hero. Tell me where, okay?" It was not a sexual move or moment, yet when he pressed his hands into my leg and kneaded the muscles, my lady parts woke up ready to go. And I meant *ready to freaking go.* "You jumped when I hit here."

He gently pushed my hamstring. I nodded, he pressed it and I jumped into the air. "Yup. There."

"Pulled a hammie. Nice." He began rubbing the muscle. "Good news and bad news."

"I know what it means," I barked, the pain getting the better of me.

"But you didn't hear the good news yet." He pouted. He freaking pouted. "I was going to say that I can take care of you."

"Damn it. I'm wallowing right now. Don't charm me." I put my head onto his shoulder and closed my eyes. "I'm cranky."

"No way." I smiled at that. He put his arm around me and pulled my legs into his lap. "Do you need me to carry you back?"

"My dignity couldn't handle that. I'll tough it out." We shared a look and I wanted to say something to describe how I was feeling, but no words came to mind. I opened my mouth to try, but I heard giggles around us. "What the hell?"

A group of girls had their phones out, snapping pictures of us and running away. "Zade...were they spying on us?"

"Fuck." He clenched his fists and his jaw turned to stone. "Yeah. They were."

"Does this happen often?"

"Sadly. Please don't let them change anything."

"It doesn't, not really," I lied. Because getting photographed crossed over being weird. It invaded our personal conversation and made me cringe. "Want to head back?"

"Can I give you a piggy-back ride for a little bit of the way?"

"You want my legs wrapped around you."

"How dare you. I'm being chivalrous and gentlemanly."

"Lies. All lies." I smirked and he winked at me. "Let's do this. If we're going to get photographed, we might as well give them something to talk about."

"That's my girl."

He'd called me *his girl*. I loved it.

Chapter Eighteen

Zade

"Remind me to tell Callie I love her, okay?" Jeff clapped my back as we left the field a couple of days later. Callie and I had opted out of running for a few days due to her sore muscle and instead got breakfast. We kissed. A lot. And I finally understood what it meant to be a lovestruck teenager. Aaron have given me so much shit that I'd nut punched him the day before. Jeff, on the other hand, had said my mood had changed for the better and something along the lines that he didn't hate being my catcher anymore. "Your shit is on fire."

"I'm *that* talented." There had been no tightness since the first day. The Pilates workouts had begun earlier in the week and I felt loose and amped at the same time. Coach hadn't sneered at me with disappointment in over three weeks and Nicole had given me a half-smile. September was looking good.

"My bad, king Zwillow. I forgot who I was talking to for a second. Dick." He punched my arm—not my throwing arm—and scoffed. "You say talent, Nicole says Pilates, I say it's Callie."

"She knows her shit." I said, pride filling my chest. She didn't act like she knew baseball—she did. It was hot as fuck.

"I know, man. She and I got into a heated debate about the best closer in baseball and when she started dropping stats from the guy's collegiate years, I kind of put my head down and surrendered." He laughed and whistled at two girls running by us. They waved, which Jeff ate up. I waved, too, because I was polite, but I was more concerned about when him and Callie had hung out.

"When did you see her?" I tried to play it off, but he knew. He smirked at me, making me have to fight the urge to smack him.

"I ran into her and Greta at the Bean. Calm down, psycho." I hated how his face mocked me, but I remain helpless. I wanted to help—hell, I wanted to *protect* her.

Instead of responding to his comment, I brought up the bonding our coach wanted us to do. He insisted we take a team trip to one of those team-building campsites. We were expected to head out for four days during our fall break the first week in October. Only a month away and we were already dreading it. Coach had a reputation for being the opposite of anything...enjoyable. The year before, someone had snuck in booze and he'd made us run laps around the lake for every ounce in the bottle. We'd never known who'd brought it, but our bets had been on the punk-ass freshman who'd made it because of his daddy's money. *Fucking Carl.*

"Maybe it'll be different this year. I don't know…campfires and shit." He sounded skeptical. He should.

"Yeah, my idea of a good time is not campfires and shit. You don't have classes tomorrow, do you?"

"Hell no. I got lucky as damn. I'm free for three days, and with that, I'm going to go decide who I'm inviting over later."

"What happened with the girls?" I asked, amused.

"Oh, well…" He grinned like the bastard he was. "They weren't too pleased about me not picking between them."

"You're a dog."

"Just because you got spayed doesn't mean that you weren't like this, too. Remember that, bro." A wash of anger filled his eyes and I became irritated. I wasn't judging him but seeing it from the outside gave me a bad taste.

I held up my hands and shrugged. "I know, man."

The awkward silence lasted until we got to our house a short time later. He hadn't changed and yet, he annoyed me, maybe because I used to be like that. He hit the back of my head, a stupid grin on his face.

"Sorry, I got defensive. Let's hash it out with Madden?" He pointed to the controllers on the table and I nodded fervently. I was itching for competition or something. I knew I needed to take my time with Callie, but to say I was tense was just the beginning of it.

"You got it."

Three hours later, we got up and stretched. We were tied and that was unacceptable. "Fuck, Jeff, you got better at the game."

"You started sucking less. That's it." He clapped my back and we roamed the fridge for food. It went so fast in the house that we weren't surprised to see none there. "Shit. Nothing but eggs."

"I take it you don't want eggs?"

"Not now. The texture weirds me out," Jeff admitted.

"Why not head to Legends for a burger?" They had great food and were just down the block. I checked my phone, deleting four texts from Veronica and two from Frankie. My fist clenched, the girls' persistence irritating me. Callie'd had a point when she'd told me the challenge she provided intrigued me. Something about how easy the girls made it... I felt ashamed for my gender.

"Great idea. I'm going to get that waitress' number this time. I can feel it," Jeff replied puffing out his chest.

"No, you're not."

"Fuck off. Let's go."

I followed him and used the walk to see what Callie was up to. I hadn't texted her all day, which was hard as hell. I didn't want to scare her, and I tried to tone it down. Even in the goddamn lecture hall where two of Frankie's brat-pack followed me, I thought of Callie.

Zade: Every strike brings me closer to the next homerun. How's that for a dorky quote? I think it has a double meaning...get it?

Callie: The joke loses the steam if you have to ask if I get it. But yes, I do.

Zade: How's your day? Jeff and I are heading to grab some food.

Callie: Nice. Greta and I are eating ice cream and watching the Walking Dead. Best show ever. I want to be Michone.

Zade: I bet you know how to handle a sword.

Callie: No matter what I say it's going to sound dirty after that.

Zade: My favorite. What are you wearing?

Callie: You never turn it off. Nothing sexy, sorry. I'm not good at this. I'm wearing an old shirt that Greta got me as a joke. It says, 'I like juggling balls'. And it has a clown on it.

Zade: Why did I get turned on by picturing you in that?

Callie: Because you flirt on the side of crazy.

Zade: I blame you.

Callie: Sure, blame me for your issues. Shit, Greta's yelling at me. I need to put my phone down. Have fun!

Zade: Can I stop by on the way back?

I asked her that knowing I sounded like a schmuck. I'd kissed her senseless after our breakfast that morning, but that hadn't been enough. Jeff was a lightweight and would only survive maybe three beers before wanting to head back. He thought he was a party animal. I laughed at the thought and waited for my phone to go off. It never did and I sighed. She must've put her phone down. The only girl in the world who I wanted to text all night had the power to ignore me. I felt humbled and irritated as fuck.

"Bro...look. It's Omega's back-to-school bash." Jeff pointed to the various girls dressed up as different subjects. The concept was cool...I dug that, but the normal excitement of seeing barely clothed girls was not the same. I nodded in acknowledgment and had no choice but to follow Jeff.

"Ladies...you are ravishing." He went up to a red-haired knockout and kissed her cheek. "Dana, damn."

She giggled and dragged her fingers through his hair. Her friend eye-fucked the hell out of me but I tried to keep my face blank. Old Zade would've winked, played it up, touched her arm or something. But now...I tried to be polite. She wiggled up to me and put her arm around me. I didn't exactly shove it off me, but I attempted to. She was a fighter, though, and persisted.

"Zwillows. I've always wanted to meet you. You're even better in person." She grazed her nails down my arm. *Gross.* I didn't know how to respond whatsoever. I nodded curtly. "I am your biggest fan, seriously. I watch you throw every single game."

Dumbass. I don't throw every game. We have a rotation. But she continued.

"You hit well. I love watching you bat, too. You're super strong."

I rarely hit. I had a designated hitter for me most of the time. Zero for two.

"Plus, I like a man who knows his way around the dirt." She purred and I fought a gag. She knew nothing about me or the sport I played. I thought of how Callie would react to her and I laughed. She took it as encouragement and a flash went off. She pressed her mouth to my cheek before I backed away as if she was on fire.

"What the hell?" I saw her friend, Jeff's latest distraction, holding up a phone. "Come on."

"Bev was dying to meet you and we wanted to commemorate it." Her expression said the entire event had been planned. All of it. They'd used us and it pissed me off. Jeff realized it, a little too late, and his face fell. He released the redhead and shook his head as we walked away.

"Fuck, man." He put his hand on my back. "Bitches."

I laughed and couldn't agree more. "It's going to get worse the bigger we get. I thought I handled it will but…who can we trust?"

"I know. I hear ya. I'm sorry that I didn't see that coming."

"Not your fault, at all. Girls do shit. I didn't eat it up like I normally would've. They were hot, but the crazy and manipulative characteristics kind of blew that." One word for that change. *Callie.*

"Agreed. It makes me question how people change when they move up. I've heard horror stories about guys changing and relishing in the attention. I don't want to do that."

"Your family will help with that. My mom and sister literally kick my ass and knock me to the ground so fast when I act like a dick face." I sent a silent thanks to both of them. I promised myself to call them over the weekend and see Zaria. We'd both been busy and we were due to hang out.

"I need to have a talk with mine to do that more." He shook his head and opened the door to Legends.

"I'm always here, too. To knock you on your ass. Just say the word."

"Always so gallant."

"Word of the day again?

"No. The goddamn romance books my mom always read. I got bored in the car once." He grinned, ashamed, and I couldn't help but laugh.

* * * *

My prediction about Jeff was spot on. He headed in the direction of our house when I went the other way, to see Callie. Her response came later, but it made me happy as hell. I quickened my pace and was at her door within five minutes. My long legs helped, but the desire to see her was motivation enough.

I knocked on the door, not giving a damn about the time. It was midnight. My mom always told me nothing good happened after midnight but I chose to disagree at that moment. Callie opened the door wearing her *balls* shirt and my mood brightened.

"Damn, with a smile like that, come on in." She opened the door and waved me in. But as soon as I entered, she held up a hand to my chest. She had a tiny frown line between her eyebrows, but her brown eyes were lit up. "For the record, this is not a booty call."

"Never thought it was. I wanted to see you," I admitted and she looked down at the ground in the cutest fucking way. "Is that okay with you, Ms. Callie?"

"Ms. Callie?" She wrinkled her nose. "I was a camp counselor once and they called me that. Brings me back to junior high."

"I'm trying out new nicknames. We'll see what sticks." I massaged her shoulders and pulled her into me. I itched to touch her. "Can I say I missed you?"

"When you have my face pressed into your chest like this, you can say whatever you want." Her voice was muffled and I squeezed her tighter.

"How was the marathon?"

"Good. I'm super into the show, but it freaks me out. I'm always a little jumpy after watching it for hours." She released her hold on me and tension lined her eyes.

"What's wrong?"

"I'm having an internal battle. Do you ever have those?" She crossed her arms, the frown line returning. The only part of the shirt I saw read *balls.* I motioned down to it with my eyes and laughed. She saw what I was looking at and rolled her eyes. "Hell. Not helping."

"I mean, if you wanted to take the shirt off…be my guest. I won't complain." I reached for the hem of it playfully and she swatted me away.

"You are my internal battle."

"How so?" I tried to hide my panic, but she must've seen my distress because she put her hand on my face. I leaned in to her, taking in her sweet smell and comforting embrace, and sighed.

"You are all sorts of crazy. I'm going to pretend you were assuming the worst. My battle is either inviting you back to my room or sending you on your merry way."

"Room. Invite me in," I yelped, happy as fuck that was what she was battling.

"Obviously, you'd pick that. The problem is, we're always together in public…where I must have some control. No promise of that happening in there. Us. Alone."

"I'm missing the problem here, babe." Her mouth quirked up at the pet name and I decided to use it as often as possible.

She bit down on her bottom lip, her nerves reeling me in. I closed the gap between us and sent a prayer to my dick to not embarrass me. She came into my embrace and I kissed her forehead, figuring it out. "You don't want to rush things, I understand. But what if I gave you a promise that I'll be really good?"

"You aren't the problem, Zade. *I* am. I lose all rational thought around you."

"I love that I'm doing that to you. But even if you strip down buck ass naked and straddle me, I won't make a move tonight."

"Why the hell not?"

"Because we haven't had a real date yet. Remember, I want to have some firsts with you, too."

"Fuck me. You're going to ruin me, Zade Willows." She sighed in resignation and I picked her up, spreading her legs around me. I kissed her, deeply and too soon, I pulled back. I kept her bottom lip between my teeth and she trembled.

"I'm now going to kiss the hell out of you, make you breathless with my name and leave you to dream about me all night."

"Too late for that."

I carried her into her room and did as I promised.

Chapter Nineteen

Callie

After a long, Zade-dream-filled night, I woke up with an inexplicable smile. Greta whistled at me when I walked out of my room to head to class. I canceled the run again that morning because my leg was still hurting, but also, I needed a little distance. Last night had changed something.

"Was it just me or did we have a late-night visitor?"

"Must be your crazy imagination. Nah, we did."

"I knew it." She clapped a couple of times, applauding herself. "How hung is he?"

"Greta!" I spilled a little coffee at her question. "I haven't slept with him yet."

"Why the hell not? I'm dying," Greta whined and pleaded. "I need to know."

"What about you and Tanner? How's that going?"

"Oh, him. Nada. I va va voomed a little bit at him the other day and the message was loud and clear. Friends. I got friend-zoned. Which, I shouldn't be surprised. This whole thing started as friends. I'm okay with it. I need to get back at it and find a new guy. So, I need you to be my wing-lady sometime."

"Any time, girl. You my main bitch." I meant it. Although I wasn't a huge fan of going out and mingling with random people, I owed Greta. "I have to run, but I'm dying to know what exactly *va va voomed* means."

"I bet you would." She waved at me. "We'll catch up. And don't think I'm forgetting you haven't dished on last night."

"Bye!" I ran out of the door, laughing, and headed to my class. I didn't dread the class like the first one after Radcliffe had gotten nasty with me, but the trepidation was still there. We had nailed the project, but the thought of making friends with him had kind of gone out of the window with the icy glares I'd gotten.

The discussion with Patz was riveting, a little off topic, but I found myself hanging on to every word. He talked about the pros and cons of everything an athlete needed to eat. He spoke about personal experiences with drinking and how it had affected his play. He spoke about the drugs and supplements out in the league that hadn't been around in his time. I took notes furiously and learned more in that hour than I had reading a hundred pages. I packed up my bag when Patz barked out Radcliffe's name and mine.

"Get up here." His tone was short and to the point. I tried to bite back the nerves because he always spoke to us in the same way. He might be giving us the best or the worst news and his tone wouldn't change. "Sit down."

Radcliffe and I shared a look, a mutual truce of sorts. "Now, you both did excellent work on the first project."

I answered first, having spoken with alpha males most of my life, with my dad. "Thank you, sir."

"Y-yes. Thank you," Radcliffe added, rather pathetically.

"I'm selecting you two for an independent project of sorts." He ruffled through his bag and handed us both a sheet with chicken scratch writing. "I'm on a first-name basis with all the trainers here and most of the coaches. They're always looking for students to help with their program, because it looks good, and because sometimes we find talent."

I faced Radcliffe, afraid to get my hopes up. It sounded like a kick-ass opportunity for an extended project. Radcliffe's face tinged pink and I waited to see what else Patz said. "Now, Ms. Williams, Nicole said she already met with you for another class."

"Yes. A shadowing program."

"Good. You made an impression. You are going to work with her and help create meal plans for the baseball team. Also, I know your dad. Great man." His eyes held a glint of a memory and a small smile formed on his face.

"He's my favorite," I added and he almost smiled again. "I would be honored."

"Good. Radcliffe, you know a lot about football, but they didn't need help seeing as the season is already starting. I spoke with the basketball coach and the hockey coach. They are vastly different, but what would you prefer?"

"T-to work with them?"

"Yes. This is an extended project, which, if done right and done well, can turn into an internship for the following year. It's a creative class. I worked the system. You don't need to head to lectures anymore.

Instead, the three of us will meet once a week and your grade will come from Nicole, for you, Callie, and whoever you decide to work with, Radcliffe."

"Holy shit." Radcliffe's polite demeanor cracked. I barked out a laugh. Patz laughed, too. "Hockey. I think I'd like that."

"Then you'll work with Greg. He's a hard ass, but he'll teach you things. Read over this. I'll email you both to meet next week. I encourage you two to work together. Now, get out."

I held on to the paper and followed Radcliffe through the door. His face matched how I felt and once we were out of earshot and in the long corridor, we jumped up and down. "Oh, my god!"

"This is amazing." He blinked a couple of times and I hugged him. I didn't care if he'd been rude before, this was fan-fucking-tastic. He hugged me back and we broke apart, smiling. "This is like a dream come true."

"I know. If we do well...we might have an internship next year. Shit." I sat on the nearest bench and held up a high five. "Nice work, Radcliffe, king of awesomeness and bad-assery."

He chuckled and sat next to me. "Same to you."

"I might be in shock." I saw the sheet had Nicole's number on it. "I have to reach out and contact her. Is yours like that, too?"

"Yeah. I'm not brave enough to call right now." He smiled weakly at me. "Can I say something?"

"Sure. I'm not stopping you. I'm too happy right now. Unless you ruin my mood." I meant it as a joke, but I saw him hesitate.

"I'm sorry for how I treated you back at the library. I feel awful about it. I'm a nice guy, really. I just... I categorized you." He hung his head low. "I would like to be friends, if you still want to be."

"I'd like that too, but if you insult me or my friend choice again, I'll beat your ass."

"I'll do my best to remember that." He stood up and shook his head. "Congrats again—this is thrilling. I should probably call my parents."

"Shit! I should too!" I pulled out my phone and waved at him as he walked away. I called my dad first, who would openly express his excitement. He answered on the second ring.

"Callie girl. To what do I owe this call? Shouldn't you be in class?" I heard the sound of a batting cage and smiled, imaging him feeding balls into the pitching machine and holding a conversation with his daughter.

"Nah, just left and I have some good news."

"All right. Lay it on me." He chuckled and I told him everything. I told him about the opportunities and how the year off had benefited me more than I could've imagined. He didn't say anything at first and I heard a cough of sorts. I forgot I was still semi upset with him. I just wanted to share the news with them.

"Dad, you there?"

"I'm wallowing like a man-child. Give me a minute." He sniffed and my own eyes stung. "I'm damn proud of you, Callie girl. Hell...I knew you were tough and determined, you obviously get it from me, but you already made a name for yourself at that big university."

"Thanks, Dad." I wiped away a tear. "I can't believe it."

"I can't say I'm surprised, hon. You might not have agreed with your mom and my decision last year, but everything happens for a reason. You appreciate everything you're going through and you don't take nothin' for granted. I can't believe my only girl gets to work with the damn baseball team." He paused, clearing his throat. "You proved me wrong, kid."

I blinked, the sting in my eyes too much. *This. This is what I wanted the past year.* The approval, the pride, the words every kid wants to hear from their idol. "Th-thanks, Dad."

"Callie girl, I know you might not understand *why* your mother and I put you through that, but damn. Bold moves require bold moves. You pushed back at us and fought us tooth and nail but look where you are." He sniffed again, turning it into a cough.

"Your dad-isms are ridiculous," I replied with a shaky laugh. My emotions were running haywire. It took me being away from home to miss the hell out of them. And maybe I'd found a reason for all their madness all those years.

"Call your mom. I need to go hit some hard grounders or something to man up. I love you."

"Love you too, Dad."

I called my mom and instead of tears, I got a lot of screaming and questions. That was the thing about my parents. They were quite different but fit each other. My dad was softening as he got older and I loved him all the more for it. I ended the quick call with the promise to FaceTime them with Greta this weekend. I practically floated to the food court. I wanted a burrito and nothing was going to get in my way—I was on cloud nine.

* * * *

"He doesn't stay on one girl long. Frankie had him for three months and that was the longest one yet. This new girl, Cal something—she won't last."

"She's too sporty. A guy like Zade needs a knockout. No offense to her. I'm all about supporting women and all that, but it's like she doesn't even try."

"I know! I know *I* can capture his attention. I bought his jersey and made it into a dress. Well, I guess some might call it a dress...it's a tad too short." The girls burst into giggles and I took a deep breath. I held my tray and walked by them, making sure to hold eye contact. I grinned at them and winked. Let them talk shit. We weren't in high school and they didn't know me. Plus, I was still so high from the opportunity to work with the team that no petty bitches would ruin my mood.

I sat down at a table away from them and waved at them, and one of them gasped. They should be ashamed. I put on the new playlist I'd made that morning. It was a sick mixture of old rock, classic funk town and eighties. I was feeling the eighties hair bands lately and the upbeat tunes put me in a better mood.

Zade and I weren't labeling anything and I figured it was best. No labels meant less pain when shit hit the fan, right? I wanted to text him everything about what had happened but figured I'd wait until I saw him next. If our history was to repeat itself, I had a feeling I'd see him later anyway. Regardless of those bitches, who didn't know he'd been with me for three hours last night. I blushed at the thought.

"Ay, yo, girl!" Aaron marched up to me, a wicked smile on his face. "Can I join ya?"

"By all means." I pulled out the headphones and noticed the stares of the girls around us. "Must you draw so much attention by wearing that crap?" I pointed to his extremely low-buttoned shirt. He might as well have left it all unbuttoned. It looked ridiculous paired with skintight black jeans. "You're dressed like you're channeling a rock star who lost his fortune."

"It works for the ladies, Callie. Trust me." He spread his arms around the chairs next to him and winked at some girls walking by.

"You are ridiculous, but you make me laugh. So, we can be friends." I eyed his plate. "*Four hamburgers? Really?*"

"Oh, yeah. This stallion needs to eat to keep his amazing stamina." He shot a finger gun at me and I laughed. "You have a nice laugh, Callie."

"Why, thank you, Aaron." We ate in silence for a minute, until one of the girls from earlier walked up to us. Aaron had a shadow of a frown on his forehead and I faced the awkward girl.

"Hello. May we help you?" I knew her type and tried to give her the benefit of the doubt, but her eyes said it all. She was vindictive and had only come for the sole intention of being mean. I *hated* mean girls.

"Hi, uh, Callie. You're all over the Zwillows Pillows Twitter and I know it's none of my business, but I wanted to let you know about what happened last night." Before I reacted, she shoved her phone in my face and I was met with a picture of Zade being kissed on the cheek. She swiped to another. Same outfit, but he grinned down at the girl with a very intimate expression. My stomach fell to my toes and not in a good way. It was a sickening swoop of nerves, but my dad's words played back to me. '*Never let 'em see ya sweat.*'

"I'm sure your intentions were just of the best quality, hun, but showing me pictures of a well-known athlete around campus…what's the point?"

"He isn't yours." Her eyes flared.

"Of course he isn't. He is his own damn person. He's not a damn pony to show around."

"Us girls have to stick together, right?" she sneered. "He'll drop you, like the others. Girl power. Bye." She walked away, stiffer than before. I side-glanced at Aaron, to catch an amused expression on his face. I released a long, drawn-out breath and met Aaron's eyes. They were on the brink of laughing, but he held back. "What? Spit it out, Aaron."

"You good?" A concerned expression replaced the amused one and he reached out his hand only to pull it back. "That was awkward as fuck."

I laughed without humor. The sour feeling in my stomach had nothing to do with the half-eaten burrito I was chowing down on. "I can handle myself. Don't worry, Aaron."

"I don't want to step on anyone's toes here, but those pictures don't mean anything. I know you and Zade are involved… I would hate to see something like that mess it up. He's seems stupidly fucking happy." His sparkling eyes were now dark. "Shit like that will probably keep happening."

"Thanks for the pep talk. I'll be okay. Shit, that came out poorly."

"You think? Damn, woman. You got a tude." He laughed, the mood lightening. "You ain't you when you're hungry."

"Ain't that the truth." I picked up the burrito again, swallowing down the warning in my head. I needed to have an intervention with all the parts of my body trying to control me, but today was not the day. "Hangry is one of the top three words I often use to describe myself. I get angry when I'm hungry."

"Damn, I like it. I'm going to use it now." He sent a quick text to someone. His phone went off and he frowned. His expression changed from forlorn to amused. "Fucking hell."

"What now?" I asked exasperatedly. Aaron was a rollercoaster of emotions. Happy, sad, amused, annoyed…hangry and now frustrating.

"You're trending on the campus Twitter. You have a hashtag."

"No, I don't." I checked out his phone and saw he wasn't lying. It read in bold words #cattycallie #calliehasclaws. "Kill me now."

"I have to say, Callie, I thought life was crazy before you, but I was damn wrong. This shit is perfect. Better than TV."

"I aim to please," I mumbled. "The past twenty-four hours, I've experienced every emotion in the book."

"That must suck. I'm only horny, hungry and ready for baseball."

"Ah, to have such a simple life," I retorted, earning a smile.

Chapter Twenty

Zade

I left the gym on a high. I threw great, almost pushing my personal best with the weights. Nicole yelled at me every second of the way, but I couldn't help it—I admired the hell out of the woman. I preferred to keep it to myself, though. Plus, if I had the ability to speak she'd think the workout wasn't hard enough. My phone went off, distracting me from my thoughts.

"Z, what's up, sis?"

"Cheery Zade is nice and all, but save some for the rest of us. You sound too happy. It's annoying. Also, can you come over tomorrow morning? My shelf broke. I need help."

"I love it when you're weak. You're nicer. But, yeah. I'll stop by sometime in the morning. I have a workout then I'll swing by."

"Thanks. Until I land that lucky son of a bitch who wins me over, I need to use you for your man card."

She made a gagging noise. "That hurt saying, by the way."

"I'm sure. So no luck with Pedro, then?"

"The mouth breather? No. He was boring as hell and only talked about his mom."

"Uh, one might say he's…sweet. Right?"

"No. Creepy. Way creepy."

"Hmm. Who was before Pedro? George?"

"The loud eater."

"Harvey?" Her online dating ranged from pathetic to hilarious.

"Without being cliché, he rivaled Two-Face. And by that, I meant two different people depending on the night." She sighed. "My life is sad. I'm married to my major, but I don't mind it. Enough about that. I keep getting weird calls."

That sounded my alarm. "How?"

"I'm sure it's nothing, but some person keeps calling asking for Zaria and insisting that it's me. I stopped answering, but they keep leaving me voicemails to call them back as soon as possible."

"Block the number."

"I did, but here's the thing. I got a letter in the mail yesterday. There was nothing alarming about it, but it said the same thing—'call me immediately'."

"Fuck. *Zaria.* Don't stay home alone tonight."

"Zade, I live in a townhouse. It's gated. No one gets in here without the code and, plus, it was mailed to my PO box. They don't know where I live."

"I don't like this one fucking bit." I clenched my fists, wanting to barge in and search for clues like I was the star of *Criminal Minds* or something.

She laughed. "Me neither. But I'm fine. We'll figure it out tomorrow when you come over."

"You can stay at the house tonight if you want. I'll take the couch."

"Eh, a house full of college guys? Hell to the no. How about this — if I feel unsafe, I'll stay with Claire's mom. She'll let us crash."

"Good idea. I prefer you aren't alone. Are you going to tell Mom?" Claire had been her roommate and her best friend for two years. Plus, her family lived in a really nice part of town.

"Am I crazy? No. She'll order a SWAT team or something and I don't want to deal with the drama. Shit, I need to go. Fourth period is starting. I'm shadowing a math teacher today. Eek!"

"Change the world, Z."

I hung up and wanted to explore what that meant for her. Calls and letters... They weren't crossing the line, but I had an uneasy feeling about it. I made a mental note to ask my coach the following morning. If anyone knew how to handle something, it was him. My phone went off with a text from Aaron.

Aaron: Bro. Cat fights are starting.

Zade: Coming from you, I have no idea what you mean.

Aaron: Callie. Girls are after her.

Zade: What the fuck do you mean?

My heart picked up and I thumbed through Twitter to see if anyone had posted what happened, but I didn't see anything. She also didn't text me. *She's fine, right?*

Aaron: We're in the dining hall. Join us. Make a scene, by the way. It'll be fun.

Zade: I hate deciphering your bullshit codes.

Aaron: It's all in good fun. We're by Chipotle. Callie's really handling the burrito.

I didn't respond and changed direction to head to the main quad. Now that I thought about it, food sounded good. The food court stood on the bottom floor of the Student Union building. It was the most accurate snapshot of who attended the university — students of every race and from various countries always hung out here. I'd only visited the lower level a handful of times and forgotten how many students went to school here. Generally, I ate at the house or at the town favorite sandwich shop off the main road of the campus. I passed a group of actors reenacting a scene, kids handing out free bibles and talking about the lord, a tightrope walker and of course, the Frisbee guys. I loved the Frisbee guys. I waved to them, their cheery faces a staple of the campus. *Everyone* knew about the Frisbee guys.

Reaching the stairs that led to the lowest level, I noticed the stares I was drawing. I wasn't immune to my looks by any means. I took care of my body, cared about my appearance, but I also knew my throwing arm was the main reason for my success. I walked toward Chipotle and smiled at the group of girls all gawking at me. One, who I recognized from somewhere, licked her lips in a grotesque way. *Ugh. I hope I haven't slept with her.*

I saw Callie and Aaron sitting at a table in the center of it all and my heart fucking soared. Like, left my chest and danced around the room before returning to me. It wasn't an unpleasant feeling, but I also didn't like losing all control. Aaron raised his eyebrows to me in a greeting and tilted his head in my direction.

"Fancy meeting you here, Z," he baited, drawing the attention of the crowd around us.

"Yeah. Happy coincidence," I threw back.

Callie's eyes lit up, but her smile was off. I needed to remedy that, like now.

"Hey, girl."

"God, you're awful at entrances." Her lip quirked, displaying one of her perfect dimples, and I plopped down next to her. I put my arm around her and the group of girls stared daggers at her. I put two and two together and figured out what the hell Aaron was saying. I wish he'd told me, but that was Aaron.

"How about this, then?" I held her face in my hands and kissed the shit out of her. I probably got a bit carried away, dragging it out a little too long, but I felt pretty damn smug at the desire on her face. "Better?"

"Damn it, Zade. Give a girl a warning." She wiped her lips with the back of her hand. It pleased me to see them swollen from my mouth. Aaron hid a smile behind his hand and motioned with his eyes to the girls off to the side. They had horrified expressions on their faces and I held eye contact with them, put my arm around Callie and sent the message clear as day.

"What's up, guys?" I asked, casually.

"Enjoying a nice lunch with our girl Callie here. Nothing too exciting." Aaron leaned back in his chair without a care in the world. "Right, Cal?"

"Right." She gave him a pointed glare and she met my eyes. Hers softened and my chest pinched. "I feel like I missed something. You don't have class today, right?"

"Stalking me?" Our inside joke made us both smile.

"Obviously. I have nothing else to focus on. But way to avoid the question. I don't know why you showed up right now, but I have something awesome to tell you." She sat straighter and her face lit up like a Christmas tree.

"Oh yeah, what?"

"Patz — you know the crazy old hockey player who became a professor?"

"Yeah, we've all heard of him. You have him this semester? I didn't realize that." I frowned, not sure why I should've known that.

"Our first assignment of the semester was to create an entire fitness plan for a fictional hockey team and the guy I got paired with, well, we fucking nailed it." She clapped her hands together and I hung on her every word. "He called us back to his desk after class today and dropped a major bomb. He hand-picked two of us due to previous experience we'd both had for an extra project. It has the potential for us to have internships next year! I get to work with the baseball team!"

"No fucking way!" I yelled, drawing more stares. "That's awesome!"

"Hell, yeah, Cal!" Aaron held up a hand, but she waved him off.

"It gets better, I think." She gave us a small smile. "I guess I never connected the dots until now, but you are all going to be seeing much more of me." I gave her a look that pretty much said, *so the fuck what*. That was the best thing ever. "I'm paired with Nicole for the year."

Aaron stood up to hug her. She laughed and pushed him away. "That's huge, Cal. Nicole is scary as hell but one of the most respected trainers on campus. She used to help in the majors but settled here because of her kid. If she allowed this, it's the best fucking compliment anyone could receive."

Aaron stole all the words I wanted to say and it pissed me off. She smiled, her face turning a little red, and shrugged. "It doesn't seem real. This shouldn't happen my first year here but it did."

"You get to hang around a bunch of assholes then. Are you prepared for that?" Aaron asked her with a shit-eating grin I wanted to smack off his face for no reason other than he made Callie smile.

"I've been doing that my whole life. Yeah, I'm prepared. Baseball is my favorite sport in the world and I cannot think of anything else I'd rather do." She held out her phone, her smile charming the hell out of me. "My dad is flipping his shit. He sent a picture of him and my mom with thumbs up. They are nerds."

"They have every reason to be proud. I don't think I've known anyone else to get this." I put my hand on her shoulder and squeezed. "I'm happy for you."

"Thanks, Zade." Her smile was different from the one she gave Aaron. That pleased me more than it should have.

"We need to celebrate, Cal," Aaron interrupted us and she nodded.

"Obviously. I'm fucking awesome." She spoke in a weird tone and gave me a side glance. "I tried to channel my inner ego, but it sounded off."

"You are fucking awesome but maybe tone it down. Between Aaron and myself, we don't need any more egos in here."

"Speak for yourself, Z." Aaron stood. "I need to bounce, but, Cal, we'll celebrate soon. Congrats again."

"Bye, Aaron." She waved at him and I pulled her chair closer to mine. "What are you doing?"

"Nothing. I wanted to close the space between us." Her bare thighs touched mine and her breath hitched. *Good.*

"Mmm. Well, I'm glad I got to see you, but explain why you're here."

"I was hungry?"

"That was a questionable excuse and we both know it. I don't like being lied to." Her dimple disappeared, a frown replacing her smile.

"Aaron texted me something weird. Even for him. About a catfight or some such? Then said, get here. I had no idea what the hell he meant, but I think I figured it out when I walked in." I ran my finger over her ear and loved how she shivered enough for me to see.

"Sounds like an Aaron thing for sure. I'm curious though — what do you think you figured out?"

"This is dangerous territory, because if I'm wrong, I am a total tool. My guess was that girls were giving you shit about me or something like that. They glared at you when I sat down."

"Pretty close." The girls were trying to hide behind their phones, looking everywhere but right at us. "You're probably making it worse. I'm going to have a target on my head now."

"Shit. I didn't think about that. I'm sorry."

"You had nice intentions. But I'm sure Aaron will tell you I can hold my own." A fire came into her eyes that I'd grown to know meant she was passionate.

"Is there more to the story?" I asked, still touching her. I hadn't broken the contact and I had zero problems with that.

She sighed audibly. "It was nothing. Don't worry about it, okay?"

"Callie. No lies or secrets. I'd really like to know why your smile was a little off when I sat down."

"You noticed?"

"I notice almost everything about you. Like how your breathing is a little faster when I touch you, or how you have a different smile reserved for me. I fucking like it."

"Well, shit." She cleared her throat. "Now, I feel foolish as hell."

"What. Happened."

"This girl showed me pictures of you from last night, a girl kissing your cheek and you looking all smug. She said something along the lines like I won't keep you and you aren't mine." She laughed, not with humor though. "I told her straight up you don't belong to anyone and pictures can mean a lot of things."

My stomach sank. I remembered the picture. The girl had plastered herself to me. It could totally be misread. *Shit.* I released her hair and put my head in my hands. "It wasn't what it looked like."

"I believe you. I do, really. You came to see me at midnight knowing you weren't going to get laid. Actions speak louder."

"You aren't mad?" I asked, incredulously.

"I think it hurt a little when I saw it, but, no. I'm not. I told you, a picture can be construed a million different ways. Plus, you know how you said I have a smile just for you?"

"Yeah?"

She lowered her voice and whispered as she patted my leg, "You have a look you save *just* for me."

"I have more than a look." I took her hand and held it in mine. "Do you have plans tonight?"

"Hmm. I don't think so. Why?"

"Go out with me," I barked, sounding like a caveman again.

"Question or demand?"

"Sorry. *Please.* Will you please go out with me?" My heart raced. This was the first time I'd asked a girl out. I know I sounded like a douchebag the size of Michigan, but it was the truth. They asked me out and dragged me to places. I must admit I hated being the one doing the asking.

"I'll think about it." She released her hand from mine and picked up her tray. "I have to head out."

"That's it? You'll think about it?" I asked, dumbfounded.

"The count's full. You can't expect a walk." She walked away, leaving me with an open mouth and laughter. *Fuck me. I'm so going to marry that girl.*

Chapter Twenty-One

Callie

I had never acted so bold before, leaving Zade sitting there, but I hummed in joy. It would make the date much more sweet. I knew I'd say yes—I'm sure he did, too—but I wasn't one to make things easy. I walked back to the apartment without any incidents, thankfully. The day had already wreaked havoc on my system and I wanted to take a bath for two hours and listen to some cool rock music.

Walking into our apartment to see Greta half-naked with a guy, not Tanner, around her, shocked me. "Oh, uh, shit."

I backed out of the door and debated my next move. I needed to get into my room but did not want to see Greta's ass planted against the counter. I recoiled and made a note to clean the hell out of that before I cooked next time. I'd give her thirty minutes until I'd cover my eyes and go back in. Luckily, I had my laptop with me and I'd find a coffee shop nearby to study.

I made the semi long walk to the Bean, a local favorite, and found a back booth. I ordered my typical coffee with peppermint and opened up my laptop to plan my following week. I had to fit the scheduled shadowing hours around my other four classes and the onsite training I did with Nicole. I still needed to call her. *Now or never.* I dialed the number and waited.

"'Lo."

"Nicole, it's Callie Williams."

"Wondered when I'd hear from ya. I talked to Patz. You in?"

"One hundred percent."

"I knew this'd work out. You have the brains and the backbone. This isn't some easy peasy flirt-with-the-team job. It'll suck sometimes."

"My dad is a college coach, ma'am, and I've seen a lot. I can handle it."

"Good. Come by my training room Monday. You have class at lunch?"

"Nope. I'm free."

"I'll provide the lunch. Bring your calendar." She barked something at someone in the background.

"Will do. Thanks. Bye." I hung up with shaking hands. My adrenaline roared. I already knew Nicole meant business and had a hell of a reputation, but the authority in her tone and the aura around her confirmed it. I wanted to start learning from her right now. My phone vibrated in my hands and I thought it was Nicole, but no, Zade.

Zade: Dinner and a movie?

Callie: Almost strike three, we'll say foul.

I grinned like a damn goon at my phone. I'm surprised people around didn't stare at me.

Zade: Fancy dinner?

Callie: Foul ball.

Zade: Taco Bell?

Callie: Ugh. Taco Bell is worse than watching the third strike go by.

Zade: Shit. Okay. Damn. But, you're forgetting I'm the pitcher and that's my job.

Callie: Yeah, yeah, yeah. You and your amazing arm. Yawn.

I loved messing with him and considered it one of my favorite activities. Bored, annoy Zade. Happy, annoy Zade. It didn't matter.

Zade: Do you trust me?

Callie: With my heart? No. But generally, yes.

Zade: I don't like that answer, but I'll work on it. I want to surprise you. Can I?

Callie: Sure.

Zade: THANK GOD. I'll be at your place at seven. Dress casual.

Before I had time to react, Greta texted me saying the coast was clear and I ran home. I needed girl advice and who better than Greta?

* * * *

"Girl, you look perfect. You rock casual like it's your damn job." She fixed my hair, somehow creating awesome braids. I'd told her he complimented them and her eyes had grown wide with ideas. I admit, they did look good. They began at the top of my head and fell loosely down my back. Greta had gotten the girly genes and I had gotten the tomboy DNA.

"What does casual even mean?" I eyed my black skinny jeans with rips in them, black booties Greta had let me borrow and a skintight green tank top that hugged every curve I had. "Am I trying too hard?"

"Try harder." She clucked her tongue at me and put her hand over her heart. "Part of me wants to take a picture of you, like I'm sending you off to prom."

"I'll murder you in your sleep if you do that."

She pointed her finger at my mouth. "Right, strict instructions not to ruin the lip stuff. Unless it's with Zade's mouth, understood?" She patted my face like a mother hen and fixed my hair one more time. "I'm freaking excited for you. Enjoy this. And if you're wondering, I'll be home, in my room, pretending I don't exist."

"Did you just quote Harry Potter at me?"

"Sure did, boo boo. I'm saying that, although I deserve it, I won't be in here being a cock block."

"We need a system like the sock or something. I still can see his ass in my eyes. Will I ever see his face?"

"Probably not." She shrugged, completely at ease with her freedom. "He was fun. We get along really well and both like each other's bodies. I'm guessing a solid friends-with-benefits situation. But enough about that. *He's* going to be here soon."

"Ugh. Yeah. I shouldn't be this nervous." I pulled the end of my shirt down because it was small. It left a little bit of my midriff bare, which was the plan, but still. My boldness from earlier had left me in a pile of nerves. A car door slammed. "Shit."

"You kill me, Cal. I love you." She pressed a kiss on my cheek and went to stand behind the counter. "If you ask me to leave, I won't. I want to see the look on his face."

"This is crazy. Insane. All sorts of wrong." I went to the door, ready to open it when he knocked.

"No, this is all sorts of right." She hopped on the counter and smiled like a freaking lunatic. "Here he comes…"

He knocked. I cleared my throat and turned the knob. I opened it and froze. Time stopped at the moment I saw him dressed in the sexiest pair of worn jeans and an old sweater. Zade pulled off the odd combination of comfort while still oozing testosterone. His eyes widened, his lips parted and we took time eyeing each other.

No one made a move first. My hand was still on the door, my feet planted in the apartment. Zade's hand twitched for a second. His gaze fell to my lips and heated over to the darkest shade of hazel I had ever seen. I gulped.

"Hey, girl," he said and the tension broke. I laughed and stepped onto the welcome mat. I spun around to wave to Greta who gave me an exaggerated two thumbs-up. When I shut the door, he grasped my hips. "Fucking hell, Callie."

I sighed into his touch as his lips grazed the spot right below my ear. If I had a weak spot or a kryptonite, it was Zade's mouth on that part of my neck. He exploited it by gently biting down. I jumped a foot in the air and he caught me. "I'm having a really hard time remembering where I'm supposed to take you."

"If it's any consolation, I forgot my own name when I first saw you."

His eyes warmed back to their sweet brownish tone and he grabbed my hand. "I left my manners back at home. I should've told you how amazing you look. Seriously, I'm going to have a hard time holding a conversation with you."

I blinked a couple of times at the compliment. He pressed his lips to the back of my hand and I gulped. I would *not* survive the night if he continued the whole time. "You fluster me."

"Good. I plan on doing it as often as I can. You ready?"

"As I can be. My heart won't calm down." I admitted the truth again and knew it was the right thing to say because the grin I got in response was enough to light up the entire neighborhood.

"This has already been the best date ever. Here, let me get the door."

"Good lord, Zade. Did you take a class in chivalry or something? You're pulling out all the stops and I'm having a hard time keeping up with you." I swooned, almost literally, when he helped me into his car. He leaned over to drag his hand under my jaw. He didn't kiss me, though, but good lord, he built up the anticipation enough to kill me.

He walked around the car and got in on the driver's side and I was enveloped in his cologne. It wasn't too much, yet it wrapped around me, warming me. I leaned back against the seat and he put his hand on my knee. Fuck if I wasn't charmed. "So, where to?"

"You'll see." He gave me a small smile and kept his eyes on the road. He seemed too relaxed, too chill for the moment. It annoyed me that he wasn't as affected as I was and it made me question everything. *Am I getting too involved? Am I being too much?* I sighed, annoyed with myself and my thoughts as we drove.

"What was that sigh for?"

"Nothing. I'm being stupid." I hated feeling insecure. It was not one of my qualities and yet my heart was frantically trying to jump out of my chest, whereas he looked like he was driving his grandma to the bus stop. But he'd held the door for me and was being polite as hell. Ugh, I despised dating. The questions. The uncertainty of everything.

"You keep biting on that bottom lip of yours in deep thought and I swear to god I'm going to pull the car over and devour you." His voice changed from polite to gruff in one second, erasing all the doubt I had. "Now, why are you frowning?"

"The nerves of dating, honestly." I didn't play games and wasn't going to start now. He squeezed my knee, the sensation stopping right around my center. I squeezed my legs together, moisture already gathering. It was an automatic response to his touch.

"I feel the same way." He moved his hand half an inch up my thigh and I bit my lip to keep from moaning. His hands were the fucking best hands ever. I didn't realize I'd let out a sound until his body tensed. "Did you just moan?"

"Sorry," I gasped.

"Fuck. I won't lie to you, Callie. I want to spend the next week exploring your body with my tongue, but tonight is our first date. I need to get through this, but if you make any more noises or clench your thighs or bite those goddamn red lips, I'm going to lose my shit."

"Should I say things from your anti-sexy list?"

"Yes. Anything. My dick is trying with all his strength to escape my goddamn pants."

I saw the evidence of his boner and I burst out laughing. The nerves took over and the laughter came harder. "He looks like he really is going to jump out," I managed to get out between laughs.

"I'm glad my dick amuses you, Ms. Callie, but you won't be laughing when you meet him."

"I know I won't. Wait. Did you seriously reference me meeting your dick?"

"Yup. I want you guys on a first-name basis."

"You named him? Holy shit." The laughter took over again and I put my hands over my stomach. "What did you name him?"

"Not important. Stop talking about him. He knows you are and he won't go away." His hazel eyes met mine and they were filled with a wickedly beautiful glint. "We're almost there."

I watched the road go by out of the window. We were in a lit-up area, filled with trees and neon lights. I couldn't be sure, but I had a suspicion. "Are we going to the batting cages?"

"If I said yes?" he asked. He was worried I didn't approve! Another little piece of my heart fell to the ground for him to take.

"Uh…best date ever. Seriously, I'm fucking excited right now."

"Good. I was worried." He patted my leg. "I figured we could have a little competition going. They have semi decent food, but, more importantly, they have games. Lots of games."

"I think we might have a problem." I intertwined our fingers. "And who the hell cares about food when we have batting cages in the distance?"

"God, you're amazing."

"You won't be saying that when I beat you at everything."

"Everything, eh?" he asked, parking the car. "That's quite the statement."

"And I meant it." I hopped out and met him at the front of the hood. "I think we're going to have to make a bet of sorts."

"Which you'll lose," he said on a fake cough, smiling when I poked him in the side. "What should we do first?"

"Honestly? This." I stood on my tiptoes and pressed a soft kiss on his lips. He didn't try to deepen it. He let me be in charge and I ended it. "I couldn't stop thinking about your mouth in the car and I know you're having an issue." I pointed to his crotch, which was still tented. "But as soon I start winning, I'm positive the attraction will die down."

"You say a lot of things, but they don't mean shit." His smile was the perfect crooked one and he pulled me against him. "Help a guy out and walk in front of me."

"Checking out my ass?" I teased and felt his length. That shut me up real quick.

"Nope. This time, I can't handle it. I need you to hide my boner from the family that's passing by."

I burst out laughing and did just that.

Chapter Twenty-Two

Zade

If I'd thought I had it bad for Callie before, it was *nothing* compared to how I felt watching her line up the winning putt in a game of mini golf. She bent low, angling the shitty putter all sorts of directions to get the best shot. I wasn't downplaying the seriousness of the situation, because if she didn't sink it, I'd win. I *really* liked winning.

"Don't mess up the angle," I said to her, but she shushed me and shoved me. I thought about distracting her with my hands and body, but she'd caught on to that right away. She'd demanded a no-touch rule during the game. I hated it, but it made me crave her more somehow.

She lined up her shot, took a slow breath and brought the putter back. The ball rolled straight into the hole. *Shit*. We'd tied. She jumped into the air, did a little wiggle and looked at me expectantly. "Take that, Z-man."

"God, you're annoying. And we can touch now, right, boss?"

"Yeah, I like touching when there isn't a game involved." She squeezed me and patted my ass. "See, love the touching."

"I can't believe we tied at air hockey, darts and golf." I kept one arm around her and held our putters in my left hand. "I'm impressed with you and disappointed in myself."

"Nah, don't be disappointed. I'm quite talented." She faced me and I captured her lips with mine. She sighed, a sound that I now put in my top favorites. "You played well. Focus more next time."

"You think you're funny. All we have left is the batting cages. You ready?" My stomach growled and she laughed. She patted it with her hand.

"I feel ya, big guy. Let's get some grub. Nothing like good ole-fashion competition to really get the adrenaline going. I'm famished myself, but I didn't even think about food with the game on the line. And I'm a really hungry person." I loved that about her. She ate what she wanted and didn't care what I thought about it.

We walked up to the cart of food. "Looks like we have the great selection of hot dogs, corn dogs and chill dogs."

"God. What a tough choice. I'll take two hot dogs." She went to grab her wallet, bless her, and I laughed. She glanced at me with a raised brow. "What?"

"I'm buying your food."

"Uh, you paid for the golf and the darts. Let me contribute something."

"You realize this is a date and I'm chivalrous, as *you* stated, not me. I want to buy it for you. I want to treat you. So, lighten up and let me." I gave her my pitching stare, the one that guys who go pro hate. But instead of quivering, she stuck her tongue out at me.

"Okay." She leaned onto the counter and blinked up at the poor sap taking our order. "In that case, may I please have four hot dogs, a large popcorn and a chocolate swirl ice cream?"

"Why stop there? Keep going."

"Nah, I'm good. That should fill me up." She waited for me to order with her hand on her hip. The little power pose made me smile. Callie was a handful, all right.

"Double the order, please." I handed him my card. "You realize I'm going to watch and make sure you eat everything you ordered out of your feminist spite, right?"

"You are underestimating how much I can pack away." She patted her belly and made a grunting noise. It was not meant to be attractive and yet my dick perked up. "And don't tell me you're one of those people with a food fetish?"

"A what?"

"You know. People who like watching other people eat phallic objects. Bananas, cucumbers, popsicles, hot dogs." She widened her eyes at me, mirth dancing in them. "You are, aren't you? You were just too perfect to be true."

Fuck the audience. I kissed her. She'd called me perfect and, coming from her, that was the best compliment ever. She gasped in shock at the sudden movement and slapped me away. "What the hell was that for?"

"You. Only you." I smiled and kept her in my arm. "And to answer your absurd question, I don't have a fetish, but I'm concerned how you knew about such a thing."

"I've heard things. That's all."

"Uh-huh." I slid my hand to her ass. I hadn't touched it yet, which I deserved an award for. I patted right where her thigh began to curve, but regretted it immediately. Her. Ass. Was. Perfect. "Does Callie enjoy people eating penis-shaped food?"

"No. I don't." She tried to sneak away from me, but I held her tighter. "I can't think straight when you touch me and I want to keep my brain the rest of the night, thank you very much."

"For the entire rest of the night, or at least while we're here?" I let her move away and her eyes heated over. She gulped.

"I'll let you know when I figure out the answer to that question."

"Fair enough." The guy passed her the box of everything we ordered. We found a table off to the side and once she had a hot dog in her hand, inches from her mouth. I dropped the bomb I was holding back. "Just so you know, Callie, I don't have a food fetish in general, but I am really going to appreciate watching you eat those hot dogs."

Her eyes widened, the food centimeters from her teeth. She thought about what to do next—I read the calculating look in her eye. "First, you have an insane talent to make the oddest things sexy, and secondly, I'm never going to be able to eat a hot dog and not think of this moment."

"Good. I like making an impression on you," I said.

She shook her head and bit into her hot dog. I'd never wished to be food before, but I wanted to be that piece. I told my brain to shut the fuck up with all the weird things I was thinking, but did it listen? *No.* My thoughts derailed, making their own way down a path I didn't want to explore. Callie, coming to games. Callie, meeting my mom and sister. Callie, traveling with me to new cities. Callie, waking up in my bed. *Fuck.* I must've acted like a crazy person, because her eyes widened in worry.

"What's wrong?" I asked her, my stomach tightening.

"Look who's here." She pointed to the parking lot and frowned. A van full of guys parked and they all walked out dressed in crazy costumes. Was she checking them out? No, she wouldn't do that. I didn't like the way her gaze heated over in their direction.

"Care to explain?"

"Aw, you're jealous. It doesn't suit you." She flicked her hand. "They're one of the lower level farm teams for the Sox."

"No way." I saw the logo on one of their shirts. *Way.* "I wonder why they're down here."

"I know. They don't play near here. Maybe a fun stop on the drive somewhere?"

"Want to go get an autograph? You're cute enough. I guess," I teased.

"Nah, I'm good." She wrinkled her nose. "I'm a fan from afar."

"You're *shy.*" I couldn't believe it. Miss *I can do anything and will do anything* was shy. The little-known fact somehow fit her.

"I'm not shy...not really. I once met my favorite player of all time when I was ten. I got too nervous and I puked on my shoes. *And* on his cleats. It was horrifying. My dad laughed his ass off and the player was cool about it."

"Who was it?"

"Paul Konerko." She bit her lip, one eye closed in shame. "And for a ten-year-old girl in love with everything baseball, he was the coolest thing ever."

I laughed and fell so goddamn hard for her. "I get it. He was awesome. I feel like I should be concerned you've had a thing for baseball players your whole life. I don't like that."

"I kind of have." She shrugged. "You're going to have to deal with it."

My mouth dropped open. She just...*damn*. I closed my mouth. "You leave me no choice."

"Don't worry, though—none have made my stomach turn into a pile of goo like you do."

"A pile of goo?"

"I'm a real romantic, can't you see?"

"Well, if it's any consolation, you make my stomach turn into a pile of goo, too."

* * * *

Now shit got tricky. The date fucking rocked. Hands down one of the best times I'd had...ever. My past had made me behave all backward. I knew all about the sex part, not the dating part and yet, we held hands in the car and I heard every breath she took. The rustle of her pants when she moved her legs to a new position had my fists tightening. I traced her hand with one of my fingers and froze at the subtle, almost nonexistent moan.

I was fucking lost at what to do. I wanted to do everything and nothing. We pulled into her apartment complex and every word I wanted to say disappeared. I parked, let go of her hand and opened the car door for her. She thanked me, looking at the ground. *Shit.* I'd put the doubt there. I'd acted like a fucking weasel in the car ride home and she probably thought I'd had a terrible time. I grabbed her hand and kissed the back. I pulled her closer, resting my hand on the back of her head. "Callie?"

"Hmm?" Her eyes were closed, her mouth parting in anticipation of the kiss I craved to give her. I held off, though. Somehow, someway, I did.

"You know how I feel about your eyes being closed." She opened them up, and I closed the distance between our mouths. If heaven had a taste, it was her. Her cherry-red lips drove me fucking crazy and I wanted to suck the red off them. It wasn't *her.*

I pressed her into the car, trapped her wrists with my hands and she bucked into me. I couldn't handle the chemistry between us and I released her mouth, only then to kiss the spot by her neck and shoulder. When I bit down and she moaned, I about came in my goddamn pants. "Your lips tonight. They were different."

"Yeah. Lipstick," she said, her chest heaving and confusion flooding her eyes at my sudden release of her mouth.

"They drove me fucking insane. The red is amazing, but I prefer these better." I traced them with my fingers and her lips trembled.

"O-h, okay." She let out another moan and stammered, "Sh-should we head upstairs?"

"Is that what you want? It's entirely up to you, babe. This date already fucking rocked. No pressure." I said the words, but prayed she said *yes.* I wanted to taste her and frankly, I wasn't ready to say goodnight.

"Yes." Her eyes became fiery again. My favorite. "Let's go before I remove my clothes out here."

"We can't fucking have that." I picked her up without asking. She let out a squeal of shock. "This is quicker. Trust me."

"I don't think so, but I appreciate it all the same. I can suck your neck now." She did. I almost dropped her.

"Shit, don't touch me yet. I have to go upstairs." I groaned when she ran her tongue down my neck. "Callie."

"Now I think you understand how I've been feeling the whole damn night. Sucks, doesn't it?" she whispered into my ear and I took the stairs two at time.

"Keys. Now," I barked at her, setting her down as lightly as I could.

She pulled them from her pocket and dropped them. Twice. "Shit. My hands are shaking."

I took the keys from her and opened the door. She went inside and I shut the door behind me. She spun around, her eyes filled with all sorts of secrets I wanted to explore. "Well..." She sucked her lip into her mouth. "Want to go explore my favorite base?"

"*God, yes.*"

Chapter Twenty-Three

Callie

Yes. Yes. Yes. Yes.

For the first time since Zade had barged into my life, my brain, heart and gut were all on the same team. It felt goddamn great to not have an internal battle going on.

"You taste like fucking heaven," he growled into my mouth. I'd always hated growling, but when Zade did it, it made me feel sexy as hell. My legs were wrapped around his waist, his dick growing by the second. He released my mouth and moved onto my neck. The combination of teeth and tongue about killed me. Combine that with his sexy growl and I stood no chance. "Bedroom. Now."

I pointed to my bedroom door and he kicked it open, literally. If Greta heard, I didn't care. She owed me. He threw me onto the bed and locked the door behind him. I lay there, chest heaving and my center screaming for attention, and Zade smiled at me. Now was so not the time for him to go all gentlemanly and shit. "Zade, if you don't get over here right now, I'm going to finger myself."

"Good god. I want to see that sometime. But not right now. I've waited too long for this, I don't want to fuck it up." Worry etched on his face and I sat up, taking my shirt off in the process. His eyes flared, the sweet color of coffee now. I went to turn off the lights but he stopped me. "No. They stay on."

"Wh-why?" I paused. My plan to seduce him had backfired.

"I want to see every fucking inch of you."

Oh.

Oh my.

His grin transformed into that of a lion about to attack his prey. He ran his hand over his jaw a couple of times while I sat there in my bra and jeans. "Would you believe me if I told you I was scared as hell right now?"

I nodded. Time seemed to have its own agenda and all I saw was Zade.

He shrugged off his shirt and sweater and matched my appearance with his bare chest and jeans. I reached out, dragging my fingers over his abs. God, they were amazing. Hard yet soft, perfect and scarred. The happy trail was *just* that. A trail I wanted to explore. He sat next to me on the bed and let me continue exploring him with my fingers. He sucked in a breath when I pinched his nipple.

"Your body is beautiful." I traced his pecs, down his stomach again and stopped when I got to his belt. He groaned and whatever patience he had, left. He stopped my wandering hands and warned me with his eyes.

"I'm going to come within seconds if you touch me." His tone left no room for argument. "I need to last. Please. Let me." He pushed me back, my body at his mercy. His fingers started at my neck, tracing my collarbone. I gasped, the sensation sending shivers through my body. He continued down my chest. His eyes caressed every part of me and my body burned in the best way. He went up to my bra strap on my shoulder and pushed it off, excruciatingly slow. He did it to the other side. Then he reached behind me with one hand and undid my bra.

"*Fuck.*" He cupped my breasts in his large hands. "I knew it. They are perfect. God." He twisted and pinched the tips, causing me to jump. "Does this feel good, Callie?

"Uh-huh," I managed. He pushed me onto my back and Zade Willows crouching over me like I was the best fucking thing he'd even seen was the hottest moment in my life. *Ever.* He used one hand to push the ends of my hair back and the other to continue pinching my nipples.

He trailed kisses down my neck, my collarbone and hovered right over my pebbled nipples. They were throbbing in a way I hadn't known was possible. "Look at me."

I did. He sucked one of them into his mouth and I was pretty sure I forgot how to breathe. "Zade. Oh."

"Mmm. Your tits are… I'm speechless." He continued sucking and swirling the tip around his mouth and, when I thought I couldn't stand it for another second, he came back up and balanced himself on his elbows. His eyes were now a color I had never seen before on him. "I cannot wait to taste the rest of you."

He slid down my body, making sure to touch me everywhere. He found the edge of my pants and he slowly pulled. "Good lord." He sucked in a breath once my pants were off and on the floor. He took his time caressing every inch of my legs and groaned when my panties came into view. I knew I'd made the right choice, going with see-through lace. He pulled them off and his smile was crooked.

"You're already soaked for me. God, I don't think I've been this turned on in my entire fucking life." He slid his hands up my thigh, not quite touching where I desperately needed it.

"Zade. I'm going to burst," I panted.

"Good. I want you to. And I want it to be for me." He traced his tongue down my stomach, all the way until he reached my center. I buckled when his mouth met my folds. Some unrecognizable noise escaped my mouth. He hummed into me. I yanked his hair in my hands, seconds away from losing all rational thought.

"Yes. So good," I breathed and clutched at the pillows behind my head. The buildup was unlike anything I had ever experienced before. He added his hands to the mix and he slid two fingers inside me. I saw stars at that point. He whispered something, but I wasn't on the physical earth anymore.

He sucked. He thrust his fingers. He moaned into the deepest part of me and I burst. It began in my toes, a tickling feeling that triggered more to follow. The feeling danced all the way to my heart and I came into his mouth. I think I screamed, maybe ripped out some of his hair, but when I saw those hazel eyes again, I came back to the present. My hands trembled from need and the aftershocks of what had happened. He pressed a light kiss on my center, the sweetest and dirtiest gesture, and moved to lie over me again. My eyes stung, tears building up at how he soft his expression was, but he didn't let me cry. He slammed his mouth to mine, possessing every part of me.

His hands roamed me. I bit into his neck when he lifted me up and he groaned. I ground against him, the taste of my pleasure remained on his tongue. I sucked it. My toes tingled and it started to build up again. I tangled my hands in his hair and he slammed me into the bedroom door.

"Fuck," he growled again. I wanted to feel him, but words were not possible. I tugged at his buckle from the awkward angle and he set me down. I fumbled with the belt buckle and ripped his pants down his legs. He. Was. Huge.

"Uhh." It reared at me and I froze.

"I won't hurt you. I promise." He pressed a gentle kiss on my forehead. He ran his hand down my body and pressed himself against me. "You are the biggest game changer I've ever seen."

"So are you," I whispered and he picked me up again. "God, I want to feel all of you."

He laid me down on the bed again and produced a condom. He held himself over me and waited. "Are you sure? You can say no."

"Zade, please." I begged and he obeyed. He slid into me, slowly, making sure I fit the length of him. I closed my eyes, because it did hurt.

"I'm so sorry, babe. It'll feel good in a second. You're fucking tight." He somehow managed to grab my ass and kiss my jaw in the process. "I'm never leaving this, ever."

He was right. It felt amazing a minute later. I arched my back, wanting him to go as far as he could. He did. He whispered all sorts of thing I knew he couldn't mean yet. I enjoyed every fucking second until we both collapsed on the bed, covered in sweat and the afterglow of sex. He threw the condom into the trash and pulled me up next to him. "Callie?"

"Mm." I had my eyes closed — sleep was close. He was warm and comfortable and perfect...

"Can I stay with you?" His voice was different...almost unsure or nervous.

"I'd like that." I relaxed at his words and snuggled closer to him. "I'm a wild sleeper."

"Fine by me. I'm nowhere near finished with you. Trust me, you'll be up soon."

"M'kay."

He wasn't lying. Three hours later, I panted, breathless from the fourth orgasm I'd had in one night. He looked like the king of the world with his pose, one of his hands under his head and his abs on full display. "Can I ask you something?"

"Just did." I felt drunk on him. Our faces were inches apart and I couldn't stop smiling, even though I was sleep deprived and would regret it the next day. "But, sure."

"Have you ever had an orgasm during sex before?"

"Hmm." I ran my tongue over my lip. "I don't think I want to answer."

"Why not? You can tell me anything." He pouted a bit. God, how he looked so damn attractive with one lip sticking out was beyond me. He was a man, and yet, that face... *Shivers.*

"I don't think I want you to know." I hid my face. It'd give him that much more power over me and I wasn't sure I liked the scale at the moment. He'd ruined me for anyone else, ever.

"Why the hell not?" He ran his hand over my jaw and tipped my chin up, forcing me to look at him. "Don't go shy on me."

"Fine." I met his eyes and worried about the reaction. "No. I haven't."

"Orgasmed during sex?"

"I've never orgasmed from a guy before," I admitted, my face warming to beat red. "Also, I've only had sex once before."

His face froze in place. Nothing moved. Not his chest, not his eyes which rested on my face. I waited, my stomach churning. I pressed my lips down together, hard, with worry. I sat up, walked to my bathroom. "I know that's probably sad, but, I never found the right person. Not saying you're the right person, because well, I guess you are. I mean, I don't regret this. At all. But I know I'm inexperienced in this area. I'm sorry." I refused to meet his eyes in the buff and shook my head. He finally moved and I ran into the bathroom and locked the door.

"Shit." I eyed my reflection in the mirror. My cheeks were rosy, my hair messy and my eyes crazier. I had a wild, satisfied expression, yet I'd made an ass out of myself. My hands shook from fear and insecurities that were years old.

"Callie. Open up." Zade spoke through the closed door but I heard the command in his voice.

"Give me a second." I wiped my face with a cool towel and unlocked the door. I might feel insecure about my sexuality, but not about my body. I didn't cover up nor did I try to. His eyes softened to the warmest color and my worries seemed stupid. No one could have anyone stare at them like…like that and not feel cherished.

"I feel like I should warn you that I'm going to be an asshole sometimes. I'm learning how not to be." He stepped into the bathroom and cupped my face. "Thank you for sharing that with me."

"You were persistent," I said to his chin.

"I reacted poorly." He waited until I met his eyes. "I'm sorry for that."

I shrugged, not sure what to say. He kissed me and I melted into him. "It's hard to be mad at you when you kiss like that."

"I'll remember that for the future. I'm bound to piss you off sometimes." He gave me a small smile. "Now, two reasons explain why I reacted that way."

"Yeah?" My voice came out breathless. He twisted us around and I saw our reflections in the mirror. He met my eyes, which was a severely underrated turn-on. He ran his hand down my left side and stopped at my hip.

"First was shock. How I found you single shocks the hell out of me. Look at you." When he tapped his fingers over my curves and muscles, he made me feel the sexiest person in the world. "The second was pure alpha man instincts."

"Don't let it get to your head." I whispered my fear and his face fell.

"Callie, I want to give you every orgasm you'll ever have." He pulled my hand and dragged me back to bed. "Now, let's sleep an hour or two before next round, eh?"

Best. Sleep. Ever.

Chapter Twenty-Four

Zade

I'd spent my first night with a girl. Like, the whole night and instead of freaking the fuck out, I relished it. I woke up with her legs sprawled around me, her hair in my face and her lips right next to mine. I found her clock without waking her up. It sat on her tiny night stand next to a picture of her and Greta from years ago. It barely read seven. *Perfect.*

I slid out from under her and used the bathroom. I had an hour before I needed to be at the field and I wanted to enjoy that hour. She stirred in her sleep a little bit when I came back. Fuck if I didn't want to wake up to this view every day. Her ass was bare to the world, perfect and tight. Her toned back stretched in a way that had me questioning if practice was *that* important.

"Are you creeping on me?" Her mumbled voice came from the pillow. "Watching people sleep is a red flag. I think it's the first sign of a serial killer."

"Um no, nut job. It's not at all. I got distracted by your ass." I walked up and smacked it before lying next to her. I put my boxers on because I needed to calm down and, also, I didn't know if my dick would handle being close to her again without waking up. He'd never let me down before, but last night had tested every limit.

"Then that makes it okay, I guess." She rolled onto her side and wiped the sleep from her eyes. She glowed. I remembered my mom saying something to my sister once and it perfectly applied to Callie. *You shouldn't have people think you look different without makeup – they should be wowed when you wear it. It should be an accessory, not a part of you.* Callie didn't need it. Ever. Her round eyes held dark lashes that framed her face in the most flattering way.

"You are beautiful in the morning." I kissed her forehead and got a smack in the chest. "What the hell?"

"You. This. Us. Everything." She grinned, dimples and all. "You're laying it on thick and I'm eating it up. I don't know what that says about us."

"Who the fuck cares?" That earned me another smile and I pulled her into my arms. "I have to head to the field in an hour. Want to grab breakfast?"

"Sure. I'm famished." She patted her stomach and rolled from my embrace. She threw on a pair of black spandex things and slipped jeans over them. She never once checked her reflection in the mirror or asked what I thought about her outfit. It was a sure sign of confidence that I admired the hell out of.

"I feel kind of slutty." I pointed to the outfit I'd worn the night before. "Same clothes. Screams walk of shame."

"You *would* know. But if the lucky gal is with you, is it really shameful?"

"Good question. I think not." I pulled on the end of her crazy hair and smiled. "I never got around to telling you last night how much I loved your hair."

"I can tell. You always touch it." She laughed at my baffled expression and threw on a plaid flannel over her Sox shirt. "I'm handling the morning after better than you. Is it safe to say you haven't done it before?"

"Very safe to say. And that I'm enjoying it thus far."

"Good. You dork." She grabbed her phone and keys and patted me on the face before leaving the room. "Shall we?"

"You're awful chipper." I followed her out of the room and blinked in shock as Greta sat on the couch with an annoyingly large smile. It surprised me how it didn't break her face.

"Morning." That one word held so many damn things. Color flooded my cheeks and Callie gave her a death stare. I nodded at her. *Fuck. This is awkward.*

"Good lord. She knew," I said to Callie as we walked hand in hand to the café after escaping Greta's knowing grin.

"Oh yeah. She totally knew. That's okay, though." She shielded the sun with her hand and wiggled her eyebrows at me. "I walked in on her going at it with a guy yesterday. She owed me."

"I guess she did."

"How are you doing?" Her question confused me. *I* should be asking her how she felt. "Don't get all grumpy at me. I wanted to make sure my player is still in the game."

Her player. I liked that. "I do recall you asking if I wanted to see your favorite base. I would've thought that would've been first, with Paul Konerko playing there."

"Excellent point. However, you showed me quite quickly that I am a fan of homeruns now." She blushed and I pulled her in for a kiss. "You and your mouth. Mm."

"Why can't I get enough of you?" I asked to no one in particular. But she answered anyway.

"It's because I'm awesome. True story." She giggled and held the door to the café for me. "After you, dear."

I smiled and my chest tightened. It must have been hunger pains. *Right?*

* * * *

After walking Callie back to her apartment and attending a brutal two-hour throwing session, I finally headed to my sister's. The trepidation I'd felt the day before came back. I clutched the steering wheel, but she was right. She'd chosen the area because gates provided an extra layer of protection and it comforted me when I got stopped three times by some form of security before actually arriving at her town house.

I pressed the intercom and she replied immediately. "Hello?"

"Yo. Open up, Z."

"Password."

"Really? I'm here to help you."

"I'm taking extra safety measures. Be proud of me. Now, password."

I thought about the crazy adventures we'd had as kids. No passwords stuck out to me except one. We'd built a treehouse—well, something that might've resembled a tree house. Our mom had kept some used cardboard and we'd somehow climbed an old tree and placed the box strategically in it to resemble a fort. We'd written *ONLY Z WILLOWS ALLOWED* and thought we were incredibly clever because it meant one of the two of us. We'd constructed the sneakiest password known to kids anywhere — *WACATT*.

Willows

Are

Cool

All

The

Time

"Fuck. WACATT." We pronounced it in a way we thought sounded French. Wah, and caught. WACATT.

"You remembered. Breaks my cynical heart. Come on up, bro." She buzzed me up and had the door unlocked for me. I entered and saw her eyeing the shelf in question. It sat in four pieces.

"What the *hell* did you do? Take a bat to it?"

"No. You know how I don't like bees, right?" She gave me a guilty smile and we both damn well remembered the summer where she'd refused to go outside. I had some lingering anger I had yet to get rid of. She'd ruined the summer between fourth and fifth grade. A lot had happened then.

"So, a bee flew in here and what? You decided to throw the vacuum at it?" I ran my hand through my hair and groaned in embarrassment for her.

"Not quite, but close enough." She held the bottom piece up. "If we glue it to the base, maybe we can salvage it?"

"I hope you weren't fond of the thing. We can't save it." I picked up the fake wood. She weirded me out sometimes. "I guess I can grill you about the letters and calls on the way to Wal-Mart."

"Yeah. You're probably right." She had her purse and threw her hair into one of my old team hats. That was the thing about Zaria, she had my back come rain or shine. She rarely missed a game and had always been the first person I went to for approval and advice. She'd let me know if I was fucking up my life. "Good news—no more calls since I blocked the number."

"Good. The letters?"

"Over here." She handed them to me. "Nothing too sketchy but rather unnerving."

I took them and flipped through them. It was basic handwriting on a plain note—*PLEASE CALL ME ASAP. SUPER IMPORTANT.*

They'd sent the same letter three times, the writing becoming more desperate. They'd left a number on the last one and I grabbed Zaria's phone. "Is it the same number you blocked?"

"Uh-huh." She sat on the edge of the couch. "Are you going to call?"

"Yup. Might as hell." I dialed the number and waited. And waited. No answer. No voicemail. "Shit."

"That was anticlimactic, wasn't it?" She was too easy-going sometimes for her own good. I guess that was one reason she'd make an amazing teacher. It took a whole lot to piss her off.

"I don't like this." I tried the number again. Nothing. "Hopefully, the person calls back."

"I have no idea what this meant or why. I haven't done anything crazy or left a trail of broken hearts like you. Speaking of, how's my favorite girl in your life?"

"Who? Mom?" I asked, causing her to roll her eyes in a way similar to Callie's. "Just kidding. Callie. Her name is Callie and she's perfect."

"Oh, dish it." She pulled her legs up to her chest. "You look lovestruck, bud."

"Let's go get you a new shelf and I'll *think* about telling you." I jingled my keys at her and she made a face at me.

"You are no fun. I wanted gossip and entertainment. I'm bored. Claire's always at her boyfriend's and I need companionship." She sighed. "And I know it must be good as hell because you really aren't that shy in talking about your...hobbies."

"And you are too intrusive for your own good." I held the door open for her and waved her out. "I got a hot woman waiting for me. Move it."

"Oh, my god. The day has come." She locked her door and glared at me like our mom. "When can I meet her?"

"Never." I said the words as reflex but thought about it. Zaria saw my hesitation and her grin matched the creepy one I'd seen on Greta that morning. "Chill, sis. You probably will at some point. I don't plan on letting her go."

"Fuck, you're serious." Her eyes widened and softened. "I love you, but I'm going to torture the hell out of you and tell mom. Between the two of us, we'll get information."

"If you do that, I'll tell her about the time you snuck out and smoked weed."

"You wouldn't. We made an unbreakable vow. Hello...what about the statute of limitation on those events?"

"Whatever you think. Mom's an adventurer now — maybe she'll dig it. Or she might be insanely disappointed and send you drug addiction pamphlets."

"Oh, god. The pamphlets are the worst." She laughed and hit my arm. "Remember when she sent you all those about getting herpes from party cups?"

"Yes, Zaria. I remember. Those scared away a potential date one night."

"Aw, poor guy. You must be very lonely." She slid into my front seat and I gave her a scathing look.

"You are a pain in the ass."

"Yeah, but you love me." She cheesed at me and rolled down the windows. "Let's blast some music and shit and get me a shelf. Yay, adulthood."

Chapter Twenty-Five

Callie

I strummed the guitar, Greta belting one of our favorites in the background. Her voice complemented mine and we harmonized in a way only people who'd played together for years could. I changed the chords to match an old Taylor Swift song and she jumped onto the couch with the remote as microphone.

I stood, speeding up the beat of the song as she twirled. I joined her for the chorus and that bled into *Teenage Dirtbag*. We jammed without a care in the world around our living room and when the song ended, I spun my guitar around to my back and jumped on top of Greta.

"OMG! Amazing."

"I know. God, I miss it." She fell onto the couch with me on her lap and someone cleared their throat. "*What the fuck?*" Greta spun and threw the remote toward the noise coming from our kitchen, made by one of the two people standing there. It smacked Aaron right in the face and Tanner bit back a smile. Then we all burst out laughing at the same time.

"I am sorry about your face, Aaron." Greta patted his cheek where a slight red mark had appeared.

"It hurt. I'm wounded. And this is my money maker."

"Oh, *okay*." I stretched out the word to make it three syllables.

"I can't say I'm mad that you left your door unlocked. I didn't realize how good you guys were." Tanner finally spoke and stared straight at Greta. Like, his eyes pierced her, but she paid no attention. *Good for her.* I felt proud of my friend for moving on when her feelings weren't reciprocated.

"We're okay." I shrugged and shared a smile with Greta. They didn't need to know we'd won Battle of the Bands one year.

Greta tsked me. "*Okay?* We're a little better than okay. Also, if guests don't want to die, they should knock next time."

"We did. You ignored us." Aaron held up his phone and shook it at us. "I got that whole thing on video and I posted it."

"Wait, why?" I grabbed for the phone, but he held it out of reach. "You didn't, really?"

"Yes. I did. I have tons of followers who enjoy my life."

"So a video of two girls playing music will help you on that front? Sad, Aaron. That's sad."

"It will and plus, you guys are cool. Don't worry. I put the hashtag you love on it." He clapped his hands and walked to the couch like he owned the place. "Now, what are you two up to tonight?"

"I'm not sure." I studied Greta's reaction and she shrugged. I hadn't heard from Zade, not that I expected to. We weren't going to be those people who spent every second together...or I told myself that all day when I hadn't heard from him. I was playing it cool. *As cool as a cucumber.* "G?"

"We need to all go out and celebrate your shadowing opportunity. It's Saturday. The nights are cooling off. Guys? See? It's settled."

"Wait, what's settled? What are we doing?" I queried.

"We are showing you what you missed while you were basking in a free year, sister." Greta put her arm around me and addressed the boys. "We'll start getting ready. We'll pregame here this time."

"Can we bring other girls? You guys are great, but I'm not getting my rocks off with either of you," Aaron said without a flicker of shame. "What? What did I say?"

"Bye, Aaron. See you later." Greta pushed him out of the apartment and paused slightly before motioning Tanner to leave. "See ya."

He walked out but gave her a scathing look. I nodded. "Yup. I saw it, too."

"He can't do that to me after he specifically told me we were friends. Ugh!"

I went up to hug her. "Remember how you said I'd be your wingman? I still am. I'll help you drive him crazy tonight."

"What about your new boo-thang?" Her mouth twitched at her creative nickname for him. It made no sense yet I liked it all the same.

"*Boo-thang* doesn't matter right now. We are going out to celebrate the amazing start to the year and I can do what I damn well please. And getting a little tipsy with my best friend sounds fun. And if we break a couple hearts, *c'est la vie*."

"God, where were you my freshman year?"

I let Greta dress me again. It had worked well the first time, so why the hell not? She chose a metallic-y silver dress that ended inches below my ass. I never wore clothes this revealing, but it kind of made me feel awesome and mature. It went well with my long hair curled by Greta and my eye makeup just a little jazzed up. Greta wore something similar, only a tad shorter and lower-cut. She had a rockin' body and our goal tonight was to piss off Tanner into making a move or to have her find a new fling. *My* goal was to be a good friend to her and enjoy Zade. My stomach swooped into back handsprings when I thought about seeing him again. I checked my phone to see if he'd texted me back. He had.

Zade: We're on our way. See you soon.

Zade: Oh, my god. Aaron showed me the video.

Callie: What?! We were messing around. It was stupid.

Zade: No. No. It fucking rocked. It's another reason why I can't get you out of my head.

Callie: To clarify, it was a good 'oh, my god?'

Zade: Hells yeah, to quote you.

Callie: I am quite quotable.

Zade: They say that imitation is the sincerest form of flattery. And yes, before you asked, I researched that.

I held my phone to my chest and smiled. He had no idea that looking up a quote to text me meant a whole lot of things I didn't want to analyze. Greta shouted for me, so I grabbed my clutch for the night and nodded to the music. "Eighties party mix? Nice touch."

"Thank you. But important question. Bra or no bra?" She struck a pose. "What do you think now?"

"I can't tell if you have one on or not. Twirl around. Pretend to dance. If you have a nip slip, perhaps try wearing one."

"Good call." She weaved and danced around the apartment, nip-slip free. I gave her a thumbs-up and she smiled. "Nice. My goal is to dance with Tanner at some point and get him to notice."

"Are you playing with fire, G?"

"Yup, and I want to get burned so bad." She widened her eyes at the 'bad' and I laughed. She was the coolest person ever. "Now, you and Zade. Are you dating?"

"Hmm." I thought about it and my stomach tightened in a knot. "Not officially, but it is safe to assume we are together."

"Not trying to lock down that label? That's pretty chill. I think you're right, though. I've seen you two and tonight will be a nice test. You banged like crazy people last night and tonight will tell you where you stand."

"What do you mean?" I bit my lip, her words worrying me. She looked out for me, but it questioned the small confidence I had in whatever Zade and I were doing.

"If he's still all over you, you're definitely an item. If he's not, it'll be out of your system. She shrugged and gave me a small smile. "He will be. Don't worry."

I jumped when the doorknob began moving. "Now you lock the door?"

"Yeah, doesn't make sense now that you mention it." She marched on over to let in Aaron, Tanner, Jeff, two girls I didn't know and Zade. My heart beat in my throat when his gaze searched for mine. His eyes lit up. Greta whispered to me, "Oh yeah. Definitely a hot-ass item."

I shook her off and was debating if I should walk over to him when Aaron stood in front of me with a bottle of fire whiskey. "This is for you, big girl on campus."

"Thanks." I took it and gave him a hug. "You didn't have to."

"I know. But I should say, I expect all of us to drink it before we leave." He produced a stack of portable shot glasses and I shook my head. I should've known better. "First ones to you."

"Yeah, okay. Pour them out." I slipped away to find Zade. He had the same intention I'd had and reached me first.

"Hey, girl." I laughed at our shared inside joke. He always greeted me this way and it made me laugh. Every. Damn. Time.

"'Sup." I attempted to be cool but everything went to hell when his lip quirked and he really stared at me. His heated gaze roamed my body, pausing on my legs, and a small scowl replaced his once joyous smile. "What is your outfit?"

"It's called a dress, Zade. Sometimes girls wear them."

"But you don't."

"*Excuse me.* I can wear a dress if I want." I pushed him away, but he grabbed my wrist with an embarrassed smile.

"Shit. I handled my reaction poorly." He ran his hand down my neck to my hips. I loved the possessive way he touched me, although he was annoying me at the moment.

"Ya think?"

"Sorry. Your dress is hot as fuck. I want to tie you to your bed and not let you leave. I want you naked and screaming my name. That is what that dress does to me." He lowered his mouth and kissed me in front of everyone. That answered any questions I'd had.

"Well, fuck. I'll ask Greta if I can keep the dress," I said breathlessly after he ended the kiss.

"I'd appreciate it. So, let's go do those shots with Aaron. He can be relentless."

"Good call. I need something for my nerves." I shivered and he frowned again.

"Why are you nervous?"

"I generally am when I am around you." I patted his chest and led him to the couch. "I'm not used to feeling all these things and I get all discombobulated."

"Yeah, I thought after last night I'd be more level-headed. I thought wrong." He sat next to me and kept his hand on my knee, like not touching me hurt him. "I'm all over the place. I want to kiss you senseless, ask you about your entire day and at the same time hang out with you. It's a lot to think at the same time and I don't know what direction to go."

"Always go with what's natural."

"I'm trying but I get all...how did you put it? Discombobulated." His lip turned up when he said it. I loved that little half-smile.

"Aw, my little player has nerves, too." I wiggled against him and his eyes became the intense coffee color I now associated with passion.

"Just with you." *Ugh. Wham, bam, thank you ma'am.* My heart upped and left me and decided to take up residence within his. My brain held a little control, but the rest of me had surrendered to him entirely.

Chapter Twenty-Six

Zade

I had issues. Right here, in a dingy bar with loud music and way too many damn people. It smelled like sweat and I wanted to punch everyone who got in my way. I blamed it on being tired, not the fact that Callie drew the stares of all the guys in the place. I clenched my beer tighter in my hand and watched Callie dance around with Greta without a care in the world. I refused to ask her to stop because she'd kill me, but I refused to take my eyes off her. She stole the show.

"Dude, don't blow a gasket, looking all grumpy like that," Aaron slurred at me, already feeling the shots he'd made everyone take. Okay, we'd willingly taken them, but he'd snuck a few more. Fine by me. I wanted to be coherent enough to watch out for Callie and try to convince her to let me stay the night. *Again.*

"I'm not grumpy." Aaron lifted his eyebrows way too high at the lack of humor in my response. I took a sip of beer and checked back on Callie. "Where did your date, err, dates go?"

"Fuck if I know. Bathroom probably. They were a little...what's the word?" He frowned at Jeff, who also had a good buzz going on.

"Annoying?" Jeff replied with a drunken smile.

"No. No. Not that."

"Catty?"

"No, save that for catty Callie. I'd put my money on her if they fought. Hands down. She has legs for days so..."

"Watch it." I narrowed my eyes at him and felt better when his face blanched. "I'd put my money on her, too."

He laughed, the tension gone. "Ah, shit. Here they come." The two girls he'd brought had ended up being exactly what Jeff said — annoying. They laughed way too much to be real, they ended up touching one of us somewhere without us knowing it and they seemed to have an agenda. I hated people with agendas. Aaron licked his lips. "Hi, beautifuls."

I shook my head at Aaron and met Tanner's knowing stare. If anyone appeared uncomfortable, it'd be Tanner. We shared a small smile and he nodded to the bar. I followed, taking one look back at Callie. Fuck, the feeling in my chest got damn near unbearable. The music pounded, lights flashing and instead of enjoying every second of it I impatiently waited until we could leave. This sucked.

"I don't want Aaron fucking up his future," Tanner deadpanned when he'd ordered the drinks. "Veronica has her claws into him and he's sleeping with literally everything. I'm fucking worried."

"Shit." I ran my hand down my face. If Veronica had anything on him…it would be bad as hell. "Are we sure he's taking all these girls back? I mean, is he just being stupid Aaron who flirts with everything with tits?"

"I thought so, too. But…he's acting erratic. Drinking more than normal, bringing home girls every night. He's shown up late to workouts, twice. When he comes, he has a lingering smell of beer or something. I sound like a fucking dad because I enjoy partying and women too but—"

"Not like that." I set my beer down and unease crept into my stomach. "Do you think coach knows?"

"Hell. I don't know. He doesn't miss much."

"We need to talk to him." *What a shitty friend I am. I should've known or seen this.*

"Yeah. Tonight is not the night for that."

"No shit, Sherlock." He grinned, then it disappeared. "I'm going to try and bring it up tomorrow, casually, but shit might hit the fan if he gets in one of his defensive rants."

"Yeah. I'll make sure to be at the house. Jeff, too."

He clapped me on the back and we got two more beers before heading back to our table. Aaron and Jeff were laughing at something and the girls were gone, thank god.

"There you are. Better check that shit out." Aaron pointed to the dance floor and I spun around to see Callie hugging some guy. Her arms were around his neck, her gorgeous smile aimed at him, whose face I wanted to break. He had his hand on her lower back, looking happy as hell. Jealousy's ugly, green and unfamiliar face reared before me. I had no hold on my reaction and let it drive me. I set my beer on the table and stalked toward them. The guy saw me first. He paled and jumped back from her. She faced me, narrowed her scary brown eyes and pressed her lips together in a flat line. I waited for her to say something, and when she didn't, I studied her, feeling stupid as fuck.

"H-hey, Z-man," the guy addressed me, nervously. Good. I hope I scared him. "I'm Radcliffe. Callie and I both have special projects. Uh, it's a pretty big deal." He held out his hand, a little shakily, and I hesitated. I had two choices here — admit I'd made an ass of myself, or go with it. I refused to concede anything to the schmuck.

"Congrats on that. That's a huge deal." I shook his hand and felt better knowing his palm were sweating a little bit.

"I came out to celebrate with friends, like Callie here. I'll get back to them. See you later, Callie." He gave her a small smile and walked away. I stared at the spot he disappeared to while Callie shot daggers at me. Before I'd worked out how to apologize, she'd walked away.

I followed her, not knowing where she was going. "Cal, hold up."

"No. I'm pissed at you. Let me calm down." She headed down a narrow hallway that led outside to the beer garden. I hated that I'd made her mad. I'd never cared before and now all the fucks I'd never given were coming back in full force. Funny how karma works.

"Callie. Let me explain." I tried to grab her hand but she yanked it away. My stomach twisted in the worst way. Her eyes were like I'd never seen them before. They were shooting fire at me and I had no idea how to make it right. "I don't want to walk away with you mad at me."

"Well, you should've thought of that before you acted like a total dick to a friend of mine. A *friend*, Zade. I will have them, guy or girl. You can't control that." She put her hands on her narrow hips and despite the terrible timing, she turned me on.

"I'm sorry." I meant it. I stared deep into her eyes and took a small step toward her. She didn't push me away. I took that as a good sign. The weight in my stomach eased a little. "This is new for me, okay? I saw you hugging him and I flipped out."

"Uh, yeah. I thought you were going to punch him for hugging me. A *hug*, Zade." Her mouth twisted when she said the word *hug* and nothing but naughty thoughts went into my head. God, I needed to get a grip.

"I've never been jealous before. I hate it." I held out my hand and lowered my voice. "Can I touch you again?"

"Fine." She sighed, but her eyes softened at me. I pulled her into my arms and my world righted itself again. "You better not be one of those crazy jealous types. They annoy me."

I kissed her forehead and pulled her back to look in her eyes. She'd told me mine were a way to see my every mood, but I began to learn how to read hers. Narrowed meant annoyance or angry. Now, they were soft and open. "How about this? I'll try to rein it in and handle it better next time. I won't tell you what to do or what not to do. That's all on you."

"Good. Because as soon as you would've tried...I would've taken off. I'm a little mad at you and you better not do anything like that again, but..."

"But what?"

"You had a little caveman thing going on." She blushed, the redness to her cheeks pretty damn appealing. "Kind of hot. But I am not condoning your behavior."

"Duly noted. I'm going to be honest with you."

"I like honesty. It tends to be the best policy." She grinned at her quote and I couldn't help but grin, too.

"I used to love coming here. Now, I've been counting down until we can leave."

"Hmm, well, we can't have that." She grabbed my hand and wiggled her eyebrows. "Dance with me."

"Eh, not a good idea." I thought about her body against mine and how hard she'd made me already. "I'm already feeling animalistic and possessive toward you."

"Animalistic I like. Possessive I don't."

"I don't want to share you." *There. I said it.* The words I'd never uttered to a girl before were out in the open. I had no idea how she'd react to that, but I did not fucking expect her to throw her head back and laugh. I fought a grin because it was contagious, but I didn't get the joke. "Care to share why you laughed when I admitted something from my heart?"

"By all means. First, you're certifiably nuts if you think for one second I have room for anyone else when you take over every sense I have." *God, best answer ever.* I grinned like a fool at that and wanted to beat my chest.

"Secondly, Zade, you have the power to remedy this situation and ensure we are exclusive."

"Were we not exclusive?" *Fuck. Fuck.* I thought I'd made that clear. "There's no one else but you."

"If you're asking, *again*, if I wanted to see anyone else, the answer is still a hell to the no." She ran her fingers through my hair, softly. "But we haven't talked about what we are. What this means. Anything like that."

"Like boyfriend-girlfriend shit?"

"Sure."

"Fine. Want to be my girlfriend?"

"Do I have to wear your watch?" An odd question, one I didn't understand.

"If you want to?"

"Nah, I'm good." She began to walk away.

"Wait, what? You don't want to be?"

"Nah. I'm good. I don't want to be your girlfriend and shit at the present time."

She had to be messing with me. She had to. I wanted to mark her as mine, forgoing all the anti-possessive speech she'd given me earlier. I wanted her wearing my jersey, watch, anything—I didn't really care. I circled her waist with my arms and kissed her neck, loving how she shivered. "Care to explain why you constantly tell me no when I know how your body reacts to me?"

"Because you asked me after reacting to someone else hugging me. It was out of a jealous fit you'd never had the experience of before." She hummed in pleasure as I continued to explore her neck. "Am I right?"

"Shit. I don't know. I want you to be mine," I growled into her ear.

"You'd better think of a better way of asking. And, if I can say, better timed." She walked away but spun around to fire back, "Plus, a *boyfriend* would dance with me."

"Ah, fuck. You're good."

"Don't I know it?"

I followed her to the dance floor because I had no choice. None at all, really.

Chapter Twenty-Seven

Callie

Waking up with Zade's mouth between my legs had to be the best morning of my life. I stretched out against him now, basking in the joy of yet another earth-shattering orgasm. "You get the best mouth award."

"That is an award I'd wear with pride. I mean, the Cy Young would be nice one day, but until then...I'll be content with this."

"Does the world know that you are actually a marshmallow?"

"Marshmallow? How so, Ms. Callie? I'm not soft and shit."

"Sure, sure." I mimicked Tanner's phrase. "For someone who doesn't do the romance and sleepovers and romance shit...you say the damnedest things."

"I do have to say that I thoroughly enjoyed my second night over here." His eyes lit up with clear acknowledgment of our sexcapades. I didn't complain though. It had been a fantastic night spent in bed together.

"I take it you didn't have a lot of sleepovers as a kid?"

"Here and there. Those were more building forts and playing superheroes."

"Sounds like the kinds I had. Tons of fun, those were."

"Uh-huh. But I assure you I never did this." He pulled me up on top of him and cupped my ass.

"I hope not," I joked, the breath leaving me when he ground against me, showing me how ready he was.

"I want to see you ride me."

"Mm. We can arrange that." I heated over, flushed from the wake-up orgasm he'd delivered, but when he looked at me and touched me like that... I got hot all over again. I grabbed a condom from the nightstand and slipped it on him. I hadn't ever been on top before, but now was not the time to be gun-shy. I straddled him, slowly sliding down and loving how his body reacted to me. His whole face tightened in pure focus and... Damn, boy.

"Fuck, Callie. Give me your mouth." He grabbed my head and kissed the shit out of me as I rocked against him. I loved being in control. It empowered me, adrenaline pumping through my veins. I pushed him back to the bed and rocked my hips. I held his hands above his head and he smiled. "I fucking love this, by the way."

"If you can talk, I'm not doing it right." I increased my speed, using my teeth and mouth to bite the places I knew he liked. Not two minutes later, his breathing picked up and he was close. He kept his eyes on mine the entire time and it had to be the most erotic thing I'd experienced. He saw all of me, held nothing back and he moaned my name as he convulsed inside me.

"Goddamn. I'm not leaving." He pulled me into his arms and cradled me against his chest after disposing of the condom. "What is it about you?"

"It's my charm and wit," I said, my mind racing from being near him.

"Uh-huh. It's more than that." He ran his fingers down my arm in a comforting and spine-tingling way. I couldn't recall ever feeling so…cherished? Admired? Loved? *Oh no. Not that word.* I stopped that train of thought before it took root in me and made me crazy. "I forgot to ask you yesterday. Can I see you play the guitar sometime?"

"Of course. I can play now, if you'd like?"

"Fuck yeah." He pushed himself to lean against my wall with a devilishly handsome smile. He made my queen-size bed seem small and unimportant. Hell, he made the whole bedroom small and boring. My heart went into overdrive, a now-constant state around him. I grabbed the guitar from the stand and went back to the bed. "I wish I had a picture of this."

"Better not even try." I pointed my finger hard at the center of his chest. I did not play the booty pics or sexting games that were so popular. Call me old-fashioned, but hell to the no. He held up his hands in surrender. "Are you ready?"

He nodded. I began with a rendition of a blend of Tom Petty songs, then into a Red Hot Chili Peppers tune and finished with the Killers. I hummed the words, not quite trusting my voice on its own. It shook around him and I sounded better paired with Greta. I closed my eyes when I played, feeling the music and vibrations from the guitar. I opened them and saw

Zade's face twisted into a grimace, almost. Suddenly, I was embarrassed. I didn't expect a standing ovation but playing music for someone meant a lot to me. It had always been a deep part of my soul. I didn't expect to see a pained expression.

The word vomit took over. "I never took classes or anything. I'm sorry. I shouldn't have played. I'm awkward. I played with Greta and I know we aren't the best but—"

"Shut up. I'm in awe of you. I'm not handling it well. Shocking. I know." His voice had an odd ring to it. I bit my lip and set the guitar down. I threw on some clothes, feeling a little too exposed at the moment, and he gnawed on his fingernail while I did it.

"You're making me nervous again."

"Not my intention. You are far out of my league and I'm a little baffled by you, sometimes. I'm having doubts about myself at the moment and that's ridiculous because I'm here with you." He glanced between the guitar and me a couple of times. "Thank you for sharing that with me. You are by far the most jaw-dropping person I've ever met and I have no idea how to keep up with you."

Damn. His. Perfect. Words.

"What's that little smile for?" The seriousness in his eyes floated away and he threw on his pants and shirt. I hated seeing his body covered up, but it was unrealistic to spend the next week naked with him. *A girl can dream, though...*

"Sometimes you say the best things." I blushed, head over heels for the guy and not wanting to accept it. "You make me smile."

He walked up to me and smiled *that* smile. He kissed me. This one spoke of things we both felt yet weren't willing to share at the moment. *Fine by me.*

"Good. Now, important question. Can I come back tonight?" he asked between kissing me. I wanted to say yes, I really did, but I shook my head. "Why not? Are you still upset with me about last night? I thought we had a great night."

"That—oh, no!" I ran my hands through his hair, my new favorite hobby. "I promised myself I wouldn't lose myself if we did this. Two nights in a row together… I don't want to fall too fast."

"Are you scared I'll hurt you?" His brows came together in the cutest act of concern. He stuck his lip out, the look I now referred to as the famous Zade-pout. "I'm falling fast and I'm terrified."

"I appreciate you admitting that to me. But let me hang with Greta tonight."

"Okay. I don't like it, but I'll respect it." He kissed my mouth again, possessively. "Can I try and convince you otherwise?"

"I'm sure you could try and eventually break me down, but then I'll be angry at myself. Trust me, your face is hard to say no to."

"But you turned down my girlfriend offer." He pouted again.

"Yup. I will again, too." I sort of enjoyed holding out on him even though my insides wanted to tattoo ZADE'S GIRLFRIEND all over them. "Figure out a better way to ask."

"Will you please be my girlfriend? I can promise you amazing orgasms, great conversation about baseball and I like playing games." He raised his brows and I shook my head. "Damn it, woman. You're going to kill me."

"Nah, you'll be okay. But I'll admit the attempt wasn't as bad as the one last night." I patted his face and threw on an old sweatshirt from one of my dad's teams. Zade eyed it. "It's from seven years ago. I loved this team. They treated me really nicely for a fifteen-year-old girl and they all signed the back, see?"

I showed him the back and he decided to put his hands on my ass. "Not my intention, but okay."

"I'm bringing you one of my jerseys." He said it without argument. "I don't like seeing other guys' names on your shirt."

"Tone down the crazy, Zade. And I think I'd like that. Now, I have ass-loads of homework and I'm meeting with Nicole tomorrow. Sorry, but I need you to leave. I can't focus on much else with your hot body in here."

"You're not helping the situation. When you say things like that, I want to stay and bother you."

"Not today, punk. Move it." I swatted at him and finally got him through my bedroom door. I saw Greta had spread her notes all over the floor and cringed. I had to do the same thing for a couple of hours later. She waved to Zade and, god, *winked* at him. I got him to the front door and he picked me up. "Uh, whatcha doing?"

"Just grabbing my little tease. I'm realizing I might be the needy one in the relationship. I hate it."

"Nah, you wear your heart on your sleeve. Mine is all up here." I pointed to my head and kissed him. "I'll see you on our run tomorrow."

"Fine. I'm mad, but I can't be. This sucks." He set me down and walked out. I went to shut the door, but he remained there. "I'm putting you on my Twitter."

"That's girlfriend-y and shit." My heart danced around and did back handsprings.

"Yup. Deal with it, punk." He left and I met Greta's knowing stare.

"I know. I'm fucking screwed," I sighed and grabbed a cup of coffee.

"You totally are. But you're handling it better than he is. God, when you turned down being his girlfriend! I high-five you, sister. You impress the shit out of me from time to time."

"I'm not trying to play games with him, but he only asked only out of jealousy. I deserve more than that." I joined her on the floor and grabbed my laptop. "I'm pretty sure I'm halfway in love with him. That terrifies me. It's only been what, six weeks of knowing him?"

"So what? When it hits, it hits. My parents married after two months." She shrugged and the thought made my stomach drop. "I know you, babe, don't overthink anything. Let it flow, baby — let it flow."

"You right. You right." I motioned for her to scoot closer. "My parents want to chat — you good?"

"Aw, anything for Mr. and Mrs. Williams."

I dialed and they picked up on the second ring.

"Hey, parental units. How's home?" Greta passed me a mug of her famous pumpkin spice latte. It was her awesome cooking talent. She made them three months a year because the fall weather had finally broken and they only tasted good in fall. I sipped mine and sighed. Damn, tasted like heaven.

"Hi, Callie girl. We're good. Busting out our old sweaters now that there's a chill." My dad put his arm around my mom and she smiled. They were very much love even after all these years. *Precious as hell.* "Hey, Greta. You look chipper today."

"I am always chipper, Glenn. Emily, you are adorable in your crewneck. New sweater?"

"Yes, ma'am. Ordered it last week. I also bought it in three different colors." My mom and Greta shared a taste for fashion. I'd missed that gene.

"Way to go. That's the way to do it. If it works, it works." Greta eyed my outfit, the old signed sweatshirt and leggings. "So, did you know Callie is dating Zade Willows?"

"Greta!" I yelled, mid coffee sip, and it went all over her. I should've felt bad, but she didn't. She burst out laughing and my parents chuckled a little bit. "Uh, I guess we are."

My mom smiled tightly and my dad closed his eyes, pinching the bridge of his nose. "How did that happen, honey?"

"No idea, actually. Just did. We aren't official or anything—"

"Because she keeps turning down his offer to be his girlfriend," Greta interrupted and I glared at her. She shrugged and gave me the most bullshit innocent face ever.

"Really, why is that? I mean, I know you need to focus on school work, Callie," my dad asked. My parents were cool enough to talk to about this stuff, but they also didn't realize how much Gage had messed me up. I thought my mom had figured something out, but she'd never told my dad because one, he would kill Gage and two, she didn't want to make it worse for me.

"Hmm. It's a little too much too fast. If that makes sense. He is an intense guy, like really intense, and I want to go slow." There. I'd admitted the real reason. "I'm afraid of getting my heart broken."

"Callie girl, you can't let the fear keep you from trying. You know this." My dad's words rang true. "Do you trust the guy?"

"Yeah. I do."

"Greta, is he a good guy?" my mom asked her.

"Yes. He's even better with her."

"Well, there you have it. Greta's word is golden." My mom smiled and a small weight lifted off me. "Now, tell us more about what you'll be doing as the side project!"

Chapter Twenty-Eight

Zade

The next week flew by. Between the running, the workouts, Aaron's intervention, my sister's letter issue and Callie, my life had never gone by this fast. I dreaded the off season, normally, counting down the days until the first game but now... Now I enjoyed the hell out of it. Now, I had Callie. She only let me stay the night twice a week, as if we were in high school or something. I hated leaving, but I needed to let her make the call. I smiled at how much I fucking needed that girl and Jeff caught me. *Shit.*

"Fuck you, man."

He laughed. "You're done."

"Pretty much." I did reps on the leg machine and grunted. Nicole and her little apprentice, my future wife, wanted me to build up my legs for more strength. I wanted to increase my speed by two more miles and they'd demanded I build more leg muscle. I felt stronger than last year, but I wasn't as confident.

They'd ordered me on a two-week break from throwing and to only increase my endurance, leg and core strength. I wanted to throw, but remained quiet. I hated sounding like a prima donna. "I don't even care though. Does that mean I'm bitch-whipped?"

"Yup. You're cuffed, bro." He wrote down his reps on the clipboard we were now required to turn in. It annoyed us, but Nicole made the rules and coach wanted it done. If we wanted to play on the field, then we did what we were told. *Talk about being cuffed...*

"Have you seen Aaron today?" I hadn't since our talk Sunday. None of us had. He'd taken it well enough but had packed a bag and left our house. He'd told us he needed to figure some shit out and he'd be back. Two days were fine...but a week? I'd actually begun to worry.

"No. I asked coach about him and he did that hand thing that tells you to shut your mouth. So I did." His eyes darkened, a feeling we all had. Aaron was the team clown. No matter the score or how shitty we were playing, he rooted for us and never got low. I admired that trait. If he made an error, because we all do at times, he shook it off with a smile and made the game-saving play the next pitch. "I think he talked to coach, though, because if any of us missed practice we'd be screamed at or made to run ten miles."

"I hope he did. I'm worried." I couldn't think of anything that would've triggered the partying. "Should we try calling his parents?"

"Yeah. I think we should. Actually, they don't live far from here. Maybe an hour or two. Want to drive down there?"

I thought about canceling my plans with Callie and knew I had no choice. Aaron was my teammate and brother. I wanted to see her, but this needed to be a priority. "As soon as we're done here, let's go."

"Cool. I'll text Tanner. Give him a heads-up." He left the machine and groaned into his towel. "Nicole and Callie are walking over here with more clipboards."

I grinned at them. Callie, already in an animated conversation with Nicole, wore a little radio and fanny pack. They were literally the most unattractive things in the world, but Callie made it cool somehow. Jeff moved to stand next to my machine and helped me write down my reps, but I kept my eyes on her. "You think they'll make us do more today? My legs and arms feel like jello."

"Speak for yourself, bro. My arm is on a two-week break and with the running, my legs feel stronger than ever." It was true. They did and I felt fucking great.

"Yeah, yeah, yeah, asshole. You're on that bitch-ass high from Callie. I want to take you out back and punch the hell out of you. Hey, Callie. Boss lady, Nicole."

"Cute, Jeff. Real cute. What's not cute is the next exercise we have for you. Move to the water tank," Nicole barked at him and eyed me. "Callie, you run Jeff through the wringer. Do what she says, Jeff—she'll report to me."

Jeff glanced at me and nodded. Callie gave me a wink before smacking Jeff playfully with the clipboard. A surge of jealousy went through me but I swallowed it down. I had no right and it was Jeff. *My brother.* Nicole watched me with a hint of a smile. "Okay, lover boy. You're with me. Finish up and hit the treadmill."

"I've been running eight miles almost every day a week," I said, not wanting to complain about running but also not wanting to run more. I might've lied to Jeff about how tough my legs were doing.

"Cool. I watched three episodes of *House of Cards* last night. Life is dandy. Get on the treadmill and wipe that stupid grin off your face." She pointed her head in the direction of the slanted one, the one I hated. It sucked ass.

"Your people skills are amazing," I grumbled to her, at which she smacked me with a towel. "Sorry, boss lady."

"Shut your trap and run." She studied a chart and watched me run for ten minutes straight. The elevation on the mat sucked ass. My knees throbbed every step and my thighs burned something fierce. I wiped sweat from my face while Callie sat on a stool and shouted something at Jeff. She met my eyes across the gym and winked again. *Fuck my life.* I stumbled a little bit and Nicole noticed. *Shit.*

She slowed down the treadmill and leaned over it. Her pretty, makeup-free face hovered in front of mine. I couldn't read her to save my life and I gulped. "Here's the situation, Zade. You're talented as hell. You have a semi-decent head on your shoulders and work harder than most people on the team. So, I'm only going to say this once. Callie told me of your involvement together. She had to."

"Okay."

"Don't mess it up." Her steely eyes told me one thing — she preferred Team Callie one hundred percent. It made me smile. If Callie had Nicole on her side, it meant Callie was *that* good.

"I won't."

"Good. Glad that's settled. Now, stop dicking around and push yourself." She sped up the machine and I knew our little heart-to-heart was over. I groaned in pain into my towel and obeyed her for the next thirty minutes. I wanted to pass out for a week when I'd finished.

"Go shower and get in the ice bath," Nicole barked at me and left. I did what she said. My pain distracted me from everyone else. I showered off the layers of sweat, threw on an old shirt and headed to the ice room. Nicole already had a bath prepared for me and I hopped in, welcoming the pain and relief. I knew I had to sit for fifteen minutes and it did wonders for my overused muscles in the end.

"Now, you play first?" A familiar voice broke through my tired haze.

"Yup. Always have." A gruff voice answered, one I knew to be Max. "If you're a Sox fan, you must love Konerko."

"All-time favorite." She walked into the ice room with a clipboard and Max immediately checked her out. My fists clenched. "So, have a seat and I'll get you ice."

"Got it." He hopped onto the table on the other side of the room and gave me a grin I had no trouble reading. *Fucking hell.* "Now, Callie, how did you get roped into this gig?"

"Hmm." She hadn't noticed me yet and continued bagging the ice to wrap him. I listened, because I had no choice, but also because I wanted to see how much she told him. "I paid a guy. You know."

"I doubt that. Nicole is a tough cookie to crack."

"That's putting it kindly. Now, sit still."

"Kind of hard when you're around me."

I held my breath.

She paused and stepped back from him. "Max. Don't even try that. Ain't going to work and you'll embarrass yourself."

"Come on. We hit it off."

"We talked baseball. I can talk to anyone, ages three to three hundred, about baseball. I'm going to be around here all year. We won't happen."

"Are you involved with someone?"

"Regardless if I am or not, this won't happen." She didn't warn him before putting the ice on his shoulder. He hissed and the sound gave me an odd satisfaction. "But, yeah. I am."

"Bummer. Lucky guy." He hissed between his teeth. "This stings."

"Your ego or your arm?"

"Good one." He laughed and motioned to his arm. "I threw too many reps today."

"Yeah, and you overextended on your long tosses." She went to grab the clipboard and only then noticed me in the tub. She paused, for a second. "Hey, Zade."

"Hey, girl." I winked at her. She blushed slightly but rolled her eyes. I guess that answered my question if she wanted to admit in the training room that we were together. "You look tough out there."

"I am tough. Also, if you aren't withering in pain, I'm telling Nicole." She went back to Max and finished wrapping two bags of ice on him. He thanked her and walked out with a smirk. She turned back to me and wetted her bottom lip.

"Will you be my girlfriend?" I tried, for the fifth time that week.

She grinned, which was the best reaction I'd had yet. I held my breath, but she shook her head. "Nah. Jealousy again. Way to be a creep and lie there."

"Would you have preferred if I'd coughed or burst out in a deep voice, 'She's mine!'"

"I guess not." Her eyes heated over for a second before business came back. "I'm okay with people knowing we're together, but I don't want it to ruin anything for me, you know? I told Nicole."

"She told me. She also threatened me." I grinned at her shocked response and put her hand in mine. She recoiled at the coldness of it. "I won't embarrass you if that's why you're worried."

"Okay. Good." She placed my hand back in the ice. "I need to go. I'll see you tonight?"

My stomach tightened at her hopeful expression and I sighed. "I can't. Something came up and some of us have to go help out a teammate. I promise I'll fill you in when I can."

"Okay." Her smile fell a little and she paused. She clearly debated with herself for a second but then left. I ached to know what she wanted to say, but I didn't have the chance.

* * * *

"Regardless of what he says or does...he needs our support." I looked back at Jeff and Tanner. We'd driven to Aaron's parents' place and his car sat in the driveway.

"Yup. We can take it," Tanner vowed. "He hasn't been the same and we need to be there."

I nodded as we walked up to the door. We'd tried to guess what had happened the entire drive up to the suburb and now our walk dragged with the weight of what we would find once we knocked on the door. Jeff rang the bell.

Aaron's mom opened the door with tears in her eyes. "Jeff, Tanner, Zade...what are you all doing here?"

"We needed to make sure Aaron, you guys, were all all right," I answered for us. She gave me the saddest look I'd ever seen but nodded and motioned us in. My heart sank. Something fierce had control of the household at the moment — Aaron's little sister sat at the table with a blank look of horror on her face. My stomach turned sour. I regretted having eaten anything on the drive over here and Jeff and Tanner's faces fell too. This sucked.

I tried to bring out my game face, the one I used on the mound, but I couldn't. We entered the kitchen and Aaron's once-bright eyes were blank. They widened, but then he barreled toward us in a hug.

My eyes stung and we all stood there. His body shook and Aaron's mom began to cry again. No one was talking and my thoughts kept getting worse and worse. Aaron lifted his head from our hug and moved on to Jeff. Then Tanner. I waited him out. Now wasn't the time to demand answers. Something was fucked up and he would tell us when he was ready.

"Let's, uh, let's go downstairs." Aaron sniffed and led us to the basement. We followed, speechless and scared. He collapsed onto the couch and pinched the bridge of his nose. "Why are you guys here?"

"We were worried about you," Tanner said in the kindest voice I'd ever heard him produce. "You haven't returned our calls for a week and we were concerned. Just know, we're here to help you in any way we can. You want to talk? We'll talk. Sit in silence? That's fine too."

"We're here for you, bro," Jeff added and I nodded.

His face crumpled again and he nodded. "Thank you. That means a lot." He cleared his throat and held up his hands. "There's no easy way to say it. My dad has stage four cancer."

I slammed my eyes shut. Waves of pain and hurt rolled over me and I knew the rest of the guys struggled too. "Fuck. I'm so sorry." Words seemed pointless as the grief took over my body. I felt lucky that it wasn't my family, but then I felt like a piece of shit for even thinking it. Then I got mad. Pissed off at the world that it could happen to someone close to me. Then I felt, regret and a sadness so deep because I had no idea how to help. Aaron gave a shaky laugh and released a huge breath.

"He had tests about a month ago. I knew it ran in the family and I learned about it once I got here Sunday. If you guys hadn't had that talk with me...I don't think my parents would've necessarily told me. They're martyrs."

"Are they operating?" Jeff asked.

"Soon. Yeah. It's around his lungs. There's a slim chance. That's what we're trying to hold on to." He ran his hands over his legs, unable to sit still. "Coach knows."

"Good. I'm glad he's giving you time. And we can get work for you and bring it back. Have you talked to your teachers?"

"Yeah. That'd be great, man. I don't want my life to stop but I have to be here." His eyes filled again. "My mom is falling apart. My sister is in her senior year of high school and if something happens...I have to come back."

"One step at a time, okay?" Tanner put his hand on Aaron's shoulder. "We're more than teammates. Let us help."

"Sure. Yeah," he croaked out. "Look, I'm not telling people yet, so can you guys keep it between us for a while?"

"Absolutely," we replied.

"Now, we packed a bag and can stay the weekend. Do you guys need food picking up?" Jeff asked. "Just my mom always told me when people were sad, the best way to help is to make sure they get fed. Is that not a thing normal people do?"

"I don't think anything about the situation is normal, Jeff," Tanner replied in a deep, sad voice. "Let's make a list. It'll take the burden off them even for a weekend."

Chapter Twenty-Nine

Callie

The high I had from working with Nicole for the week slowly diminished as I still hadn't heard from Zade. The clock struck midnight and my texts remained unanswered. I didn't voice my concern to Greta because I hated insecure girls and didn't want to be annoying. But that didn't stop the pit in my stomach from forming. Greta and I ate a fucking delicious dinner, curtesy of me and a new recipe I wanted to try out, but even the *Walking Dead* marathon didn't help the unease.

I checked my phone again and nothing new popped up. I tossed it on the couch, out of reach. I didn't need to check it a thousand times and get worried over and over. *He'll text when he can. He isn't playing games.*

"Lover boy texting you too much?" Greta asked, popcorn falling out of her mouth.

"Opposite, actually. I hate that I keep looking. What?"

"I don't like that. Why isn't he responding?"

"I have no idea. He canceled our plans for the night and mentioned something about helping a teammate. I'm assuming it's about that."

"Then it's best to trust him. He's halfway in love with you, babe. Try not to worry. I know it's easier said than done, but I have a pretty good read on him." Her kind eyes softened. "Want to continue the marathon and fall asleep out here?"

"You read my mind, sister. Distract me with chatter. How's the situation with Tanner? I haven't seen you two hang out since we went out that night." I paused, trying to think if I'd really seen him outside the training room. "I really haven't seen any of the guys instead of Zade."

"Me, neither, but I'm okay with it. I think," she sighed sadly, "that I built up this thing in my head where we were friends who became lovers. I love that story and desperately wanted it, but I think we'll remain friends. Distance is good sometimes." She ate more popcorn. "I feel crazy, though, because sometimes he'll look at me with these bedroom eyes, but if I try flirting, they shut down and he'll act like I'm his gross little sister."

"I don't think you're crazy. I've seen some of the looks, but if you're okay being friends then do that. You're beautiful, one of the best people to be around rain or shine, and you ain't got no time for silly games with that hunk of meat."

"I love your way with words." She snuggled next to me and snatched up the remote. "Let's pretend we're in the same world as Rick and Daryl and Glenn. Why are they oddly hot?"

"I have no idea. Must be good TV." I laughed and decided to be perfectly content hanging out with my best friend and binge watching my new favorite show.

* * * *

I woke up with a crick in my neck and Greta's legs on my stomach. We had indeed fallen asleep watching the fourth season and it'd sort of helped the worry I had. *I wanted slow and casual, damn it. Slow and casual doesn't cause worry or panic. Shit.* But, too little, too late.

I checked my watch and decided to go on a run. I needed the escape, with or without him, to clear my head. The thought cheered me up and I went to grab my phone and put on running shoes. I had zero texts and zero calls. *Fine. That's fine.* We'd talk when...when we'd talk. *Go with the flow. Be cool.*

I headed to the trail but not to where we met. I decided he'd pissed me off. Regardless of what had happened, he could've sent me a one-word text to check in. A *hey, I'm not dead* text.

I'd started mile four when the mad moved to betrayal. What if he'd decided he wanted nothing to do with me and called it quits? He wouldn't ghost me, right? He'd tell me. *Stop inventing problems. He isn't a total dickhead.*

Mile five, I decided I hated myself when I over-analyzed things and I needed to get a fucking grip. I loved life here. My classes were intriguing, working with Nicole blew every expectation I had and I had great friends. Yup. Life rocked.

Mile six. Back to being pissed.

Mile seven. My brain woke up and yelled at me. I'd chosen to trust him and I needed to do that until I had no reason to. Trust was the bottom line. Luckily, I had enough homework and hobbies to keep myself busy for the day, and I needed to focus on anything but him.

With a new resolve, I ran back toward my apartment…and my phone went off in my hand. *Zade.* My heart leaped into my throat and I answered on the first ring. "Hey."

"Oh, my god. Hey, Callie. I'm fucking sorry." His voice sounded gruff, like he'd gotten no sleep, and every worry left me. "I swear I wasn't ignoring you."

"Is everything okay?" I slowed down to a walk.

"No. Well, I'm fine, but shit is a mess." He sighed and I pictured him running his fingers over his hair. "I can't tell you, babe. I want to, but it's not my business. Did I wake you?"

"No. I went for a run today. I needed to clear my mind."

"Shit. I probably caused that. I'm sorry, again. Are you mad?" He grumbled something in the background and I chose to trust him. It was a tough choice, because it left the possibility of getting hurt. I chose it anyway.

"I'm not mad. I'm worried though. We haven't gone that long without talking, and naturally, I assumed the worse."

"I know. I'm sorry again. If this were reserved… Let's say you are handling it better. Look, I don't know when we're coming back, but I'll come see you as soon as I can, okay?"

"I'd like that." *I couldn't say much else, right?*

"Thank you for understanding. I gotta run."

I said goodbye and although the call calmed my stomach, my unease remained. He must've known because I got a text from him.

Zade: I miss you. I wish you were here.

I smiled at his words. I smiled a whole lot.

* * * *

It wasn't until Sunday night that I heard from him again. They say distance makes the heart grow fonder and it rang true. I hated the saying, though. Greta won the award for the best friend ever in his absence. We ran errands and made a game of it. It took my mind off *him* for a good part of the day, but whenever I let my thoughts get away from me, thoughts of *him* took over. I even met with Radcliffe for an hour over coffee and we compared notes of our first week. We made plans for the same time the next week.

I'd just begun cutting chicken into pieces, planning a mushroom-stuffed chicken meal before our Sunday night shows came on, when the door pounded. Greta barely acknowledged the sound and I raised my hands, covered with chicken goobies. "Can you get it?"

"Sure." I didn't turn to look, but I heard Greta laugh. "It's for you, babe."

"Yeah?" I didn't have time to register who it was before Zade seized my face in his hands and kissed me like he hadn't seen me in months, let alone two days. He smelled like a scent that was now pure Zade. His mouth claimed mine. My head spun from the worry and how much I'd missed him. He ended the kiss but kept his hands on me. He stared down at me with love...or lust...or something. "Hey, there."

"Hey." He released my face and this time his breathing came out ragged. He leaned on the counter and noticed my hands awkwardly held in the air. "I came at the right time, eh? I'm starving."

"Hmm. You are assuming an awful lot that you can barge in here and eat our food. This was hard earned, you know."

"I deserved that. Look" — he ran his hand through his hair — "I don't have to eat. But can I stay? I want to be around you. I'll help. Just name it." The vulnerability in his eyes at that moment would've gotten me to agree about anything. Legal, illegal, good, bad — it didn't matter. Something had happened, clearly, and I needed to be there for him.

"I'd be mad if you left." I smiled and nudged him with my hip, hands still gross. "Now, I need to finish with these breasts because I hate chicken goobies on them."

"Chicken goobies?" His mouth lifted at the sides.

"Yup. Goobies. The weird coating you get on your hands when you touch raw chicken. These! These are goobies!" I held my hands near his face and he laughed, deep and rich in timbre.

"Only you could make the word goobies sound sexy." He lowered his voice and Greta yelled something like "yuk" from the living room. I laughed and, gross hands and all, he pulled me into a bear hug. "I'll let you finish cooking. Tell me about your weekend."

"Hmm. Nothing too eventful. Errands, homework, the whole crazy college life at its finest." I grabbed the chopped-up mushrooms I'd sautéed earlier and began stuffing them into the breasts. I avoided his stare but knew he watched my every move. "I missed you."

"Was that so very hard to say?" he asked.

"Sort of. This weekend really tested me." I put the chicken in the oven, washed my hands and turned to really look at him. His eyes had bags under them. His bright eyes were sad, only lightening when he looked at me. I hopped onto the counter, making my face level with his. He fit between my legs and touched me. He didn't push me but waited for me to speak. "This is big for me to say, okay?"

"I'm listening." He pulled the ends of my hair in a familiar way.

"I realized something. I'm not a big fan of big words, but I trust you." He fought back a smile and the light came back into his eyes. "I went through every scenario of where you were and why I hadn't heard from you. I went through every emotion. But in the end, I realized I trusted you. I have no reason not to and I want to really give us a shot."

He wet his lips and brought them to mine. He opened my mouth with his tongue, telling me I'd said the right thing. I moaned into his mouth, putting my arms around his neck. He pulled me to him and I felt his hardness. I giggled. He slowly pulled his mouth from mine and gave me a skeptical look. "I must be doing something right if you're giggling."

"Nah, you're doing *everything* right."

"So are you, Callie. So are you."

Chapter Thirty

Zade

I left Callie's the next two mornings in a better mood than when I'd gotten there. I wasn't sure if I'd entirely won my case that it was okay to stay there more than two nights a week. She'd melted in my arms when I'd asked if I could come back later, so I called it a win.

Our house changed to a sullen and stifling mood. Aaron wanted us to continue on as if things were 'normal' but that wasn't possible. He'd lost his spark and was glued to his phone. I didn't blame him. I'd have handled it even worse if it were my sister or mom. He hadn't touched a drink since he'd gone home and if there was any silver lining, it was that. I walked into the house and found him watching ESPN with a blank stare. "Hey, man."

"Hey. How's Callie?" His eyes were sad and red. He admitted he'd barely slept the past nine days. "Did you see Greta? I haven't told her yet and I haven't responded to any of her texts. I don't know what to say."

"They're doing good. Worried about you, though. Greta asked me if you were okay and I told her some bullshit excuse about school work or something. I don't think she believed me, though." I enjoyed seeing a small smile on Aaron's face.

"She texted me last night and said she's there for me. It meant a lot." He sighed and went back to watching the TV. "They're good people."

"Yeah. They're good people." I joined him in watching baseball highlights. "Are you going to tell them?"

"At some point, yeah. But I'm trying to figure out how to continue living a normal life. My mom thinks I can just…be here and enjoy college. I feel guilty if I even have a moment of joy. My dad…god. You saw him. He's broken." He squeezed his eyes shut. "I couldn't talk to him without breaking down."

"I'm know I'm not your parents, but your mom is right. You need to try and enjoy what you can here. Life is way too short, man. Your dad wouldn't want you suffering. You need to be strong, tough and bring laughter and shit to people. That's why you're damn important to our team. Jeff, he leads with a calming presence. He'll make the calls and be the silent strength. Tanner uses his quick brain and speed to help us. I throw okay now and again, but Aaron, you are instrumental in our success."

His eyes lit up and he nodded, clearly wanting me to continue. I didn't talk a lot about emotions. I was a broody, temperamental pitcher, but my role had begun to shift. I needed to be a leader on and off the field. I'd never had the urge to lead, per se, besides throwing well. But now, it felt right. "You play the game like it's the best thing in the world. You fucking love it. You shake off errors like it's no big deal, which, let me tell you, takes a hell of a lot of talent. You laugh and cause shenanigans in the dugout. You make the tough losses a little less tough. I know when I get a homerun hit off me and I want to kill someone, you come up to me and say the stupidest fucking thing, but it works. I need you on the field. You need us now."

He swallowed. I continued. "You need to do that for your family. You relieve tension and make people laugh. Your mom and sister, hell, your dad, too, they need *that* Aaron."

He shied away from me when I finished. I let him react to the words I didn't know I had inside me. I clapped him on the back. "You'll get there, to that place again. Take your time, though. It's a lot to handle, your dad and family. But let us know what we can do to help."

I headed to my room to actually do some homework that I'd avoided the past week and an idea came to me. The half marathon. We raised money and now... Now if I managed to get more people to run it and raise awareness, we might be able to donate to cancer research. *Yes!* A wave of purpose and excitement ran through me and I called my coach.

"Yeah?" he barked instead of a nice hello.

"Coach, it's Willows. I have an idea to help Aaron." I shut the door to my room and told him my idea and plan. He agreed and got it into full motion. I went online and began researching different products and ways to raise money. I could *finally* help Aaron's family.

* * * *

We had a team meeting Wednesday. We were told to show up in running clothes and be early. All of us were there before Aaron, per the plan. Coach saw me and came up to me to clap my back. "This is good of you, Z. I'm proud of you."

"Thank you, but, it's all for Aaron." Jeff joined us with a grin and wearing the shirt we'd had made. It wasn't anything special, just said *We play for him.* It had Aaron's dad's initials on a baseball and no one besides us knew what it meant. Coach told us everything. He announced it in a somber tone and the pride I felt for my team overwhelmed me. The seniors stood up and made speeches about how to support him. Freddie, the starting third basemen and captain, explained what he'd gone through with his aunt. And Max stood up and told us about his cousin.

None of us had known all the suffering we each had in our families and it opened my eyes. We'd gotten along before as a team, but not like this. This bond went beyond teammates. The new recruits, freshmen who were cocky as hell, kept their heads down, at a loss. Max and Freddie threw out the shirts Jeff and I had designed and ordered overnight. We all put them on and coach broke down the training schedule for the half marathon, which had become a team requirement.

"We'll start raising money tomorrow. Today, today is about Aaron and supporting him. Now, news might break because people can never keep their mouths shut, but right now is the first step in our journey this year." He put one foot on the bench, meeting every one of our eyes. "It isn't the success that shows real character of people. It's moments like this that define us. What do we do when our teammates, our family, our friends need us? Do we run and cower? Do we avoid them with the fear of saying the wrong thing? No. If you're on my team, you won't do that. We come together. We use one another to build him up."

We nodded something fierce. We heard Aaron come into the locker room and we waited. Waited until he came into view and saw us all wearing our shirts and the stupid wristbands that coach had ordered and I almost broke down when his jaw began to shake. No one made a move and I fought the urge I had to swallow down the pain. I went up to him and hugged him.

Then Jeff did.

Then Tanner did.

The rest of the team followed and, when we'd all had our moment with him, coach went up and did the same thing. "Now, go run seven miles. Z, you lead the team. You've been training longer. I don't want to see any of you in here until you're done. And Aaron, every cent we raise is going to cancer research."

"Thank you, sir."

"Thank your teammates. Now, get out." He walked out and I led the team to go run seven miles. Sweating out emotions had never felt so fucking good.

* * * *

I planned on showing up at Callie's after my afternoon class, but she never replied. A canal of emotions opened up and I had no idea what to do with them. Unable to see her, I drove to my sister's. I knew she would barely have gotten home from student teaching but I didn't want to be alone with my thoughts. Aaron met up with Greta, explaining everything to her, and the others all went out to drink some beer. I could've gone with them, but I wanted to be around family.

"Hey, Z. Let me up." I buzzed her door and heard her surprise. I took the stairs two at a time and hugged her when she opened the door. She let out a grunt and pushed me off. "What the fuck is going on?"

"I have no idea. I'm a fucking mess inside." I let her go and plopped onto her couch. The shelf we'd bought at Wal-Mart matched her eccentric living room. "Can I chill for a bit?"

"Duh. But explain what happened. I mean, I love you, bro, but we don't express ourselves too much. We're Willows."

I laughed and ran my hand over my jaw. "I know. That's the problem. I'm not used to showing emotions like I have the past four or five days."

"Is this all about the girl I have yet to meet and am pretty pissed about, still?" She joined me on the couch and crossed her arms. "Not fucking cool, bro."

"Yes. No. Part of it. Aaron's dad was diagnosed with stage four cancer. We just learned about it and it's a fucking ride."

"Oh my, oh god." Her cheerful face fell and she put her hand on my arm. "I am goddamn sorry. God, I can't imagine what he and his family are going through."

"It's rough. Hardest thing I've ever seen. We drove to his parents' house Saturday because we had no idea what the hell was going on. He'd missed practice and meetings for a week and up and left the house. The team is running in the half marathon now to raise money."

"That's a huge sign of support." She nodded a couple of times. "Can I run, too?"

"Hell yeah. I can get you a shirt." I showed her a picture of the shirt we made. "It's not the best but—"

"It's amazing and you're turning into the leader I know you to be. Zade, I'm proud of you. I generally am but stepping up and organizing it for a teammate… This is why I know you'll do big things in the world. I am really fucking proud to call you my brother."

"God, go back to insulting me or something." I swallowed the lump in my throat and playfully punched her arm. "I need to drink beer, smoke a cigar and watch *The Godfather*."

"You afraid your man card is slipping away?"

"Yes. God, yes. It's awful. For someone who pretty much skirted through life as baseball, family and parties, the whole thing is a new experience for me."

"It's about a time you grew up. Just saying." She stood up and pulled *The Godfather* from her movie stand. My sister still had a fucking DVD stand in the world of streaming. She liked to think of herself as old-fashioned and I wouldn't be shocked if she had a VCR somewhere in the place. "Should I get tissues or can you get through the movie without getting upset?"

"Fuck. Off." I laughed, order restored in my life. The tightening in my chest felt uncomfortable again, because I was thinking about how much I loved my sister and how glad I was that she sat in front of me, perfectly healthy. Sometimes life wasn't fair.

Chapter Thirty-One

Callie

My body burned. Not the good sexy kind either. My legs burned, my arms were stiff and I had the beginnings of a headache. Why Nicole had thought it would be a good idea for me to do a workout perplexed me. But I'd done it. I regretted it as I began hobbling back to my apartment for some much-needed rest. I had been going since six that morning and I hadn't gotten the best night of sleep due to Zade and his wandering hands. And mouth. I smiled. *This is working out.*

"Hey, Callie. Wait up." Aaron jogged toward me, a tortured expression on his face.

"Aaron. Long time no see." I went in for a quick hug and he patted my back. "What's up?"

"I'm sure Zade already told you, but I wanted to tell you for myself because we're friends, I think." Zade hadn't told me anything. "My dad, uh, well, he's battling cancer now and it doesn't sound good."

"Oh, Aaron." My mouth slammed shut hard, the pit in my stomach hurting for him. "I'm sorry. I know it doesn't mean anything but I feel it anyway." I put my hand on his arm and closed my eyes. "Is that why you've been gone for a while?"

"Yes. I'm not really telling people. Please don't say anything."

"Of course, and Aaron, we are definitely friends." I pulled him into a hug again and he squeezed me. "How can I help? Anything?"

"Not that I can think of. Oh, actually, just don't treat me differently. I need you and Greta to be the bright, happy faces you always are. I don't think I've told you how much you cheer me up. I can't handle sympathy right now."

"You got it, dude." I punched his arm, another small smile breaking out. My heart broke for him, but I didn't let it show. I wanted to be a friend to him and he wanted it to be normal. I could try to be normal. "Want to go find some hot girls or something?"

He laughed. *Score.* "I appreciate your willingness to be my wingman, but not today. Another time, perhaps."

"Can I at least make you dinner or something?" I knew food helped in any situation. The tiredness went away, knowing Aaron needed support. Who would've imagined that guy I thought was robbing the apartment my first day here would have become such an important friend?

"Yeah. I'd like that. Let's go get Greta and you can come back to our house. Unless you had plans with Zade."

"Nah, he can wait. I'd rather help you out right now."

* * * *

Aaron put on some reggae and chatted with Greta in the other room. I heard her cry and I left to head into the kitchen. They had been friends longer and I couldn't imagine how Greta was handling the news. I thought I was loyal but Greta took it to the next extreme. She'd not only help me bury a body, she'd plan the kill in the first place and do it for me without asking. It was a beautiful and frightening thought. My throat clogged again with emotion, the desperation to help trying to claw out.

I opened the bags of food we'd brought over from our apartment. I had no idea if I should cook for all six of us or not. I hadn't heard from Zade all day, but I hoped I'd see him soon. He'd broken down the wall of only two nights a week. I had to agree — it was silly to try to hold my feelings back when they were already spiraling out of control.

I decided to make tacos. They were easy to make a bunch of and who didn't like a taco? I'd begun cooking the meat when Tanner walked in. He gave me a nod and I expected him to leave. He didn't. He sat down and eyed me. "Yes, Tanner?"

"Are you cooking only for Aaron or...?"

"Meaning, you want some?" These guys swarmed around food like Greta swarmed around sales.

"Yup. Shit smells good."

"Yeah. I'll make enough for like thirty tacos. But you guys are buying my groceries next time. I cannot afford to feed a house full of testosteroned, muscle-bulging meat heads." I began cutting up tomatoes and peppers and he laughed. Tanner was a good guy and I understood what Greta saw in him, but she shouldn't be waiting around for him to realize how awesome she was.

"Meat heads. Love it. Did Zade tell you what he did?"

"Uh, in what context?" I paused, once again assuming the worst.

"For Aaron."

"I have no idea." I hadn't talked to him yet about it at all and a part of me was irrationally hurt he hadn't told me. But it was Aaron's situation, not his. And I admired his loyalty to his friend. That spoke volumes, way past my wounded ego.

"He got us all shirts that support Aaron's dad and he arranged with our coach for all of us to run the half marathon. We're trying to raise a couple grand and donate it to research on cancer in his dad's name." Tanner's voice flooded with pride. "He's turning into the leader and captain that I knew he had the potential to be all along."

I paused, his words hitting me hard. Tanner wrapped his arms around me in a tight hug. "Thank you, Callie. For giving him a chance. For doing whatever it is you did to him, because he's changed for the better."

"Uh, not sure what to say here. I don't think I've changed him. I think he's always been that person." I fought an odd sting in my eyes. *Must be allergies.*

"No. The fact you don't see it makes me smile." He patted my head in a brotherly sort of way and left the kitchen. It overwhelmed me. Aaron and Zade…and now Tanner. These rambunctious guys were messing with my head.

I continued prepping the food and let my thoughts slide to Zade. He'd stepped up for his teammate and after witnessing the bonds teams could have, I knew in my core that he was going to cement his future in baseball. Talent gets a person noticed but personality, loyalty and character take it to the next step. I dropped the bag of lettuce and went to pick it up.

"Not that I don't appreciate the view, but why haven't you responded to any of my texts?" Zade's voice broke through my cooking haze and he leaned against the door frame. He belonged on the cover of magazines with the tight shirt, loose jeans and dancing eyes. The eyes that were checking me out head to toe with a desire that should've been sated the night before.

"Hi." I blushed and waved the bag of lettuce I'd picked up. "I haven't checked my phone all day. Were you mad?"

"I thought you were ignoring me." He pouted that lip again. *Kill me.*

"Come on, why would I do that?" I set the bag down and went to him. "Are you being insecure in our relationship?"

"We don't have an official one because you keep turning me down. Hey, I like your outfit. A lot."

"This old thing?" I ate up the compliment. I hadn't tried to wear anything sexy but apparently my yoga pants and low-cut sweatshirt worked for him. "Thanks."

"Girlfriend?" He dragged his hand down my face and collarbone with hopeful eyes. I shook my head and he growled. "Damn you, Callie Williams."

"It's too easy. Shit. Now that you mention it, I have no idea where my phone is." I walked over to my backpack I lugged around all day. I preferred a backpack over a purse. It had more pockets. I carried first aid kits, books, water bottles, extra shirts, shoes and Advil. A purse had no business trying to fit all that in it. I dug through the front pocket where I normally kept my cell. "Shit."

"Not in there?" He snuck up behind me. There was something about that position, his height over me and closeness that gave me weak knees. "When did you use it last?"

"I think the training room. Or maybe my morning class." I sighed. "Guess I'll have to get a new phone tomorrow."

"Stay over tonight. I don't want to worry about you." He slid his arms around my stomach and kissed behind my ear. Warning bells went off inside my brain, my heart and my body. *Fuck.* I loved him. It hit me hard, fast and without reason. His love for his sister, his loyalty to his teammates, his concentration on not wanting to mess up his future... I was done for. I tensed up at the realization and he noticed. "Why so tight?"

"Uh, nothing. I'm fine." I tried to escape his embrace but he held on tighter. "The food."

"It won't burn." He turned me around and cupped my face. "I can read you like a book, babe. What just happened?"

I blew out a long breath and met his hazel eyes. "I guess I realized how amazing you are and how lucky I am. It scared me."

"You, lucky?" He laughed and ran his finger over my lip. "Cal, while I appreciate hearing you say that and it makes me real fucking happy, don't for one second think that you're the lucky one. I'm the luckiest son of bitch there is."

I scrunched my nose at his words and decided to go with honesty. I held my breath, my body tense as hell, and told him, "I think I'm falling in love with you."

"Cal, I surpassed that weeks ago. I didn't want to scare you."

"I'm fucking terrified." My heart raced and although we didn't say the words, the feeling remained. "I heard about Aaron's dad—"

"All the more reason why we shouldn't hold back. You never know." He kissed my forehead and frowned. "I'm sorry I didn't tell you. He asked me not to."

"Don't apologize for that. Ever. I understand. He told me earlier today and that's how I got roped into cooking dinner for everyone here." I backed out of his embrace and went to stir the meat. "Honestly, I feel like a house mom right now. I'm cooking thirty tacos where Greta and I probably only eat six total."

"You're sexy as hell cooking, though. It makes me feel manly and taken care of." He sat at the table and watched me. "I'm getting a Fifties housewife vibe."

"Yeah, lose that vibe." I threatened him. "I cook because I'm good at it and I enjoy it. As soon as it's expected, I'll burn you."

"Duly noted."

"Knock it off with those sexy eyes. I need to continue to cook and it's for Aaron, not for your dick."

"I like knowing my sexy eyes distract you."

"Great. Another ego boost for you." I finished draining the meat. "You know, make yourself useful and get out some bowls and shit."

"Yes, ma'am. Anything for you, dear." He swatted my ass and handed me the dishes I needed. Jeff walked in next with a big smile. He tried grabbing some of the meat and I hit his hand with the spoon.

"No."

"Come on, just a bite."

"No. I'll hit harder next time. It's almost ready, you barbarians."

Jeff joined Zade at the table and they snatched the food like feral dogs who hadn't eaten in days. *Their poor mothers.* I imagined the grocery bill these guys needed, let alone giving birth to the monsters. I shivered at the thought. Zade kept smiling at me and Jeff eventually called him out on it.

"Why are you smiling like a fucking fool?"

"I got a girl who can do it all. Cook, knows baseball and is dynamite in the bed."

"*Zade!*" Jeff high-fived him and I threw my hands in the air. "Boys!"

It wasn't until hours later, when Zade and I were lying in his bed, that I brought up what he'd done for Aaron. The lights were off, we'd spent an hour fooling around and now I lay in his arms with him stroking my bare back.

"Zade, what you did for Aaron…I'm proud of you." I pressed a kiss to his chest and he hummed in pleasure. "Just when I think I can't fall any more, you surprise me." He pulled me tighter to him but didn't reply. We continued to lie there and after a full ten minutes of silence, he spoke in a rough voice.

"When we drove up to his parents' house and heard the news, the first thing I thought was how fucking thankful I am that my mom and sister were okay. Does that make me the worst fucking human being ever?"

"What? No!" I propped myself up on my elbow. "I think it's perfectly normal to be thankful that your family is okay. You never think of something like this happening to you or someone you know. It's always someone you're acquainted with. You never think it'd happen to someone close to you. So, don't feel guilty. Please don't."

"I hate how it's breaking him." He squeezed his eyes together in pain. "I saw their family and the cloud of doom they all carried. I wish I knew how to help."

"You are helping." I put my hand on his face until he opened his eyes. "You are helping by being his friend, by rallying the team around him and caring. I'm really fucking proud of you."

He kissed my palm and I felt it all the way to my heart. "I'm glad you're with me, Callie. So fucking glad."

"Me too." I crawled on top of him and kissed him. It was slow and passionate. We moved together as though we were made to fit into one and I did my best to show him how much I loved him. I wasn't ready to say the words yet but my body was.

Chapter Thirty-Two

Zade

Things were getting back to normal, if there could ever be such a thing. I heard nothing more about my sister getting odd letters or calls. Aaron went home every weekend, but he laughed a bit more each week. The team had a lot to do with that. He never found himself alone. If it wasn't Jeff, Tanner or me playing video games with him, it was Max or Freddie taking him out. The only downside was that I now trained with the team in the morning instead of Callie. She continued to run and became more determined to run the race because all proceeds were for Aaron's cause.

Nicole worked the hell out of him and I think we were all proud to see him channeling his frustration into the workouts. Within one week, he benched more than he had before and broke his personal best in the clean and jerk. He was going to absolutely kill the ball when the season started.

On my way to pick up Callie, I mulled over my two plans. The first, to fucking give her my jersey to wear. She continued to say no to being my girlfriend, but we both knew she was. I liked the game she played and how she challenged me on everything. She kept me on my toes and it was time to take it to the next level — meeting my sister.

I whistled to myself and laughed at how I had become one of those happy-assed punks I used to make fun of. They'd had it right all along. Nothing was going to ruin my mood, not even the group of girls walking toward me with a determined look on their faces. I smiled politely at them but they stopped right in front of me. "Excuse me, ladies."

"Zwillows, can we interview you really quick for our blog about you? We work for the university paper." An eager girl, with wide eyes and maybe a hundred pounds. "It won't take long."

"Five minutes." I checked my phone and knew Callie wouldn't care if I arrived a little late. Actually, she'd probably make fun of me for getting interviewed. "I have plans."

"Thank you, Zade. First off, tell us, how is the team handling the news of Aaron's family?" she asked and held the phone in front of my face with a hopeful look. I didn't recall Aaron sharing it publicly yet and I had no idea how they knew. I wasn't going to give them anything and a protective surge flowed through me. People were low as hell to use someone's pain to get a story.

"Well, we're a team. We win together and lose together. Not much more to say about that." She tried again with a new question and I didn't hold back this time. "Listen, if you're looking to get answers about something that doesn't concern you or anyone else on campus, try someone else. You're being rude and intrusive."

She jumped back and fixed the glasses on her nose. "I apologize. I didn't realize how protective you were of the team."

"They're my family." I pushed past them, but she ran after me with her damn phone. "What?"

"Can you address the rumors that you're currently seeing a new student, Callie Williams? The paper wants to do a dating profile for some of the major athletes as an entertainment piece."

I laughed, but not with humor. "They aren't rumors. I'm with Callie."

"You are a known player on campus—how did she catch you?" I stared her down, now outright annoyed. She cowered a little bit. "Your fans want to know what she did."

"She was herself. Now, I'm late for a date with her. Interview over." I walked faster, her short legs not able to keep up with me, and I ran up the stairs to Callie's door. She answered on the first knock and I stood, speechless. All thoughts of the interview flew out of the window with her standing there, looking like she did. She wore a skintight red dress and had her hair curled in waves. "Oh, my god."

She smiled, her dimples coming out against her red lips, and shrugged. "So, you like the dress?"

"Fuck our plans." I stood, frozen unable to believe how I'd gotten this lucky. She never wore dresses. Just once I had seen her in them and I was going to have a hell of a time not looking at her legs or the way it fit her curves just right. "God. You're unreal."

She blushed and I felt like a million bucks. "You clean up nice, too. You really fit that jacket."

"Thanks. Really a raving compliment." I laughed and pressed a light kiss to her cheek. If I started on her mouth, we wouldn't make it past the door. "Are you ready to meet her?"

"I'm nervous, a little. I've never done this before." She sucked in her bottom cherry-red lip. "Where are we going?"

"It's a quaint little place about five blocks away. Want to walk there?" Her shoes clacked and I saw her wearing heeled sandals. I moaned. Her strong calves were quickly becoming a weakness.

"Hells yeah. It's perfect outside." She went to lock the door and I forgot about the gift I'd brought her. I shoved the bag at her without a word, looking like a weirdo. "Uh, what's this?"

"For you." I wanted her to like it. I needed her to like it. "I know we aren't boyfriend and girlfriend." I paused "But I want you to have this."

"Hmm. I'm intrigued." She pulled the jersey out of the bag and her eyes warmed. "Aw. Your jersey."

"I've never given one to anyone before."

"I'll take good care of it." She hugged it against her. "I love it."

"I'm glad. Now, promise me you'll wear only that later? It's one of my top fantasies."

"What's your top one?"

"Me. You. Pitcher's mound. I'd probably get kicked off the team."

"And I'd lose my opportunity with Nicole." She placed the jersey on the counter with care before heading out with me. "It might totally be worth it, though."

"Oh, fuck yeah."

* * * *

"You're real!" Zaria met us outside the restaurant and eyed Callie as if she had a damn alien growing out of her head. I glared at her, but she didn't notice me. She went up to Callie and hugged her. Callie laughed and gave me a questioning look over my sister's shoulder. I shrugged. Zaria was her own person and was going to do whatever the hell she wanted, regardless of what I thought. "It is nice to *finally* meet you."

"You, too. Zade talks about you a lot. I pictured you differently, though."

"How so?"

"I don't know…more mother-like. You're stunning. Like this one." She pointed to me and continued, "I prefer not to stroke the ego too often. I need to insult him really quickly to go back to normal."

"Ha ha ha," I mocked and pulled her into my arms. She leaned against me and smiled like I was the best thing in the world. Zaria saw it and nodded at me. I didn't need her approval, but knowing I had it felt pretty fucking good.

"I like her already." She opened the door to the restaurant. "Now, are you going to be all gross and hold hands during dinner?"

"Nah, I hate that." Callie answered and I rolled my eyes. "Zade will try every so often, but I stop it."

"Good for you. Stick it to him." They shared a laugh and I decided I didn't want them being friends. The two of them against me did not sound fun. "So, Callie. Tell me everything about yourself."

"Uh, not sure how to start that." She gave me a worried look and I held up my hands.

"I won't be any help. I think it's best if you ride her out. She'll calm down eventually."

"Okay. I'll be more specific. How did you get Zade to be your boyfriend? You're the first girl I've ever met and trust me, this is a huge deal. He's been a bit of a commitment-phobe for some time." She sat across from us at the table and smiled at our waiter. She crossed her arms and stared at Callie, waiting for her to answer.

"Actually, he isn't my boyfriend."

"Wait, what?" Zaria looked at me with raised eyebrows.

"Yup. You heard her. Why don't you explain that to my sister, dear?" I said sarcastically, hoping she'd feel bad enough to agree to it.

"Well." She bit her lip for a second, clearly debating how to answer my sister. "I keep turning him down."

Zaria tilted her head and watched the two of us. "Why? Aren't you two together?"

"Oh, we're together." I answered.

A mischievous grin took over Callie's face. "As you probably can see, Zade can be a little...overzealous and the first time he tried asking me was due to being jealous. I wanted him to ask me because he wanted me to be his girlfriend, not to prevent another guy from looking at me."

"That makes sense. Continue."

"And his attempts got lazy. We'd be eating dinner and he'd ask. I'd politely decline. He'll try to lay on the charm, but I'm tough. I've held out this long — another week or two or four won't kill him."

"God, I get it now. You're perfect for him. Mad respect for you to hold him off this long. When he doesn't get what he wants, he gets a little…what's the word?"

"Crazy? Insane? Barbaric?" Callie answered and I decided they should not be hanging out again.

"Yes, all of those."

"I'm glad you two are having a hoot talking shit about me," I sulked. Callie patted my arm in a condescending way but kept her hand on me, which made me feel a little better.

"Having a hoot." Callie laughed. Hard. "We are going to be talking about where the hell that came from. Good lord."

"It's not talking shit if it's true and it's not behind your back," Zaria said between chuckles. "I'm enjoying this much more than I thought. Let's do this again every week."

"Hell to the no," I replied and Callie smirked.

"Don't pout, Z," Zaria ordered and Callie squeezed my knee under the table. I clasped it and kept it there. I shouldn't complain. My two favorite women were getting along. "Now, let's get some food."

The rest of dinner went by without a hitch. Zaria generally made fun of me and told stories from my wild youth. Callie laughed her ass off and I took it all because I was a gentleman. We bade my sister goodnight and she and Callie hugged a little too long. When they broke apart, I didn't like the way Callie's eyes had mischief in them.

"Care to share whatever my dear sister told you?" I put my arm around her and tucked her right where I wanted her for the walk back.

"Nope." She squeezed my side and laughed. "I loved her, by the way."

"Yeah. I think that feeling is mutual." I pouted and she pinched my lip with her fingers. I jumped back, surprised at her action. "What was that for?"

"Your bottom lip pout drives me wild. I want to suck it and shove it into your mouth."

"Mm. I like it when you say suck."

"I'm sure you do. Oh look, there's a park. Want to see if they have a pitcher's mound?"

My dick jumped at the thought. "Are you fucking joking right now? You better not be."

"Let's go look." She ran toward the fields, stumbling a bit. "Damn it, I'm taking these shoes off." She bent over, one arm on a bench, removing her shoe with the other and her beauty amazed me. Once she had her shoes off, she ran toward the park and I had no choice but to follow.

"I didn't know about this field." I looked around at the dark, secluded park and saw that she'd run into one of the dugouts. The whole place stood surrounded by trees and abandoned sidewalks. I chased her, unsure where she'd gone. I walked into what should be the guest dugout and she jumped me. I caught her and wrapped her legs around me. "There you are."

"Mmm. Something about you…on a field. I'm a little needy." She began to unbutton the top of my shirt. I cupped her ass under her dress and realized she wasn't wearing anything. I sucked in a breath and she laughed in my ear. "I'm offended you only now realized I did that."

"Fucking hell." I pushed her against the fence. "You are the hottest fucking thing, ever."

"Right back at you, babe." She slid down me, nipping at my now bare chest. "Have you ever gotten off on a field before?"

"Uh, no." I lost my train of thought. She'd somehow pushed me onto the bench, her hands at my buckle. "What're you doing?"

"I want to give you another first." She undid my pants and slowly dragged her tongue over my dick. She crouched on her knees. In a dugout. With my dick in her mouth. *Dream fucking made.* I fisted her hair into my hand, ready to explode. My dick throbbed, hard as hell. She did things to me that I didn't know she knew how to do.

"Callie, baby slow down." I saw stars. Literally saw fucking stars. She came up, a wild grin on her face and straddled me. "Oh, my god."

She kissed my neck, biting on it enough to have me buck beneath her. She had all the power. I would do anything she asked. "Do you have a condom?"

"Fuck. No." I moaned into her neck, smelling her hair and pulling her against me. "I'm sorry, babe. I didn't think."

"It's okay." She pulled back and waited until I met her eyes. "I trust you."

"Are you sure?" I shook at the thought of entering her without anything protection. I had never done it. Ever. The thought of it just being us... I shook with need.

"Yes, Zade." She slid onto me, nothing between us. She dripped, soaking wet, all for me. I gulped at how tight and perfect she felt.

"Fuck. Fuck." I lost rational thought at that point. She rode me in the dugout, the field in the background, and I had the best orgasm in my entire life. I sat there, her remaining on top of me, and floated. I hadn't dabbled in drugs before but I imagined the high felt just like this and I got it. I was fucking high on Callie. "Uh. Words."

She laughed and pressed a light kiss on me. "Hottest sex ever."

"You think?" Her eyes still held their heat and I winced at my thoughtlessness.

"You didn't go, did you?"

"Nah, the angle prevented it, but trust me, this topped the charts." She slid off me and I set her on the bench. "What are you doing?"

I quickly redid my pants and hovered over her. "I can't have you not satisfied. That wouldn't be fair. You just... I'm never going to forget this moment for my entire life. The least I can do is repay the favor."

"Yeah? How so?" she whispered and I lifted up her dress, exposing her. She sucked in a breath.

"God, you're gorgeous." I stared at her, bared to the world. I wanted to make her fall apart with my hands. I'd done it before, but in the moonlight and on the diamond? Second best moment in my life. "Do you like it when I touch you here?"

"Y-yes."

I traced her inner thighs, drawing small figure eights without being in a hurry. Her legs bucked, her eyes shutting the closer I got to her center. "Your body is fucking responsive. I love it."

"Mm," was her only reply. I took that as a good sign. I used my pitching hand to slowly enter her. "Do you like this, baby?"

"Yeah." She bucked against my hand and I gently swirled around her clit. She trembled with need already and it wouldn't take much. Every arch of her back and tightening of her body made me fall more for her. I desperately wanted to drag this out, draw every ounce of pleasure from her. One orgasm didn't cut it. I wanted more, all of them. I leaned over her, pressing small kisses down her neck and biting my favorite spot on her. She jumped and I increased the pace.

"You close, baby?"

"God, yeah." Her hot breath hit my neck and I bit down on her ear. She convulsed around my hand, body shaking. She trembled beneath me, her moans and sounds echoing off the dugout walls. It was hot as fuck. "*Zade. Fuck.*" She continued to shake and I held on to her, letting her ride it out. With a final moan of my name, she stilled, wide-eyed. "Holy shit."

I laughed, pressing a soft kiss against her temple. "You aren't done yet, Callie."

"Huh?" Her voice was sluggish. "What do you mean?"

Instead of answering, I lowered her back on the bench with her legs wide open. I used both hands to flirt with the inside of her thighs. "I want you to come again."

"Yeah?" Her interest piqued. "I'm up for trying."

"You will. Trust me." I lifted her hips, bringing her center to my mouth, and added my tongue to the mix. She tasted like heaven and our love-making earlier and I moaned into her. She. Was. So. Hot. I nibbled and flicked and sucked until she fell apart in my mouth.

After her second orgasm, I picked her up and set her in my lap. She rested her head against my shoulder with a small yawn and I felt more content at that moment than I'd thought possible.

"I'd say tonight made it to my top favorite nights," I said, breaking the comfortable silence.

"One might say it was a homerun of a night, eh? We really knocked it out of the park?" She laughed at her own joke and my chest clenched.

"God, I'm laughing at your jokes. What's wrong with me?" I kissed her temple.

"You're trying too hard. I won't be your girlfriend." She laughed and I couldn't help but join her. I loved this girl and I needed to figure out the best way to tell her.

Chapter Thirty-Three

Callie

"Yo, G, I have a dilemma of sorts for you. I need advice." I whipped up scrambled eggs and brought them to her on the couch. Thursday had crept up and I had the only class I disliked, the lecture.

"Hit me. I got knowledge." She held out her hands for the plate. "Gimme."

"So, you know how I have that class today?"

"Sure. So what's the dilemma?"

"Well, it's a huge lecture hall. Maybe three hundred students or so. Tell me if you think this is weird or I'm overthinking it."

"I'm listening."

"Zade is in that class, but I never told him I also had it." I closed my eyes, not wanting to see Greta's reaction.

"Okay. Why?"

"In the beginning, I wanted distance from him. This was before we became a thing. Then, the next couple of weeks I didn't really see him there and thought maybe he transferred the class. He used to have girls follow him everywhere, still does, but he sat by them and at first, I wanted to see if he continued to."

"Because you didn't trust him in the beginning." She nodded as she put it together. "You want to tell him now, but it'll look bad, like you didn't trust him the whole time."

"Yup. Bingo. Things are pretty fucking perfect between us. I'm in love with him, but I can't say that and tell him about the class. He'll think it's a ploy or something. And I think I'm going to ask him to be my boyfriend. Make it cute and shit." The idea had come to me a couple of nights after our dugout frenzy. I'd told Greta about it and she'd said it was the hottest thing she'd ever heard of and I couldn't have agreed more. I wanted to officially be his girlfriend or whatever after that.

"Yeah. I think he'll handle it okay. I mean, you guys are grossly obsessed with each other. He'll get over it. Tell him what you told me. Truth is the best." She gobbled up the rest of her eggs and eyed me. "What?"

"You are quite pretty when you eat." I patted her shoulder and laughed. "Thanks for the advice. Maybe I'll mess with him in class. Text him creepy things."

"Knowing him, he'd probably like that. Text sexy things, though. Get him amped."

"Good call."

"Let me know how it goes, lover girl."

An hour later, I sat in my usual spot, in the back without anyone around me. I scanned the room, unable to find Zade. *This is odd.* I generally knew where he sat by the crowd of people around him. Other people gravitated toward him. I couldn't blame them. He was pretty damn awesome.

Callie: Hey, girl, hey. What's going on?

It said he read it, but didn't reply. Damn, maybe he was doing something. That made sense. A couple minutes went by and I saw him come into class. He looked mad. I tried another one.

Callie: I like your jacket. It's sexy.

Another read but no reply. Maybe he'd seen me and gotten pissed. *Shit.* I wouldn't mess with him today. I'd tell him after class, in person. He'd never ignored my texts before... My stomach dropped. Something must be wrong. I tried my best to focus on the bullshit lecture but it did nothing for me. I took notes and about fifteen minutes in, Zade ran out of the lecture. A girl I recognized from one of their parties followed him. She stopped at the top of the stairs, looked me up and down, winked and kept going. *What. The. Fuck.*

I didn't like it, but I wasn't going to let a petty bitch fluster me. I needed to be better than her, even though I thought about kicking her face in for a good ten minutes. I knew I wouldn't be able to focus on class anymore so I texted Greta instead.

Callie: Mission aborted. He saw my texts and ignored them.

Greta: Maybe he saw you?

Callie: Thought that too, but he ran out mid lecture without seeing me. Also, some skanky girl I've seen at their house followed him out and winked at me.

Greta: Uh, ew. Did you flip her off?

Callie: Nah, didn't think fast enough. She ran out of there before I did anything. Am I panicking over nothing?

Greta: Everything seems a little shady, but I'm guessing there's an explanation. There has to be.

Callie: Should I go over there? Ask?

Greta: If you feel like you need to. Again, shady, but not another alarming.

Callie: Okay. I hate this uncertainty. God, when I'm ready to tell him I love him...I get all the paranoid thoughts and shit.

Greta: Call him and see what's up. He'll have an answer that'll make you feel better.

I left the lecture hall, unable to focus at all at that point. I had a sinking feeling of dread. My sixth sense knew something happened. Like, something major. I couldn't pinpoint what or why, but I knew. I tried calling Zade, but he sent it to voicemail. *This. Is. Not. Good.*

My heart raced and my hands shook. I sent him a text asking to talk.

Zade: I can't talk now. In class.

My heart sank. He'd left class. He'd lied. Lied to me. The nerves and worry I had shifted into a sick sense of betrayal. Old Callie would've cowered and gone back to her apartment to cry with Greta. New Callie—she had more confidence and wanted answers. Fine. He wanted to lie. There'd better be a damn good reason.

I marched over to their house, determined to figure out what the hell had happened. I knew he was inside — my body somehow tuned into his. I knocked on the door. The bitch answered with a knowing smirk.

"Callie, right?" She opened the door a couple inches and slid her head out. She smirked with a sneer on her lips. "You really stood no chance. He never belonged to you."

She pushed it open farther, walked past me and down the stairs. I watched her head down the road, my stomach clenching. *What the hell does she mean?* I went into the house and up to Zade's room. I knocked on the door, questions bursting through me.

He opened up with hard eyes, ones I had never seen directed at me. They softened a little bit, but confusion took over. "Callie?"

"Yes, Zade." I strode into his room, fuming with anger. "Expecting someone else?"

"Wait, what? Why are you here?"

"Why did some girl leave your house? Why did you lie to me?"

"What? I didn't lie to you." He ran his hands through his hair, pulling on the ends of it. "A girl? Veronica? *Please.*"

"Answer the question, Zade," I demanded, my heart breaking.

"Which one?" His eyes, dark and angry, narrowed at me. "I don't understand why you came over here. I told you I was busy."

"No, you told me you were in class. Which, by the way, surprise — I have the same class as you and I watched you leave. With Veronica or whatever her name is behind you."

"*You're* in the sports psychology lecture?" He drew his eyebrows together and his eyes turned cold. Ice cold. "Hold the fuck up. You mean to tell me we've had a class together this whole time and you didn't tell me?"

"Yeah. I planned —"

"Why, Callie? Because you didn't trust me and wanted to spy on me?" His eyes were now almost black with anger.

"At first, yeah, but —"

"I can't believe you. I can't fucking believe you. You *still* don't trust me, do you? After everything we've done..." He squeezed the back of his neck, his entire body tensing and I got pissed.

"Let me finish." I raised my voice this time. "I didn't tell you in the beginning because I wanted distance. Then, I couldn't figure out how to tell you without assuming you'd think the worst. I planned to tell you today and mess with you a little bit, but you ignored my texts and ran out."

"I have a lot of shit going on right now, Callie, shit not connected with you. So, forgive me for not telling you every fucking thing that's happening the second it happens. I assumed you trusted me enough to tell you when I was ready. But apparently I expected too much of you. You need to leave."

"What?" Color drained from my face. "Why?"

"Because I have somewhere else I need to be and I don't want to deal with you right now." He snatched up his wallet and keys and glared at me. "I won't do this with someone who doesn't trust me after everything we've been through. I fucking love you, Callie. But I won't put myself through the pain if you can't trust me."

"I do trust you." Tears welled up in my eyes and anger, fear, pain and betrayal all coursed through me. Tears fell, the salty taste mixing with my words. "You ignored my texts and when I got here, I saw her leave the house and she — "

"Exactly. You assumed. You think I'd throw us away?" He shook his head a couple of times, pinching the bridge of his nose.

"I didn't assume anything. I got a bad feeling in my stomach something happened and I wanted to make sure you were okay." My voice shook now.

"Yeah. Everything is great. Can't you tell?" His tone was unlike anything I had heard before.

"Why are you speaking to me this way? You've never spoken to me this harshly before."

"Yeah, well, when you invest a lot of time in someone you see a future with and you find out they were spying on you? Following you? Not a good feeling. I'm going to talk how the fuck I want to talk."

"I get you're mad, but there's something else. I *know* you, Zade. What's going on?" Concern took over now I saw the signs. His hands shook, his jaw tensed and he seemed on the defensive. I knew I'd pissed him off, but his reaction worried me.

"Not really your business, is it?"

"I hoped to tell you today I loved you," I admitted, looking at the ground. It wasn't the ideal time or moment but I couldn't back out now. "I planned to text you all during class and mess with you and tell you. I mean it, Zade."

"How dare you throw love at me?" He shook his head and his nostrils flared. "I can't believe you. I don't believe you." He hit the wall with his fist. "Fuck! I've shown you every day how much I love you and you...you use it against me?"

"Zade, please!"

"God, I need you to go. I can't look at you right now."

"You don't mean it."

"I do." He met my eyes, his dark and hurt.

I watched him with my chest clenching. I waited a second longer and saw my answer. I gulped, darted out of the room and walked out of their house with as much dignity as I could. The tears hit hard, unlike any crying I had done before, and by the time I got to my apartment, I wanted to crawl into bed for days.

Greta waltzed in an hour later, spying me on the couch shoving mint ice cream into my mouth. She put her arm around me and took the spoon for herself. "Good shit."

"Yeah. The best. I should only date ice cream."

"You really can't go wrong with it. It's a perfect relationship, unless you're lactose intolerant. Then the relationship might be a little toxic."

I laughed, the sound painful. "I'm not sure if I messed everything up or whose fault it is. But I'm pretty sure we broke up."

"Fuck. I'm sorry, babe." She squeezed me harder and gave me silent comfort. "Did you go over there?"

"Yup. He lied to me and wouldn't tell me why and he accused me of not trusting him. It's not that I don't trust him. I wanted to understand."

"I get it, girl, I would've, too. Maybe he'll come back and grovel?"

"I don't think so. His eyes... They were pissed. Like, majorly pissed at me. But we both need to say an apology and I don't think he sees it that way."

"This is your first fight though. You haven't learned how to fight yet. My parents always tell me that you need to figure out how to fight as a couple because it's bound to happen. Don't give up hope yet, kid."

I laughed and snorted at the same time. "I hate feelings. They suck."

"That they do. That's why I chose to bottle mine up real tight. Probably not healthy in the long run, but hey, it works for me now."

"Love you, G. You're my best friend."

"You too, Callie girl. You too."

Chapter Thirty-Four

Zade

I drove to Zaria's clenching my fists on the wheel. My hands hurt by the time I arrived. I took deep breaths. My heart hurt. My head pounded. Too fucking many emotions. I couldn't believe Callie didn't trust me. I wanted to beat the shit out of something because she'd broken my goddamn heart. I needed her now more than ever. But, no. She didn't fucking trust me. My hands shook. I hadn't had time to explain anything when I'd gotten that text from Zaria saying I needed to get there immediately. She'd received a letter from our father. *Our fucking father.* I couldn't breathe with the anxiety I felt.

I parked at a terrible angle and ran up to Zaria's place. She buzzed me in instantly and opened the door without a word. "Where is it?"

"On the table."

"It arrived earlier today, right?"

"Yes. I read it twice. You need to, too. Then we'll talk." She put her hand on my shoulder and pushed me into the chair. "Take your time."

"I don't know if I can handle it, Z." I clenched the edge of the chair. "I'm skeptical."

"Read it."

I opened the letter addressed to Z. The pages were bent and discolored, as though it had been sealed for a long time. The front of the envelope had an odd signature on it. "Is this really from him?"

"Yes." Her eyes filled with tears and I squeezed her hand.

"We'll get through this, no matter what."

"I know."

Dear Zaria and Zade,

If you're reading this, then unfortunately I've been lowered into the ground. This may come as a shock to both of you but I have been following your successes throughout most of your lives. There was a reason I left and a reason your mother raised you without a father. I had been abusive, irresponsible and unstable. I had a cocaine addiction and didn't get clean until about ten years ago. By that time, I had already started another family. I have three children with my wife, well widow, now, Janine. David, Rachel and Mally. Too much time had passed to try and ask for forgiveness and that alone lies with me. I could have tried, but I chose not to out of guilt. This letter is a way for me to have peace, knowing I can help you out a little. Please, if anything, do not get upset at your mother. She protected what belonged to her and knows little of anything I'm telling you.

I want both of you to know two things. The first, your mom did a hell of a job raising you. You are both wonderful human beings and are such a gift to society. Zaria, you're going to change the lives of thousands with your teaching and Zade, I cannot wait to watch you from up here to see what you do on that mound. I have no right to say this to you, but I am proud of you both.

Janine knew about the both of you and encouraged me to reach out to you multiple times, but my fear held me back. Fear of rejection. Fear of facing things I wasn't meant to face. I am sorry I chose to be a coward and I never got to know you both besides the outside looking in. She will probably try and meet you both. I have no right asking this of either of you, but please, don't push her away. She is a strong woman and saved me from myself.

My last wish, which you can ignore or accept, is for both of you to be at the reading of my will. I left you both something that you can either keep and use for the future, donate to a charity if you wish or throw away. I know you might do that and that's okay.

I am sorry for the pain I've caused you. I cannot tell you how much I am and I let my fears rule my life. If you meet your half siblings, please don't take out your anger at me on them. They were born without knowledge of you both — again, my doing.

Thank you for reading this. I am sorry. I've held nothing but love and pride for you both and your mother. Until I see you guys again, Dad.

I reread it. Two more times. Zaria continued to hold my hand and waited for me to react. I remained silent a little longer, unable to comprehend the gravity of the situation. "I don't know what to say."

"I don't either. Should we call mom?"

"Yeah. Yeah, I think we should." My eyes stung but I swallowed the emotion down. "She'll know what to do."

She did. We talked to her for two hours. We all cried and mourned a man we hadn't seen or thought of in years. *How do I mourn someone I never really knew but who had a huge impact on my life?* I couldn't. My mind broke into a million pieces at the thought of it. Mom told us stories of how they'd met and the problems they had. There were five years of bliss until the addiction took over. It seemed our mom had kept his addiction from us all these years to shield us from pain, and I couldn't fault her for that.

"Was there a number or someone to call about the reading of the will?" My mom asked, blowing her nose.

"No, but I'm going to call back the number that tried getting hold of me." Zaria wiped under her eyes and I put my arm around her, comforting her the best I could. "Should we go? We have half siblings. I can't believe it."

"I know. I can't either." I felt numb to it. We had other siblings. Other children made from the same man. I didn't know if I was angry. Sad. Mad. Pissed. Shocked. Or all of the above.

"I cannot decide that for you guys. Do you want me to fly home? I can take a couple of days."

"No, Mom. Stay there. Keep being superwoman We'll see you, as planned, for Thanksgiving. We can get through it. You raised pretty awesome kids."

"That I did." She sniffled again. "You can take my advice or leave it, but hear me out, okay?"

"Of course, Mom," I said, rolling my eyes. The action reminded me of Callie and my heart stumbled all over again. "What is it?"

"I think you should go. This opened up a can of worms I never thought would be opened. You might not realize it now or next month, but this might hit you in the most unexpected way in a few years. Or when you have kids or something. I don't want you to have regrets. Your father did, and I've had my fair share."

"I think I want to go. I want to meet our half siblings." Zaria peered up at me through her lashes. "What do you think?"

"I have too many what ifs going on, but I agree with mom. I have no idea what he left us, but I won't take the money. I'll donate every cent to Aaron's family. I won't touch it. Mom, you raised us and I'm not taking money from a stranger who was a sperm donor." I hadn't realized I had so much anger until that moment. "I'm pissed, now."

"I know. I am too, Zade. But you might regret it later." Her voice remained calm, but her eyes, the same as mine, filled with emotion.

"I'd never let Zaria go alone. And, yeah, I'll meet them. But, I won't accept anything from him. I don't even know his damn name."

"Zamon. His name was Zamon."

"Is that why we have weird Z names?" I asked, having been curious why we were named that. I'd asked my mom countless times growing up, but she'd said they were pretty. I'd always accepted the half-assed answer.

"Yeah. Yours means popularity and origin. Zaria, yours means blossom or princess. He chose the names." She wiped her eyes, sighing. "Are you guys going to be okay?"

"Yes. We'll hang out tonight," Zaria said, sniffling again. "Thanks for taking time to talk to us, Mom. We love you."

"I love you, too. Both of you. You're the best part of my life. No matter what happens, know that." She blew us a kiss and promised to call the next day. I went to Zaria's chair and collapsed into it.

"I want to get rip-roaring drunk and feel nothing."

"No. I won't let you." She sat on the floor, legs crossed. "This is a lot to process. Give it time."

"I'm not dealing with only this. I'm done with Callie, too." I bit the words out like they hurt saying. "She doesn't trust me."

"Uh, are you on drugs or something? None of what you said made sense. That girl loves you. What the hell happened?"

"It's too much to explain. She doesn't trust me. End of story."

"Zade. You better fucking tell me what happened. If you think you can give me half-truths, think again. The entire time we talked to Mom I thought how lucky you were that you got to talk about this with someone you loved. You found someone who matches you. Why throw that away?"

"What makes you think *I* threw it away?" I fired at her, but my heart clenched that she didn't have anyone to talk to. She had her friends, sure, but she didn't have a Callie...

"Because I saw her look at you when you didn't, dumbass." Her eyes blazed at me. "What. Happened."

"I headed to class, no issues. I saw Callie text me, but I saw your text, too. The one that only said call me ASAP."

"Yeah, you said you were in class. I said I got a letter from dad and to get over here when you could."

"I never replied to Callie during that time because shit, hearing from our dad is fucked up." I ran my hands through my hair. "I mean, fuck. You don't get a text like that every day."

317

"Right. Keep going."

"She texted me but I didn't read it. I couldn't. So I said I was in class. I went for maybe ten minutes but ran home. I would've told her eventually, but, as I said, I was preoccupied. I ran back to the house and one of the damn cleat chasers who has been targeting me all year followed me back. She let herself into the house until I screamed at her to get the fuck out. She finally went to leave."

"Ah, shit. Callie?" Zaria grimaced.

"Yeah, apparently she had the same class as me and refused to tell me this whole time." I gripped my hair. "I can't decide what I'm madder at. She said, at first because she wanted to spy on me. Or maybe the fact she followed me back to the house and assumed it had something to do with Veronica."

"So, what happened then?"

"We got into it. I yelled at her that she didn't trust me. After all this time, I've showed her day in and day out she changed me. Then, she drops that she was going to fucking mess with me that day in class and tell me she loves me. It's bullshit. She wouldn't have followed me back or hid the fact we were in class together all semester if she really trusted me." I scoffed and threw one of her pillows onto the floor in protest. "We yelled a little and I told her get out. I didn't want to deal with her or see her face."

"Jesus, Zade." Zaria sighed and gave me a sad smile. "That's really fucked up and a total misunderstanding."

"Yeah. I see that now, but I can't get over the fucking fact she doesn't trust me."

"You need to talk to her. I don't want you throwing away something over something minor. Look, I get the class thing pissed you off, but is that worth breaking up over? What if you saw her running out of a class and she ignored your text? What would you do?"

"Probably follow her," I admitted, realizing her words made sense. "Ah, fuck."

"Yeah. Dumbass. What if you showed up and a guy left her apartment and when you asked her about it, she told you to... What did you say to her? What if she said she didn't want to deal with you or see your face? How might you feel, Zade?"

My stomach dropped and not in the anger kind of way. More like, *I was the biggest dipshit on the planet* kind of way. She nudged me. "How would you feel? Answer me."

"Furious. Worried. Pissed."

"Yeah. Does that mean you don't trust her?"

"No." I said in a small voice.

"Go to her."

I thought about it. I wanted to see her, desperately, and make sure I didn't ruin the best thing to happen in my life. But things had been said and we needed to cool off. "It can wait, I'm not leaving you alone tonight. Today was...a fucking ride."

Her face softened and I knew I needed to wait to talk to Callie. "Today is about family."

"Thanks, bro." She hugged me, quickly. "I appreciate you."

"Now, maybe not rip-roaring drunk, but how about a couple beers? I need it."

She nodded. "Let's go. I don't want to be here. There's a pub down the road. We can watch baseball or something. It's not my favorite sport, but it'll do." She slid a sly glance at me.

"Sis got jokes. Okay." I held the door open for her. "You can help me think of ideas to get Callie to forgive me."

"Yeah, you're going to need all the help you can get."

Chapter Thirty-Five

Callie

In bed, I went through my Zade phases again. Hurt, then anger, then sadness, then...regret. I tossed my phone up and down. I wanted to mope and vow to never love again, but even thinking it made no sense. My life had millions of moments, good, bad, sad and amazing, and regret had no place. Sure, I'd missed Zade every second since I'd arrived home but I had no regrets. I sat up and logged into my laptop. *I might as well channel my inability to sleep and get some work done.* Nicole wanted, no more like demanded, that I personalize every exercise plan based on the athlete's bio. I wanted to wow her, despite the possibility that the assignment might never be used.

I grabbed the first profile and gasped when I saw Zade's name. I sighed and decided maybe I shouldn't work. I twirled the phone in my hands a couple more times and jumped when it went off. My heart raced, wanting it to be Zade but also not sure what I wanted to say to him.

Zade: Can we talk? I'm sorry.

I read it and clenched my teeth. We needed to talk. I saw that the clock already read midnight. *I might as well.* I wasn't going to be sleeping that night anyway.

Callie: Sure.

Zade: Thank god. I'm outside your place.

Callie: Be right down.

I threw on an old sweatshirt and ran down the stairs. He leaned on the hood of his car, looking like a better version of James Dean. He followed my movements as I slowly walked toward him. My heart beat out of my chest. My palms sweated and I fought the dual urge to smack him and run into his arms. I wasn't sure which one I wanted to win.

"Hey, girl." He gave me the crooked smile and the worry in his eyes stood out. I took a spot next to him on the car, not touching him, but also close enough to feel his heat.

"Hey." I crossed my arms over my chest, unsure what to do or say. He was here and that mattered. I fought a smile and gave up. "This is awkward."

"Agreed. But come here. I need to hold you."

I went into his arms and hugged him something fierce. We needed to talk everything out, but in that hug all my pieces were put back together. He smelled like home. He ran his hands up and down my back and pressed a good hard kiss against my head. "I love you, Callie."

"I know you do. And I love you, too. I have a lot to say but don't know where to start."

"I do too. Can we go up and lie down together?" He pulled away and smiled down at me with hope in his eyes. "I need to fill you in on everything that happened, but I need to be with you tonight. We can talk in the morning. I promise I'll tell you everything."

"I'd like that." I took his hand and we walked up the stairs. He took off his shirt but kept his pants on and tucked me next to him. I sighed, content and not as worried about the future anymore. Tomorrow we'd talk. Tonight I wanted to sleep with him by my side.

* * * *

I woke up tangled in Zade's arms, my face pressed into his strong chest and yesterday's events unraveled before me. He stirred and I held on to the moment a little bit longer. I knew we would survive the talk, but I dreaded it nonetheless.

"Morning, babe." He stretched and wiped his eyes before rolling over onto one elbow. "I slept like a brick."

"I think we slept through your class. It's past ten. Didn't mean for that to happen."

"It'll be fine. I haven't missed one yet this semester. I'm due." He ran his finger down my neck. My body betrayed me with a shiver.

"I hate to sound cliché, but we need to talk." I smiled at his guilty expression. I knew what he preferred to do and it didn't involve clothes.

"Yeah. Yeah. Yeah. Look, I need to apologize, first and foremost, for how I treated you yesterday. I was a total asshole and out of line. I understand if you want to put me in the doghouse for a while. I deserve it."

"Thank you for acknowledging your asshole-ness." I poked him in the chest. "If you ever do that again to me, I'll kick your ass."

"You should. I'll never do that again. I had some issues I dealt with yesterday, which we'll get to, but it didn't hit me until my sister and I were drinking a beer last night that you'd said you loved me."

"Yeah, you ass. I do. And, I had this whole thing planned, too." I rolled over and mirrored his position.

"What were you going to do?"

"I'm not sure you deserve to hear about it." I paused dramatically and felt a shadow of shame. "Look, in the beginning of what we started, I wanted distance. I stood no chance against your charm and humor. I chose to not tell you about that class because I knew you'd smother me."

"You're right."

"See?" I laughed. "Then, when we started being together, we were running and spending nights together… I didn't want my classes to have something to do with you in case something went wrong."

"Protecting yourself. I get it."

"Right, and soon after…I fell in love with you. It's scary as hell." I gulped, emotion coming into my voice that I wanted to hide. "I planned on texting you dirty things and asking you to be my boyfriend. I know we've had this joke going on for weeks and it's fun, but then I realized I wanted the label. I wanted to be your girlfriend."

His eyes softened to that warm coffee and cream color and he took hold of my face in a slow kiss. I closed my eyes, tasting him and enjoying the slow build-up. I pushed his chest though. "No, no hanky panky yet."

"Hanky panky?" He chuckled. "You want to be my girlfriend—I feel like I won and I want to claim my prize."

"I don't recall you asking me."

"Uh, you admitted to wanting it. That kind of makes it a thing."

"Nah, try harder." I winked at him. He made a sound in his throat and positioned himself on top of me. His elbows were on either side of my face and he stared into my eyes. He gently kissed my forehead, each eye and finally reached my mouth.

"Callie?"

"Yeah."

"I love you." He bit down on my favorite spot. "Will you please be my girlfriend? I'll watch Sox games with you. I'll help you cook and support you in anything you do. I'll never question what we have or take it for granted. I see you in my life. You've become my best friend."

A tear leaked out of my eye and he smiled down at me as though I was the best thing in the world. "Damn, my allergies."

"Cute. So, your answer?"

"Yeah. How could I say no to that?" I grabbed his face and kissed him. I kissed the hell out of that man and did it some more. It was slow this time. As if we had all the seconds in the world, and I guess we did.

Our looks were a little longer, our touches were a little gentler and when we crashed together...my heart said *game over*.

Naked and a little breathless, I moved to lie on his chest. "I trust you completely. I'm sorry I didn't express it enough."

"I know that now. I needed an outlet for some anger and you were up to bat." He ran his hands through my hair and sighed. "I fucking love your hair."

His compliment warmed me. "Thanks, Zade."

"I need to tell you about what happened yesterday." I lifted my head and saw pain etched on his face. "It's a head trip."

"I'm listening."

"Zaria received a letter from our father. I haven't seen him in nineteen years. I don't remember him." He ran his hand over his jaw and I frowned. I knew this wasn't going to be a good story. "He died."

"Shit." I hissed and closed my eyes. "I'm sorry."

"Yeah, I didn't feel as bad as I should about his death. I think mourning someone you didn't know is complicated and hard. He wrote us a letter and when I ran out of class yesterday, it was because Zaria texted me to get over there ASAP."

"You should've told me there was an emergency! I would've helped or something."

"I know, shit. I should've told you or asked for help. I handled it really fucking badly. My sister had been getting weird calls and letters in the mail and it freaked me out. I'd been worrying about someone stalking her and to find out it is someone delivering the letter of my dead dad? It fucks with you."

"It would fuck with anyone." I smoothed my hand up and down his arm, needing to touch him and give him any strength I could.

"He had another family. Has another family. We have half siblings. Three of them." He spoke in broken sentences and my heart hurt for him. "He wants us to meet them, I think. I can't really tell. There's a reading of a will and he said he left me and Zaria something. I don't want a cent though. Zaria doesn't either." He stopped talking and tilted his chin toward me. "What are you thinking right now?"

"Hell. All sorts of things. I'm sad that you have to go through this. This has to be really hard. I think you can always donate money or set it aside to figure out later. This is like a huge Band-Aid being ripped off."

"Yeah. You aren't kidding."

"Do you want to meet your half siblings?"

"I don't know. Zaria does. I don't care enough. Am I awful?" He fisted my blanket in his hand and sighed. "He wrote that he was proud of us. That he'd been following us growing up but stayed away out of cowardice. What kind of life is that? He had two kids and he never did anything for us, until he died. That's bullshit."

"It is bullshit. I don't think you are awful at all. As I said, I think this is going to take some time to digest and you don't have to make any decision right now."

"Yeah. Zaria said something like that. She's a more understanding person than I am."

"Or, you care a whole lot about how your dad hurt your family and made you have to be the man of the house. Or, you can't understand how he did that because you would never abandon anyone no matter your situation. But, Zade, sometimes life has a really funny way of working out."

"What do you mean?"

"'Life is a highway, and I want to ride it all night long,'" I joked.

"Did you really just lyric advise me?"

"Yup. Did it work?"

"Not at all. Dork." He laughed and I considered that a mission complete. "How is this good? I don't see any good in it yet."

"Zade, your family might grow three more people. You could help your dad's legacy, however much you hate it, live on. You might be a role model for your newfound siblings. You get to decide what to make of this. If you want to go in guns blazing, then go for it. This is your life and your prerogative. But, as the face of Zwillows Pillows, I think you should take the classy route."

"You *would* bring that up."

"Of course I did. My boyfriend has a fan club and I'm not president."

"I can talk to some people. Get you a membership card," he teased, laughter coming back into his eyes.

"Nah, I get the real thing. I think I win. This is way better than the pillow cases with your face on them."

"No fucking way—they don't have that, do they?" He pouted again.

"My birthday is coming up. You now know what to get me."

"You're ridiculous, but you're mine."

"Yeah, I guess I am." And I liked it.

Epilogue

Zade
Five months later, first game of the season

I held my breath. We were two outs away from beating our rivals. I stood against the fence, my hands above my head. Zeke, our closer, struck out their biggest hitter. We cheered, the stands going crazy. He had two more outs to go.

"Let's go, Zeke!" I shouted, adrenaline pumping through me. Coach stood to my right. He always led with a silent strength and never showed emotion. I'd thrown a shut out for eight innings and he'd hit my back. Luckily, I spoke 'coach' and knew I'd done a hell of a job.

Zeke threw his sick curve, the batter getting a piece of it. He pulled it, not connecting well and it bounced to Aaron at short. He backhanded it, shot the ball to first and got the out.

"Yes! One more, baby!" I hung over the edge, some of the bench guys and other pitchers joining me. I smiled, noticing their wrist bands. We'd decided all upperclassmen were going to wear them for Aaron's dad, and the rest of the team caught on. I looked into the stands, seeing his dad and family there. He'd had his surgery over Christmas break and seemed to be doing okay. They were waiting to see if the cancer had spread, but Aaron had finally figured out a way to deal with it. Well, the best he could. No one could get over that.

Zeke threw two pitches, the count 2 and 0. He needed to change speed, throw the hitter off. Jeff motioned for a change up behind the plate. He threw it but missed his spot. The ball soared into the outfield. Tanner sprinted toward the fence. I stood, waiting with the rest of the crowd to see if he caught it. He jumped, arm outstretched to full length and he gloved it. We won the game.

"Yes!" I jumped over the fence and stormed the field with everyone else. It felt fucking great winning the first game of the season, but to our rivals? *Hell yeah!*

"Way to go!" I jumped on top of Zeke's back, Jeff hugging us, too. Aaron laughed, all of us enjoying the moment. I snuck a glance out to the stands. Callie and Greta jumped up and down, along with Zaria and our half siblings. She didn't look as comfortable as Callie, but she cheered her face off nonetheless.

We shook hands with the other team and met in the locker room for our post-game talk with coach. He celebrated our success and made a plan for the next game. We dedicated our win to Aaron's dad and I showered as quickly as I could. I wanted to go see my girl.

She waited by the fence, her hair in braids, and proudly wearing my jersey. I hopped the short metal fence and took her in my arms. "Hey, girl."

"You threw great! Your arm — it looks amazing. You totally increased your speed by at least two. I swear there were some —"

I kissed her, shutting her up. "I cannot tell you how much I fucking love seeing you in my jersey. Favorite thing ever."

"I'll make sure to wear only your jersey when we get back." She wiggled her eyebrows at me. "I like making you beg for it."

"Good. Only time I'll beg, too." I put my arm around her, fitting her right into me. She took my hand in hers. "Did I tell you I'm proud of you, by the way?"

"*You* proud of *me*? Hello…you pitched your ass off. I'm proud of *you*, Zade." She leaned her shoulder into mine, grinning.

"Yeah, but seeing your parents in the stands, supporting us. You." I felt my heart grow in size, with pride and happiness I didn't know I could feel. "You worked your ass off and get to come back here next year. Things happen for a reason, babe, and I know your year off sucked —"

"But look where it led?" She finished my thought. "I never thought about it that way. I don't know if I would've liked freshman Zade."

"You wouldn't have. He was a dog." I admitted, pressing a kiss to her temple again. "But I love you and nothing else really matters."

"Ugh, you and your words. Today is a double whammy. Meeting my parents first, and your half siblings. You ready for that?"

"With you by my side, yeah. I can do both of those things," I admitted, damn well knowing the truth. She made me braver. Stronger. Better. Happier. And cheesy apparently.

She rolled her eyes at me but her dimples came out in a smile. "I'm proud of you. This is the right step. I can feel it."

"I'm glad you're here with me. I couldn't do this alone." I confessed the weakness to her. Somehow, there had been a transfer of power throughout our relationship. She made me stronger and weaker at the same time. I opened up to more things. I talked about more things. When Zaria and I had gone to the reading of the will, we'd found out we'd each gotten ten thousand dollars. She'd donated half of it to a cause she felt passionate about, a scholarship for students. I split mine in half, part of it going to cancer research for Aaron's dad and the other half to help youth in the community go to baseball camp. I donated it under the name Zamon.

"No. You could. You have Zaria and your mom has been amazing about it. But all the same, I'm glad I'm with you." She waved as we approached Zaria. "You got this. Just don't make an ass out of yourself."

"Great advice. I really needed that," I deadpanned.

"I figured." She laughed. "Never forget how awesome I am, okay?"

"Challenge accepted, baby, challenge accepted," I whispered into her ear and she pinched my ass. With Callie by my side, life was good.

Want to see more from this author? Here's a taster for you to enjoy!

Cleat Chasers: The Game Changer
Jaqueline Snowe

Excerpt

Greta

Action movies are full of shit, feeding us fake information our entire lives. For instance, when a fight breaks out in a bar, there's no Mark Wahlberg look-a-like to rescue the damsel in distress. Second the sound of flesh hitting flesh is repulsive and meaty. There are no wooshes or bangs or ka-pows. Nope. It's just disgusting.

I cringed at the smack and crashing of a fist meeting the face of my date. That's right. I always picked the *best* of the best when it came to dating and tonight was no different. Todd, who had blood dripping down his eye, chin and nose, had made the bold decision to ask me out. I'd accepted, like a fool, and would live to regret this night for all eternity.

"Where is my money, Todd?" The broad-shouldered man with a beard longer than my hair pummeled his meaty fists into my date's face. "Where the feck you keepin' it?"

No response. Burly Guy didn't like that. He grunted, swung his arm back past the table and hit Todd square in the nose. *What happened in my past life for me to witness this?*

No one got up to help. No one moved. They all watched with half-smiles on their faces and I knew in the pit of my stomach I needed to get the hell out. Like, ten minutes ago. I slowly slid my trembling hand into my purse to find my phone, but Mr. Burly heard me. He whipped his face toward mine, the terrifying glint to his eyes making me gasp. I gulped, the fear suddenly *very* real.

"You know this fecking asshole?" he barked at me. Countless gazes followed his voice and now stared at me. They wanted a show and I was *so* not the person for the role. My chin trembled as I shook my head.

"N-n-no. I j-just met him tonight." I clutched my phone to my chest. I would use it as a weapon if necessary, although I had no fucking clue what damage I could do on this beast of a man.

He ran his fat tongue over his lips and studied me. I stood stock-still, my spine straight as a rod. "I think it's time for you to go, doll. My boss ain't gunna like me lettin' ya leave, but your blonde hair don't fit in here. Get the feck out and don't come back."

I nodded, glancing one more time at Todd. My gut screamed to get out, but I had been raised Catholic. *Do I leave my epic failure of a date to get killed? Do I call the cops?*

Mr. Burly thought I took too long and put his grimy fingers around my wrist. I squealed, yanking it out of his touch.

"Get gone, girl." He kicked open the door and threw me outside. I stood on a rundown street with one streetlight working correctly. The others flashed and made a high-pitched buzzing sound that sent chills down my spine. "Fuck. Fucking. Fuck."

I called my best friend with shaking fingers and snot running down my face. Oh, did I mention I had blood on me that wasn't my own? I gagged, looking at the splatters. The phone rang and rang again. I loved Callie to death, but if that bitch didn't answer right then, I would get her for it. Big-time. Because what the fuck? It appeared the downward spiral my life had begun a month ago still had a way to go before hitting pure rock bottom. Nothing topped this story, as long as I got home alive.

"*Give me my fecking money!*" A booming voice traveled through the closed door. My longtime sixth sense had sent warning after warning all day and I'd chosen to ignore it. *This is my own damn fault.*

I gripped my phone tighter and took a deep breath. *Count to eight. Make a box with your breathing.* It did me no good and my fingers still shook. After three failed calls to Callie, I called the other number I knew by heart. Aaron Hill answered after the first ring with his obnoxious and playful voice.

"G-spot, what's crackin'? Finally calling me for a booty call?" His voice had the power to make me smile and roll my eyes simultaneously. This was not that time.

"I need you to come get me." My voice shook as the shouting picked up. Why had I let Todd convince me this place was cool and a '*real biker bar*'? Standing alone on the dark country road made it feel more like a place where girls went missing than a legit biker hangout. *I fell for it. Dumbass.*

"Where the hell are you?" His good-natured tone shifted and I imagined his steel eyes going dark. "It's past midnight. Shit, G, are you alone?"

"Uh, pretty much." I sent him the address while still on the phone. "I texted you the place. I'm calling in my favor."

"Jesus, Greta." He let out a string of cuss words. "Why the *fuck* are you all the way out there?"

"A date gone bad." Shame filled my chest, regret chasing it. The feelings had my throat closing. Tears weren't far behind.

"Goddamn it. I'm on my way. Stay on the phone with me. I swear, I'm going to wring your neck. I hate this shit." A door slammed—he'd just gotten into his car. After a minute of silence, he sucked in a breath. "Are you at Dirty Matt's? Please say no. Tell me no, right now, Greta."

The neon signed mocked me, *Dirty Matt's*, blinking over and over. "I'm at Dirty Matt's."

"Jesus Christ." His deep voice got so low, so calm, I made a vow to end all my plans for dating. His anger and disappointment in me were well deserved.

I gulped. Ever since my childhood best friend Callie had found love the year before, I'd wanted to try it. She'd fought it, but seeing how damn happy she had been all year and how she'd grown into herself had motivated me. I was damn happy for her and in no way jealous. I just yearned to have the closeness she had with her boyfriend, Zade.

Okay, so all the longing and searching had led me to a series of bad, awful and miserable dates. Not one had clicked. Not one had ended with the promise for more. And, not one has ended with a guy acting like a gentleman. Apparently, I had a stamp on my head that read, *I tend to date losers.* And, now, I could add I dated felons. It was the *only* explanation I could muster why Todd had brought me here, and why they'd beaten the shit out of him.

"I'm twenty minutes out and I'm beyond pissed at you. You know the rep this place has? Do you?" His deep voice held nothing but rage and worry. I closed my eyes and leaned against the wall. I had known about the reputation, but I'd wanted an adventure. Todd rode a motorcycle. He had tattoos and looked as good as sin. I wanted, even an inkling if possible, of the happiness Callie felt. *Is that so bad?*

Yes. I shivered.

Aaron's shaking voice pulled me from my self-pitying thoughts. "Greta! Did you know and still go there?"

Shit. He was past mad. "Yeah."

"Why? Tell me why. I know shit hasn't been great for you recently, but stop with this self-destruction crap. I can't watch you do this."

The squealing tires informed me he was close. His dark SUV sped down the road on a mission, the headlights showcasing how wretched this place looked. He pulled up to the spot right in front of Dirty Matt's and threw open his door. He stormed out, his anger evident on his handsome face.

"Aaron, look—"

"You asshole," he said, yanking me into his arms. "You worried the hell out of me. I lost ten pounds on the drive here."

"Aaron," I managed to squeak out before he pressed my face into his chest. "I'm okay."

"Just, let me be."

So, we stood like that for at least three minutes. His ridiculously large frame towered over me, but not in the way Mr. Burly back there had. Aaron was different. His body was sculpted from hours and hours in the gym. My arms barely fit around his middle, but I tried anyway. He squeezed me one last time and broke our hug. His gray eyes still held on to some anger, but relief took over. "Thank you."

"You're welcome, G." His lips turned white while he glanced at the sign. "Now, get in the car."

I obeyed, not foolish enough to piss him off even more. He opened the passenger door and glared at me until I buckled myself in. Without a word, he shut it and pinched his nose walking to the driver's side. His cologne clouded the car, the pleasant aroma of wood and leather comforting my nerves.

My body shook, the adrenaline wearing off. Aaron must've seen, because he turned on the heat despite the high July temperatures. I understood him well enough to let him stew. We had been close for over two years, but last year things were different. His dad being diagnosed with cancer had made the Aaron we all knew and loved change and we had grown closer and closer. Callie was my girl for life, but I couldn't envision a future without knowing Aaron would be there. He understood me, respected me and pushed me to be better. He was allergic to feelings and emotions while I was forever giving up on men. Our friendship worked.

He drove the silent, dark path back to campus, one hand on the wheel and the other repeatedly making a fist. I blamed myself for his anger. He had enough to worry about and now picking me up... Remorse filled my chest and my eyes stung. "I'm *fucking* sorry. I'm an idiot. I don't know why I went there. I wanted to have an adventure or something."

He nibbled on his bottom lip, keeping his expression blank. *Shit.* Instead of remaining silent and letting him deal with it, I'd decided to ramble. Rambling was a favorite sport of mine and I couldn't stop.

"He had a motorcycle..."

"I thought he would be a winner..."

"I want what Callie and Zade have..."

"I didn't realize he was a felon or something and would get the shit beat out of him…"

"I had no fucking clue I would get manhandled…"

"Excuse me. What did you just say?" His jaw tightened.

"I didn't have a clue—"

"No. You said manhandled. Someone hurt you?" His grip on the wheel tightened and I swallowed, loudly.

"Not hurt, no." I tucked my arms further into myself. A bruise had already formed and Aaron was in no state to know that. "Forget I said anything."

"I swear to God, Greta." He pulled off the road and stopped the car. He shook, his large frame tight with pent-up rage. I wanted to crawl into a hole. Pissed-off Aaron could scare the boogeyman into retirement. "Don't fucking lie to me. Are you hurt?"

I shook my head, but kept my arms crossed. His gaze flicked to my arms, and without asking, he grabbed them. I closed my eyes and knew he'd seen the bruise when he sucked in a breath. My lip trembled.

"Take off your shirt. I might have another one in the back." He released my forearms and turned to grab something in the back of the car. He was too calm, too well-behaved. It freaked me the hell out. I expected him to lose his shit and break something. Calm Aaron was new.

"I-it's okay." My voice shook again.

"No," he growled at me. "You have blood on you. Take it off now. I'm getting rid of it."

He waited, staring daggers at me until I took my blood-soaked shirt off. He wasn't lying. He whipped it out of my hands and chucked it out of the window. "I can't find my gym bag. Take mine instead."

Aaron Hill taking off his shirt should be photographed and made into a calendar. Or, better yet, a promotion for a porn video. He had always been hot as hell, and this was so not the time to ogle my friend. But I was human and his muscles rippled as he tugged off his shirt. "Put this on, Greta. Don't argue."

I didn't. I took the warm black shirt and put it on. It was three sizes too big, but I felt loads better. It wrapped around me like my favorite childhood blanket. I sniffed it unabashedly and closed my eyes. Sleep took over, and it wasn't until we pulled into Aaron's driveway in the early hours of the morning when I woke up.

I yawned, not sure why he hadn't dropped me off at my apartment. He ran his hand down his face, getting out of the car without a word. *Okay then.* I followed suit and tried not to stare at his back. His beautiful, sculpted back. "Aaron, why didn't you drop me off?"

"We need to ice your bruise. I have stuff here." His clipped tone told me he still wasn't happy with me. I couldn't blame him, though. "Come on."

He put his hand on my shoulder, guiding me into his home without making a sound. I walked toward the kitchen, but he shook his head and pointed upstairs. The floor creaked with each step and I made a vow to myself then and there.

No more dating.

No more being a dumbass.

I am going to focus on school and my friends.

I needed to save as much money as I could, ensuring I could return my senior year, because one of the things that had triggered my spiral was my dad losing his job six years before retirement. My parents had had to sell our childhood home, retire three years before they'd planned, and most of their money had been spent helping my brother with his nasty divorce. Shame consumed me again at how selfish and foolish I had been. My eyes stung and I clenched my jaw, hoping to stop the waterworks.

I planned to delete my online dating apps and have someone change my password as soon as I woke up the next day. Tonight had crossed a line. Too fucked-up.

"Go ahead and sit on the bed. I'll get my kit." He held the door for me and disappeared down the hall. Aaron's room fit him well—baseball legends and pinup models plastered on the walls. Clothes scattered across the floor made it appear messy, but I knew the closet was organized by colors. The bed welcomed me, the exhaustion of the night taking me. I lay on it, just closing my eyes for a little. I would leave after I'd iced my bruised arm. Dreams began to take over when I felt the softest touch on my cheek, like a feather.

"Greta?"

A deep, hushed voice forced me to open my eyes and Aaron's gray ones were inches away from me. "Hm?"

"Sit up for a second. You can sleep right after." He nudged my leg with his arm and sat next to me. He was still shirtless, the handsome devil. He carefully put my forearm in his left hand and used his other to hold the ice against it. "It hurts me seeing this bruise on you."

I closed my eyes at his honesty. I leaned into his shoulder and sighed. "I'm so embarrassed. And sorry. And I hate myself a little right now."

"We all make mistakes. Hell, you knew me when I went on a bender. You stood by me when I drank every night, slept with countless women, and chewed my ass out the one time I tried drugs. I haven't forgotten that."

I groaned into his shoulder. "I would do it again if I had to."

"I know you would, G." He laughed softly, the first time that night. I'd missed that sound.

"There it is. I wondered if your laughing part broke."

"Okay, no need to be dramatic." He picked up the ice and hissed at my arm. "Promise me something."

"No need. I already made a vow to never online date again. No, to never date again. Or at least for five years. Don't worry. This will never happen again."

"It better fucking not." His hand came around my leg, squeezing my knee. "Promise me you'll call me if you need help. Any time. Any place. You're one of the most important people in my goddamn life."

"Okay." I met his gaze and winced at the intensity in his eyes. "I promise."

"Good." He yawned, taking the bag off my arm. "I'm going to sleep. I'm beat."

"Uh, should I call a cab?" I hesitated.

"Don't be a dumbass. Sleep here. You've crashed on the couch countless times." He leaned back, fluffing up the pillows and rolling over. *Damn those back muscles. I want to bite them.*

I pushed myself up to head downstairs when his arm wrapped around me. "Uh, Aaron?"

"Stay here. My bed is huge. Don't make it weird."

He pulled me back onto the bed but kept enough distance between us. He must've sensed my trepidation because he rolled over and mumbled, "You mean too much to me to try anything. Go to sleep."

Home of Erotic Romance

Sign up for our newsletter and find out about all our romance book releases, eBook sales and promotions, sneak peeks and FREE romance books!

About the Author

Jaqueline Snowe lives in Arizona where the 'dry heat' really isn't that bad. She enjoys making lists with colorful Post-it notes and sipping coffee all day. She has been a custodian, a waitress, a landscaper, a coach and a teacher. Her life revolves around binge-watching Netflix, her two dogs who don't realize they aren't humans and her wonderful baseball-loving husband.

Jaqueline loves to hear from readers. You can find her contact information, website details and author profile page at https://www.totallybound.com